# Ghosts and Strangers

# Ghosts and Strangers

# Emyr Humphreys

seren

seren is the book imprint of
Poetry Wales Press Ltd
Nolton Street, Bridgend, CF31 3BN, Wales
www.seren-books.com

ISBN 1-85411-299-6

A CIP record for this title is available from
the British Library

*The publisher works with the financial assistance of the
Arts Council of Wales*

Front cover image: detail from 'Veronica II'; back cover image: detail
from 'Veronica I', both inkjet printed linen, 610 x 560 mm, by Karen
Ingham from her *Death's Witness* exhibition

Printed in Plantin by Bell & Bain Ltd, Glasgow

# CONTENTS

# LADY RAMROD

## I

I never liked dogs. When I was twelve my father moved to a new parish and there were kennels beyond the hedge at the bottom of the back garden. Those awful creatures used to howl and bark all night and I had to sleep with the window open because my father had spent time in a sanatorium in his youth and was obsessed with the condition of our lungs. There wasn't much my father could do about the dogs because he was the anointed agent of peace and tranquillity in the neighbourhood. The kennels were run by three women who wore breeches and leather leggings. If I stopped to stare at them on my way home from school they would slap a whip against their leggings and make me run off.

Ah, my father. On earth and now in heaven I trust. What age did he belong to? I grew under his shadow like a beetle in the bark of a tree. I have a large photograph of him, backed with cardboard. He is standing on a carpet of artificial grass wearing a top hat. The stillness of his gaze can still develop into a threat. He was fond of asserting that life was a ceremony. My existence was governed by the need to please him. My sister Dyddgu could achieve that blissful state without any effort at all. She moved in the warm air of his unstinting approval so that her feet barely needed to touch the ground. So much beauty and accomplishment were already destined for great things. The Rectory was darkened with doom and disaster when she stormed off to live in South America with an impecunious polo player. She left behind a devastated rural dean with only my mother and myself as insufficient comfort. I worked like a Stakhanovite to carve out an academic career he could take pride in.

So why am I about to kiss a dog? And what has a pasteboard photo of my father in a top hat got to do with it? It could make a fancy detective story if only I had the literary talent to pursue it. The truth is I have little imagination and a profound aversion to detective stories. Life itself always ends up with a corpse. So what is the mystery in that? Escapist reading is no escape. Whodunit? I did it. Just study my father's top hat.

He was a quarryman's son. That meant he ate the bread of a man who earned his living swinging from a rope in all weathers and from time to time plugged the rock face with dynamite to obtain suitable slabs of slate. Among such photographs I have of this grandparent is a faded blob half hidden by the euphonium he played in the village brass band. He was a serious man. A teetotaller devoted to God and Education to the extent that he never really distinguished between them. He worked himself into an early grave in order to send my father and his two brothers to college. The brothers were brilliant. One became a professor in Australia and the other ended up as a Labour peer. What could be more wonderful? My father was less brilliant and never reached those heights. At a crucial point in his career he switched from chapel to church like a climber who changes a hold to make an easier ascent. And he never looked back. On the other hand you could argue he never looked forward either. He rather lost touch with his family. I suppose it was a sort of inward emigration.

A country parsonage is an ideal place for a man to gnaw on the bone of frustrated ambition. He took his duties seriously. His stall in the cathedral was deeply cherished. It does not become a child to find fault with her parent's shortcomings since she is bound to inherit them. As a Warden I carry out my duties with a ritualistic sternness that stems directly from my father. I like gowns and head-gear. I enjoy treading red carpets. These are the things I assume he would approve of, so that by extension they might incline him to approve of me.

Even the most single-minded need modes of relaxation. My father's hobby was buying second hand books. There were rooms in the rectories to be furnished: there were outhouses in which to store dead minister's libraries bought cheaply from their widows. There he could sort them at his leisure and even conduct a modest business among collectors. He was no great reader but his activities indirectly fed my appetite for the classics. No one else in our grammar school sixth form took Greek and Latin. It helped to make me a minor phenomenon and helped to restore the self-esteem of a retired classics master who was conscripted to coach me.

My mother believed I studied too hard. She was a farmer's daughter and a wonderful cook. Too much good food and lack of exercise made her fat. She nursed a secret fear that she wasn't quite what her upright statue of a husband wanted. She knew he believed life was a ceremony and if he had required it, she would have retired to enable him to acquire a more appropriate partner for the great dance. I can see now that it is from this subdued woman that I inherited my own distinctive shade of humility.

In the Rectory kitchen my mother's diurnal unease was intensified by my father's moody obsession with social and ecclesiastical connections; and by my lack of a boyfriend. I was straight and thin and wore spectacles and I had developed a sharp tongue which she felt discouraged local boys from knocking on the Rectory door. Her joy therefore was unconfined when I brought Marcus Mostyn home in the Easter vac of my second year at St. Anne's. And my father was instantly intrigued by Marcus's surname. He established that Marcus was an authentic descendant of that Thomas ap Richard ap Hywel ap Ieuan Fychan, Lord Mostyn, whose display of 'aps' so exasperated Rowland Lee, that ruthless President of the Council of the Marches, that he ruled that these pedigree obsessed aristocrats should assume forthwith either their last name or that of their residence. Marcus was made welcome by my parents to a degree that soon embarrassed me. My own status was marginally improved, hovering between agent and instrument. Since Dyddgu's abrupt departure I had never seen my father look so contented. He took to nibbling nuts, rubbing his hands and occasionally even humming through his nose.

I need to think of Marcus as he was then more than as he is now. There were his eyes to begin with. Large, clear, brown, canine, begging to be placed at the centre of the universe. I could see myself in them. I could swim in them. Warm pools of unflinching sincerity. Then there was his wide mouth and his nimble feet. They were intimately related. He liked to sing and dance. He loved to be popular and to entertain. He was very pleased with his thick black curls. They finished off the picture rather like my father's top hat, always in need of a brush to be kept in good condition.

He was never startlingly intelligent. I needed to help him with his essays. His law degree was poor but there was a place for him in his father's practice. It was his craving to be popular that stranded him on a television mast in the winter of 1974. He used to confess close to my ear that he wanted to be a person who would make a difference. I trembled to his touch and was thrilled to be the guardian of his secret ambitions. He gave me a leather bound

edition of Elizabeth Barrett Browning's *Sonnets from the Portuguese.*
He said it used to belong to his grandmother. Agnes Rowlands, my
best friend at St. Anne's, said they were awful mush. She could
have been right but I never felt quite the same towards her again.
*How do I love thee...* All that business about depth and breadth and
height seemed burning truth to me. It is clear to me now that an
intelligent woman in love is condemned to endure an additional
anguish: her finely tuned critical intelligence is obliged to live with
the seismic turmoil of her feelings bereft of any power to control
them. This may well be an aspect of the human condition that has
received insufficient attention.

Through me Marcus became involved with the Language Society.
I think he must have been looking for a protest movement in which
he could exercise what he believed was his talent for leadership:
become a person who would make a difference. In my eyes there
was no need for him to prove himself a hero; but to become a
leader he needed a following. And in those heady days the only way
to lead was from the front. There were always others prepared to
make greater sacrifices: at a certain point you could see a queue of
young men and an even longer queue of young women lining up
to be sent to prison. I suppose I must have been too scared of my
father to join the queue. For a brief tempestuous period, Marcus
exercised his eloquence to reach extremities it had never reached
before, and as a climax he climbed the television mast to a height
of three hundred feet, and had me quoting in my heart that this was
the height my soul could reach if only our two souls were up there,
standing up erect and strong. To this day I have a lingering guilt
about having sent him up and let him down.

He broke the law, his enemies said, because he was too terrified
to move. It was up there he discovered that he suffered from vertigo.
Although he was wearing mittens his fingers were frozen to the
struts of the mast. Furious committee members declared he had
brought the protest into disrepute when the police had to request the
fire brigade to get him down. His links with the Language Society
were finally broken when it was revealed that his father's influential
friends had pressed certain establishment buttons and he was let off
with a caution.

A temporary failure does nothing to impair the driving force of
the will. Marcus's desire to make a difference became an article of
faith in the little sanctuary where we two were as closely involved
as two parts of the same body responding to the urge of one will to

manifest itself. We understood no ambition could ever be fulfilled without attaining some kind of a hold on that slippery element so inadequately defined by the word 'Power'. Marcus's will throbbed beneath the surface need for words. I put a lot of effort in helping him compose his speeches. His personal assets were a melodious voice, a pleasing presence, and a repertoire of gestures that conveyed indomitable sincerity. He convinced me that if there was to be a Tory revival, it was vital that he should be a part of it. He had to be at the right place at the right time in order to ensure that this little country of ours would not lose out in the upheavals that were bound to come. It was my loving privilege to help him make a difference.

## II

I sit as still and neat as a flower arrangement reading my book in the departure lounge. I am as early as ever and Marcus as ever is late. He has so much to attend to. It has become his habit to bound up, out of breath, his tongue visible and his eyes glittering with the prospect of some new triumph, as assured of his welcome as any mythological harbinger of another spring and a new beginning. He will have some breathless variant of his humorous membership of the eleventh hour club available on the red tip of his tongue. He puts me on a higher plane in this regard: his dear schoolmistress trained by time tables, above the squalls of ambition that spin him about like a weather vane. I have begun a scrapbook of his activities and achievements and often when he is late he brings with him some new item to add to my collection. At school I have an arrangement with the caretaker's wife that allows me to check on newspapers and magazines before they are dispatched to the wastepaper collection.

He appeared with a young woman on his arm. She holds on even as they stand in front of me and I keep my finger in my place in my book. Marcus is as jovial and as confident as ever.

'Chrissy,' he says to the girl on his arm. 'I want you to meet Llinos. The best friend a chap ever had.'

She is offering me her hand and I can't easily take it because my finger is wedged into my place in my book. What I would have liked best would have been to sit down and carry on reading. But Marcus's wide smile suggests I should be flattered by the introduction and I do my best to respond. My intelligence tells me that

Chrissy is a feather-headed blonde with buck teeth, but Marcus's large eyes are begging me to think of her as an innocent child in need of care and protection and to think of his career.

We fly off together, Marcus and I. We sit next to each other in the economy class. This is life above the clouds, free of the mundane concerns of the earth beneath: duties, obligations, rota and registers. Our bodies are lifted up: why is my heart not lifted as well? I don't really feel well enough to ski. Later in the hotel bedroom at La Clusez, Marcus takes my hand in both his, – which is where my hand always likes to be, – stares soulfully into my eyes and tells me he is going to marry Chrissy. With a sincerity that would break my heart if I allowed it to break, he swears in a husky whisper that this would make no fundamental difference to the beauty of our relationship. I had to believe that. Lord Lychor, Chrissy's father, was not one hundred percent convinced of Marcus's loyalties. In the potentate's eyes, he had a past to live down. And by a tortuous reasoning spelt out by Marcus to which I am obliged to nod my head, those lingering doubts and hesitations would only be dispelled by Marcus marrying Chrissy. Of course things would have to change on the surface. No more holidays together for example. But we could write and telephone to our hearts' content: keep in constant touch, practice private devotions in a code to which the only key lay in the depth of our hearts. In the most practical sense, he would need an intellectual direct line to the wisest and cleverest woman it had ever been his privilege to know and cherish. I knew him better than anyone else; better than he knew himself. I knew how impetuous and impatient he could be: how easily he could get carried away on some quixotic impulse or other. A career was a thing to be nurtured and managed. He would always need me to manage and encourage it. His success would be our joint reward. He smiles and squeezes my hand until I smile too.

## III

My problem as opposed to my pain was how to tell my father. A passion for genealogy had overtaken his interest in second hand books: absorbed it rather. He moved into manuscripts and anti-quarian books and he would go to great lengths to chase up anything that might add to his knowledge of what we had all begun to call laughingly 'The Mystery of the Mostyns'. At sixty he had given up hopes of preferment. He took to cultivating a reputation for eccentricity and declared himself a mystic. This took the form of ritual observances rather than intellectual effort. There were cromlechs to choose to visit on foot, either at sunrise or sunset. He drove my mother to new depths of dejection by becoming a vegetarian and living on a monotonous diet of matzos and milk puddings. His sermons consisted of ever longer quotations that he barely understood and he made the congregation recite the words of hymns instead of singing them. The organist resigned and the bishop set in motion the means of his early retirement.

By chance an opportunity of release from my dilemma occurred and I took it. I was appointed deputy head of Sefton Hall School for Girls in Yorkshire. I informed my father that I had decided to put my own career first instead of marrying Marcus. At least his rage and disappointment was directed at me rather than at Marcus. And I suppose a sufficient fragment of my pride was saved. I did what I could to assemble a fresh attitude for my father. He had to take pleasure in Marcus's burgeoning career from a benevolent distance: and my mother had to believe that the poor boy had married Chrissy Lychor as a consolation for having lost me.

In my new job I allowed myself to be programmed by my duties. They provided a comforting numbness. I was cool in corridors and a degree of detachment added to my authority. After school I relied on a schedule of study of Latin and Greek texts for my own benefit and an amount of sixth form marking in excess, the headmistress told me in the friendliest possible manner of what a deputy headmistress is usually required to do. I caught a glimpse of myself in the mirror one morning and realised with alarm that bordered on horror, that I was beginning to resemble my father both in appearance and in manner: that steady gaze of reserved pride, and the stiff back, that reliance on routine disguised as ceremony.

Agnes Rowlands re-entered my life more or less at her own insistence. Her natural scepticism had been swept aside by an eruption of evangelical religion. I was wary at first that her approach might have been dictated by a concern for my soul rather than the desire to renew old friendship. She was certainly more cheerful than I remembered, married, ordained in the Anglican church, the mother of two small children, and given to outbursts of laughter that seemed meant to reassure, in spite of everything that all was well. She was still intrigued by her own transformation from analytical chemist to married priest.

When I confessed to Agnes that Marcus sometimes travelled up to Yorkshire so that we could spend the best part of chaste weekends polishing his speeches, she told me roundly that I was daft as a brush. This time I didn't take umbrage. I began to temper my chronic infatuation with a trace of detachment. I looked at what had happened and what was happening as though these were events that had taken place in the ancient world. I told Agnes that I had put Marcus in a toga and transferred him to Rome and this made her laugh so much she spilt sherry on her cassock.

Marcus was keen that I should not lose my links with North East Wales. After all it was his power base and there were good reasons why I was suited to serve on quangos connected with education and the arts. I began to attach too much emotional importance to committee meetings and fleeting visits. I was nominated to a sub-committee charged with the preparation of the opening of an Art Gallery extension. This had a special sweetness since Marcus also attended. Making any kind of plans that involved both his voice and mine was a rare pleasure to look forward to. There was a last inspection before the official opening in the late spring. I made a great effort but I arrived late. In the entrance hall I heard Marcus's voice reverberating in the empty gallery.

'So our Lady Ramrod hasn't turned up.'

It was a sharp thrust to realise he was talking about me. Because of my upright carriage and positive walk he called me 'Lady Ramrod' behind my back. For how long had he been doing that? I snatched at the first scrap of comfort. It was a stratagem: a hostile attitude cultivated to provide a cover for out true relationship. Rigid with anxiety I struggled to remember how he assured me that our refined loving friendship remained the guiding star of his career. I needed to know who he was talking to. I crept up and stood trembling behind the half-opened door.

'Bit of a pest to tell you the honest truth,' Marcus was saying. 'I suppose you could say she had a bit of a thing about me. Still has. It can be bloody nerve wracking. On the other hand it has its uses. And of course it keeps Chrissy on her toes.'

That intimate chuckle. All I could see in the crack between the door and the wall was the back of a man wearing a dark overcoat and a bowler hat. It wasn't anyone I knew. This was how he could talk about me to any one. I raised up my arms and pressed my lips against the cold wall to prevent myself from crying out in pain. I felt trapped in my own frame. There could be no escape. With my arms still raised I moved like a wounded insect to the front door. Somehow I reached my little car. I drove back to Sefton Hall and took to my bed. I never told anyone, not even Agnes of the source of my breakdown. It was more fitting that people should think I was overworked and suffering from nervous exhaustion.

## IV

The practice of concealment can penetrate into the depths of one's being. I told Agnes that in bed I had regressed further back than the womb and achieved a consciousness as condensed as an amoeba. But all that was no more than a defensive smoke screen. There were my parents to worry about. My father's compulsory redundancy impending and nowhere in particular to live since they had never owned a house. A career you could say is a course of continued progress until you begin to stumble: and I had stumbled until both my knees were too raw to kneel on.

Agnes came with salves for raw knees. She brandished an advert from a *Higher Education Supplement*.

'Tailor made for you,' she said. 'A classical scholar who is also a woman. Llinos, I said. The moment I set eyes on it. Deputy Warden of Plas Mathwy Centre for Advanced Studies. Only ten miles from my parish. You've got to try for it!'

She pounded the pillow of my bed and helped me fill in the application form. Could I do it? 'Of course you can,' she said. 'Nothing to it.' Enlightened organisation, an awareness of classical heritage, a particular responsibility for the welfare of women researchers and a positive passion for the arts.

Retreat or Advance? The interview restored my self-esteem because the Warden knew about my work on the hexameter in the Annales of Quintus Ennius. To Agnes's immense joy and shouts of I told you so, I got the job.

I was resolved it should be a new beginning, in idyllic surroundings. When I arrived there were circles of daffodils under the tall beech trees and the promise of spring in the air and a pair of buzzards circling over the cottage allocated to the Deputy Warden. I looked out of the window in the half furnished living room and sensed that I could be happy here. The Warden was a civilised man absorbed in the mysteries of the languages of Gaul and Early Britain and fast cars and frequent continental visits. He was more than willing to delegate authority to his deputy. I thought of Marcus's designation and decided to live up to the name. Lady Ramrod divided her attention between her duties, keeping an eye on her ageing parents and cultivating a deeper interest in the arts. At Plas Mathwy there were regular concerts and exhibitions and conferences and Lady Ramrod needed to be knowledgeable and discriminating. And there was an academic world still male dominated to face up to. The price of my authority was eternal vigilance. In those bristling thickets there was no knowing how many Marcuses lurked. There were delectable moments when I could wander through the gardens and the woodland paths and around the lake and imagine myself a great lady for whom all this arcadian elegance had been laid out.

When I first saw him I thought he was one of the gardeners. He was squatting in front of the torso of a dead beech tree. He seemed entranced by the new world growing out of it: fungi, moss, new plants, new homes for insects, small animals, shy birds. He was shy himself. Some kind of pastoral god capable of whispering in sacred groves. He was outlining shapes in the air before he realised that I was watching. He mumbled an explanation. Something about the poetry that lies dormant in the shape and pattern of rooted forms. It was all a mystery. But not, it seemed to me, even in that first instant, as great a mystery as the man himself. I took to him at once. He seemed a being as unworldly and gentle as a tutelar spirit of the wood.

In reality he was Tibor Gale, a research fellow in Sculpture who had the use of the barn on the edge of the estate on a three year tenure. He had emerged from a suburb of Birmingham in the grip of a thirst for nature and art. I was fascinated by his voice and his accent and his gestures and everything he had to say about image making. We seemed to meet by accident and then took walks together. One tree or other would hold our attention. There would be a beech and he would compare the trunk to an elephant's leg in thickness and colour: and the branches he said twisted the air to create patterns of light and shadow that caught in the right moment were as solid as the wood itself. Not to be outdone I measured the girth of an oak by attempting to wrap my arms around it. He stood behind me. I closed my eyes and waited for him to wrap his arms around me.

I don't believe he was aware of his own beauty. When I first saw him naked I wanted to speak but all I could do was tremble in his presence. This was a real man: simple, smooth and finished and sufficient in himself. I realised how inadequate Marcus had been smothered in his petty little ambitions, white and flabby as a plucked chicken. Not that Tibor was without ambition. It took me time to realise how much it consumed him. He spoke of cutting into the void in order to create a fresh connection with the mystery and miracle of the world. Nothing could be more ambitious. It was a case of Jacob wrestling with an angel, only to discover that he was wrestling with himself. What could be more difficult than creating *ex nihilo* and what could be more like a godsend and a blessed gift. He had no need to manipulate and impose his will on other people: he needed all his energy and powers to impose his will on himself.

Of course he was almost ten years younger than myself. Eight years, nine months, and nine days to be exact. It was a case of counting the ways again and not so much the height and depth as the sheer length. The marvellous thing was we could make a joke of it. As an inspired artist in the last decade of the twentieth century there was no need or obligation for him to get married but that is what we decided to do. We wanted it for our different reasons. My dear mother was seriously unwell and I had to contemplate the prospect of looking after my father. He would have expected it. Dyddgu was far away and I was the dutiful daughter who had once worked so hard to please him. What else did I exist for except to darn his thick socks and brush his clothes and make his meals? Patriarchs are never truly reconciled to their daughters growing up. Leaving their service is in itself a misdemeanour. I snatched at my chance to become protective of Tibor. He was my young genius and he wanted me to look after him. He said so. He believed my devotion would revitalise his flagging inspiration. Not that I believed it was flagging. Wood and stone responded to his strength and I was willing to sit and marvel as new images of life emerged from inanimate matter.

## V

Artistic temperament of course he had to have. How could he be an artist without it? There was silence he needed. And isolation. Long walks in the woods without me. Long walks on the hills. Unaccountable absences. He needed despair as a spur. I understood that. I was too ready to understand. I reasoned that if artistic endeavour was so central to his existence I should make it central to mine. *Pictoribus atque poetis / Quid libet audendi semper fuit aequa potestas.* Poets and painters not to mention sculptors have always an equal license in daring invention. I meant it to bring comfort to his struggle. Instead it made him furious and threatening. How dare I quote at him in a language he couldn't understand. How dare I talk so much in any case? I realised my fondness for quotation got on his nerves and it was a pedagogic habit I had to break.

I was unimaginably slow to realise he had a drink problem. There were bottles hidden not only in the barn but also in the woods and hedges and their whereabouts were related to routes he took for his solitary walks. The stuff was there to assuage the dissatisfaction and the disappointment he felt in his own work. There was a sense, I dimly grasped, in which destruction was essential to creation. The frightening thing was the destruction was aimed as much at himself as at his materials. There were moments when I thought I understood. He would stretch out his arms and say 'Is it a bridge or a cross I want to make?' He was burning with questions to which he could not find the answer. I was appalled to realise the extent of the ambition that threatened to engulf him. It was a phenomenon I had never encountered before and I tried to smile when I saw the extent to which it dwarfed Marcus Mostyn's pathetic little manipulations.

I longed to do something to console him. In the silence of the night I could hear the beating of his heart. There was a silence of the day too which he imposed on me. For a whole morning I would move about the cottage engaged more in harvesting a few chosen words which I could venture to offer to him rather than housework. I struggled with concepts like 'extrovert' and 'elemental' and 'affirmation'. Which was it to be? The grand force of self-expression or the monumental confidence of public art? I struggled to crystalise a fluid situation: to formulate his dilemma in sufficiently simple terms that would help him to choose his direction. A moment of inspiration struck when I proposed an exhibition. I would help him organise it. We would choose a date, a deadline and he would work towards it.

For a few weeks we were blissfully happy. As far as I knew he abandoned the bottle. He began to talk at length. It was exciting to see the world through his eyes. Everything new and fresh. He allowed me to share something of his primary love of wood and stone and metal. Every day became an exploration. When I looked at him I felt my own image tremble as though I were looking at myself reflected on the surface of deep water. In the same reflections

I saw the sky darken. Any attempt at a cheerful or encouraging remark and the sky grew darker. At dinner I suggested brightly that if things weren't going so well, we could postpone the opening date. His response was to sweep his plate of food to the floor with the back of his hand and to march out into the night.

At first I felt that if it brought him any comfort I didn't mind him beating me. It was better that he should hit me than cut off his own ear or go screaming mad seeing the world around him dissolve into a cyclone of spirals. Then some atavistic impulse made me start to fight back. For a time Tibor seemed to enjoy this. He was bound to triumph of course, and have me on my knees whimpering for mercy. He enjoyed even more smashing up the kitchen and this presented a range of problems I was not prepared to endure. Before our final encounter, I secreted a lacrosse stick behind the sofa and early in the fight, before he had warmed up I suppose, I delivered a blow to his wrist that more or less broke it. The public explanation was a stone on a shelf in his studio had dropped on his wrist.

## VI

I know it is an exaggeration to say that love and hatred are two sides of the same coin. He was beautiful and I adored him. There were moments when I was so alive to his touch, I was like the string of a bow drawn back ready to fly into some form of ecstasy. I lay helpless, and he hung over me like a hawk that worships its prey before it devours it. Then there were these dark days when he took to crouching like a wounded minotaur in the darkest corner of the barn. Animals don't use metaphors. They lurk inside the cage of their instincts feeding hatred and insecurity on fear. When I bring him food on a tray he hurls anything that comes to hand, a bat, a boot, a chisel, at my defenceless head. However, since it is his left hand, he always misses. I am bold enough to laugh and say he needs more practice. At the same time I am sorry for him. He sits at his work table trying to make a design with his left hand and he looks as beautiful and as pained as a Piero della Francesca St. Sebastian. His verbal abuse most of the time is mumbled as though he half hopes I will ignore it. He is always hungry so I can salve my uneasy conscience by feeding him well.

It was also a time of anxiety about my parents. My mother died as she had lived, as if she were intent on giving me the least amount of trouble. Losing her was like an earth tremor: an external warning of the fundamental instability of all existence. Her lifelong concern was for my father's wellbeing and peace of mind. She was quite willing to die first. By ceasing to exist she facilitated his transfer into one of the best rooms of Archbishop Edwards's Residence for Retired Clergymen. When she had gone I realised for the first time that, sequestered in that sequence of draughty rectory kitchens she had acquired a peace of mind far beyond anything I could hope to attain. I had to adjust myself to a role that would be acceptable in the public domain. The Warden and his wife, Agnes and her husband, the people with whom I was obliged to be in regular contact, committee and quango persons, who mixed with the likes of Marcus Mostyn, would all report that I was an extremely efficient deputy warden married to a handsome but sullen artist younger than herself, and therefore a woman who had a lot to put up with. I had not the slightest wish to be pitied, but I wanted people to know how difficult it would have been under the circumstances for the Deputy Warden to make a home for her retired clergyman father who had his own eccentricities. In public you could tell the Deputy Warden bore her burdens with fortitude. There was no relaxing the straightness of her back or her purposeful gait where each step advanced on the other as if there were a future to conquer and colonise.

## VII

My father is playing chess with the former Suffragan Bishop of the Windward Isles. He is in a good position and he raises his right hand in a greeting which is also a warning that my arrival should not interrupt the game. I have baked him a cake and I take it to his room on the next floor. As I admire the view through his bedroom window I realise that my father is more contented now that I have ever known him. He has made friends with the suffragan bishop and and asthmatic Archdeacon and he is pleased to tell me that he is fitter than either of them and usually beats them at chess. He has special walks in the grounds and he keeps appointments with particular trees. He claims each one of them have something to say to him. I tell him Tibor has broken his wrist. He takes very little interest. He is collaborating with the Archdeacon on a series of essays on the Thirty Nine Articles for the House Magazine that they are pleased to call the *Thirty Nine Steps*. 'Read all about it' my father says so jovially. Late in life he has learnt to chuckle.

I sit in the lounge downstairs while the chess game continues its snail like progress. My father is so scared of losing, his hand hovers for minutes on end above a piece before making a move.

*'Man is of his own nature inclined to evil, so that the flesh lusteth always contrary to the spirit: and therefore in every person born into this world, it deserveth God's wrath and damnation...'*

Ah, so now we know. They meant the flesh of course. The birth-sin. Since you can't be born without flesh it also means us. My father and the suffragan bishop playing chess, Tibor nursing his wrist and trying to make images on paper with his left hand. Are they, to a greater or a lesser degree, forms of concupiscence and sin and therefore of the nature of sin? Oh dear.

'Llinos.'

My father is resting on his bed and munching appreciatively a piece of Dundee cake. I don't know whether or not he intends to share it with his new found friends and fellow clergy.

'Are you still in touch with Marcus Mostyn?'

What a silly question. How do I answer it? Agnes's grinning husband Raymond serves on a quango for tourism and hill farming which Marcus chairs. Raymond seems to think I am dying to know whatever Marcus gets up to. What I wanted to tell him but didn't was a year on a hill farm would kill them both off, the gregarious Raymond, with whom I put up for Agnes's sake and the skinny self absorbed Marcus. So what do I say to my father?

'He's as important as ever,' I said.

My father is oblivious of the sarcasm, absorbed as he is in his own design.

'There must be lots of Mostyns in the world,' my father was saying. 'Like those Scottish clans Americans are always fussing about. I think I could claim to having made a pretty comprehensive survey of the Mostyn pedigree. What I am thinking is why can't your Marcus find the finance to publish my researches? And indeed, publish it in America! There must be dozens of Mostyns all over the place.'

'My Marcus.' That was the moment when I realised the gulf between my father and myself was too wide ever to be bridged. I could have been standing on some barren quayside waving him goodbye, engulfed in my own solitude. As I stood there I became aware of meanings and perceptions making themselves apparent and even more aware of having no one to share them with. At home if I made an effort to speak to my disconsolate husband he made an even greater effort not to listen. I was isolated enough to be transformed from a person into a thing.

## VIII

I brought him vegetable soup and fresh bread. It wasn't exactly bringing forth butter in a lordly dish but I had no intention of hammering a nail into his temple either. It was a peace offering. His wrist was getting better and it was time we talked.

'Bloody Lady Ramrod.'

I almost dropped the tray in my hands. It wasn't his usual mumble. It was as loud and as clear as a church bell.

'Lady bloody Ramrod. I should have ramrodded you and that's a fact. Got away while the going was good. Look what I've got to put up with. A woman twice my age. Old enough to be my mother.'

He relapsed into his usual mutter and I never felt so injured or so helpless. I seemed beset on every side. Where had he heard the name? Who gave it him? How did he know. I was the victim of a conspiracy. It came from Marcus but how was it transmitted? There were devices planted everywhere broadcasting the unpleasant name in a penetrating whisper that I had failed to hear. He used it with such fiendish glee. That suggested he had just heard it. I saw a book on his table about the decline of the democratic ideal. That was Agnes. She brought it. She had been here. She and Raymond. They were all in it together. I fought off a fit of paranoia that was making me shake. At all cost I had to maintain my dignity and self respect. I could not allow my back to bend.

We were in church when I tackled Agnes. It seemed the appropriate place to be. She claimed to have a passion for rood-screens in out of the way parish churches. Agnes was always enthusiastic. Raymond sat in the car well wrapped up. It was a cold autumn day. She was lighting a candle when I asked her.

'Agnes. Did you tell Tibor I was called Lady Ramrod?'

She put the back of her hand to her mouth to stop herself laughing.

'I'm sorry,' she said. 'It sounds such a silly name.'

'Did you tell him?'

I could see in the light of the candle she was blushing.

'Of course I didn't.'

Quite a flat denial. And yet she knew something. It was probably Raymond. He had been standing in the doorway when Agnes took Tibor the book, full as she was of christian sympathy. I could hear Raymond saying it. 'Where's dear Lady Ramrod?' I could see the smile of delight on Tibor's handsome face as he registered the name and saved it up to use against me. In a world of people like this, who could you trust?

## IX

I cannot tell whether or no he regards it as my fault, but Tibor has fallen out of love with wood. He wears a leather band around his wrist and carries an iron-headed hammer in his hand to strengthen his arm. He communicates with me intermittently like an engine that splutters rather than starts. His bottles are still concealed and he appears to have convinced himself he has given up drinking.

'I'm going to begin in the beginning.'

When he feels like making a pronouncement he can speak quite clearly.

'I'm going to start again, thinking with my hands.'

That could only mean intense active silence. He would have nothing to say to me. He has entered into a feverish correspondence with a man called Terry Duden who began as a sculptor in the same year as he did. Duden had given up sculpture to become an architect on the grounds that he needed more space to explore himself. He wanted a monumental presence, he said, and he wanted Tibor to join him to provide his structures with what he termed 'organic decoration'.

'What about nature? What about those frozen presences in wood and stone that Tibor Gale has been sent to uncover? What about seasonal patience and determined pursuit of solid sunlight?'

I am not afraid to taunt him any more. We live like civil neighbours, who can indulge in intermittent communication. We recognise but don't know each other. I have acquired a detachment which is based on the meticulous execution of my duties, a fastidious attention to the neatness of my appearance and a heightened awareness of the true nature of natural justice which I would like to expound at length if only there were someone at hand to listen.

I received an urgent message from my father. A sequence of

cairns were being excavated in the Denbighshire uplands and he had to see them. It was presumed to be a Bronze Age cemetery with an intriguing system of small standing stone circles interwoven with curials. My father as usual had his own theories. He wanted to bring the Bishop of the Windward Isles on the trip. To my relief the Bishop couldn't face it. In between elaborating a thesis about the genetic need for ritual that had persisted among the inhabitants of these islands for at least five millennia and showed no sign of diminishing in the future whatever shape or size technology took, my father was also excavating the personality defects of the Bishop and the Archdeacon. They were too timid he said, and had no talent for leadership. There were also disagreements with the Archdeacon on the true nature of Works of Supererogation (the Fourteenth Article). However he was happy to report that all three of them were equally opposed to the ordination of women. It was such a freakish notion it wasn't even mentioned in the Thirty Nine Articles and my friend Agnes would be better employed in the Salvation Army, for which my father had some regard, or some evangelical sect. He was very tiring to be with and there seemed to be more sheep than stones among the excavations when we reached them. There was a chill breeze blowing but this did nothing to deter my father from chatting away and making his wild exposi- tions. I returned to Plas Mathwy exhausted: to find my husband gone.

X

He must have been planning his flight for some time. There was nothing of his left in the Barn. In my cottage there was a hasty note to the effect that I would be far better off without him. He had gone to Portugal. In the Alentejo, there was a happy combination of marble quarries and a burgeoning demand for luxury holiday homes. These homes and gardens he would help design and embellish. Duden and Gale would be famous yet. 'In any case,' he concluded. 'You withdrew, so I've withdrawn.'

I did not appreciate the full meaning of that sentence until I visited my bank. He had left £50 in our joint account and absconded with the rest which was almost £15,000.

This depressed me. If only he had asked I would have given it him. I had loved him. We had meant something to each other. This was a mean revenge for breaking his wrist. In the end, on what did human relationships rely on? Things were better in the animal world. Sharks didn't eat each other. And there are myriads of them, all shapes and sizes, gliding around two thirds of the earth's surface. Why are humans so intent on making each other miserable? Or is it just me?

I put this to Agnes on one of those useful occasions when the grinning Raymond wasn't tagging along. Of course she knew Tibor had gone for good, but not about the joint account until I told her. She was outraged. She stormed about the room waving her arms. She even shook her fist. I should get Marcus on to him. I needed a good lawyer. I needed justice. Marcus was just the man. When she calmed down I shook my head.

'It's love I want, not justice,' I said. 'What's wrong with me? Why can't I have it?'

I could see Agnes standing in the middle of the room looking at me as though I were the answer to my own question. A helpless, hopeless ultimately stupid creature, crying for the moon, and incapable of standing up for her rights. As soon as it could decently be done she left me to my own miserable devices.

XI

At the end of the month the Warden, rubbing his hands with unconcealed delight, was obliged to attend a conference at Bourg en Bresse concerning the Coligny Calendar. My back was obliged to stiffen. I was in charge. This meant several extra chores including welcoming an incoming seminar on the European Monitory Union. It would be my job after dinner on Friday evening to deliver a cheerful chat on procedures in this establishment, together with a brief lighthearted survey of the history of the house and the gardens. This was a duty the Warden carried out to perfection. He enjoyed doing it. I couldn't say the same for myself but I took pains to prepare and do it as well as I could.

Friday lunchtime I sat alone in the dining hall going over my speech and nibbling a piece of dry toast. I had no appetite and I could almost feel myself getting thinner. Carol and Myra from the kitchen staff were watching me through the serving hatch. They weren't unsympathetic. They knew of my travail and trouble. And whenever I gave them the opportunity they went out of their way to show a special interest in my well-being. They could see now I had eaten nothing. It was Myra, the fat one, no more than twenty years old, who came up to my table and even dared to put a hand on my shoulder.

'Warden,' she said. 'We want to give you something. Carol and me.'

I sighed and looked up at her. She was smiling in the most benign fashion, her eyes almost hidden by her plump cheeks.

'It's Bob,' she said. 'You'll love him. He's a cocker spaniel. Carol's old uncle gave him to us. We're not allowed to keep him. But we thought you'd love him. He's lovely, honestly. As good as gold and ever so loving. Will you take him?'

And I took him. Which is strange because, as I said, I never liked dogs. He's made a difference to my life. We're going to have our photograph taken together. He'll be in my arms.

# GHOSTS AND STRANGERS

## I

For the second time the man on the dusty platform sat down on a bench to change his socks. Perhaps he was as bored as I was. At least he was something to look at as I lurked in the interior of the railway bar. Rowena used to say that I wasn't exactly buzzing with intelligence but I was quite good at observing. It gave me pleasure when she paid me the compliment of taking account of my observations. Even in her last illness she would hold her head to one side and draw all sorts of sharp conclusions from my simple recitals. She said she had little faith in human nature, and that's why she married me. Not for excitement. I was a calm sufficient person who excelled equally in innocence and innocuousness. She always took her time over delivering verdicts and judgements. They were designed to reverberate. Strange how softened is the edge of the voice I can still hear.

It was feasible that the fellow nurtured an interesting obsession with the condition of his feet. I notice a flute peeping out of the side pocket of his capacious blue haversack as he rummages around for a change of socks. I am curious to see his face but not curious enough for me to leave what is left of my drink. It had been hot work marching up to the abbey to admire its massive and austere beauties. I was most intrigued by the ninth century Carolingian chapel so dwarfed by the vastness of the twelfth century structure. From force of habit I amassed details to present to Rowena back home before I remembered she was no longer around to comment on them.

*Go off and educate yourself Gwion. And while you are at it you can infect the world with your innocence. I'm leaving you all my money to do it.*

How old was he? I needed to move at least beyond the broken pin table for a better view. Little else here to observe. Across the tracks an abandoned shunting yard with dry weeds, rusting trucks and a derelict warehouse. *Avoid Florence, she said. It's nothing but a tourist trap.* Seek out gems in out of the way places. This was out of the way alright. A junction had become a terminus and the terminus scheduled for closure. I stumbled here through carefree ignorance. Did he know where he was going as he changed his socks? For lack of a fresh coat of pink paint a Fascist slogan was making a ghostly re-appearance on the station wall: 'Work and Obey'. Rowena would have liked that. I could hear her say it. *Get going, Gwion. You don't need to work or obey any more. I've seen to that.* I really can't get over how much I miss her. She was never all that affectionate, and people used to say behind my back that I was only a servant promoted to third husband. But I knew she liked me and you could say as I wander about spending her money I'm really lost without her. Just lost. Not even a pilgrim in a foreign land

Is he a man accustomed to be noticed or is it my boredom investing him with glamorous attraction? The age could be mid-thirties, determined to remain youthful. The hair straight and dark falling over his eyes. He pushes it back with an angry gesture. He wears a long thin raincoat with a certain careless elegance. A hint of desperation in the quick movements of his head, looking up and down the line. Has he got to the end of his tether as well as the end of the line? Should I go out and engage him in conversation? About the weather. The heat abating and the autumn mist assembling. Over the way a solitary railway worker is burning leaves. He looks listless and redundant. The last train had left. White faces and waving hands vanishing into the distance. Maybe the socks fellow would take out his flute and oblige with a melancholy tune to mingle with encroaching evening mist?

As I watched him he broke out of his trance and he made a move. In the abandoned lethargy of the place this was quite exciting. The female attendant was still asleep in her cubby hole, sheets of newspaper on her lap. He rapped the glass surface of the counter with a coin. I prepared to smile in a friendly manner but he did not notice. I took comfort in my obscurity: a lay figure propped up in a corner, in the kind of seat a local would occupy, merged into comfortable anonymity to watch the passing show. At the moment he was all the passing show there was. Underneath his lightweight raincoat he was wearing linen shorts that reached below his knees. His legs were thin and his feet in trainers looked extra large. The socks were white. I decided he was an Englishman. Ready to be assertive and yet uneasy. There were bags under his eyes which looked prominent and bloodshot. His boyish cheeks were flushed. He drank with unseemly haste and returned to pacing up and down the deserted platform from time to time pushing the hair out of his eyes with the same impatient gesture.

I lacked the imagination to speculate on his origins or his purposes. *Stick to observation* Rowena used to say, *and leave the speculation to me.* He may well have been in some kind of trouble but it was well outside my capacity to guess what. All I could conclude was that he was in an even more self-absorbed state than myself.

I would be better employed attending to my own paltry arrangements.

My base camp as I liked to call it was at the Bellavista, an imposing new establishment on the road to Pienza. All my stuff was there including my modest motor car which lay indisposed in Angelo's garage. With Rowena's money I could have bought a bigger and better one: such an expenditure would have been beside the point. I was in no hurry. All I required was a modest mileage from one place of interest to another. Since I was on my own with time and money on my hands the need to send away for an obsolete engine gasket was part of the enjoyment. I had exhausted the interest of my immediate surroundings within a few days and decided to venture further afield by public transport. I took all the hazards and vicissitudes in my stride. It didn't matter at all that I confused the way to San Galgano with the way to San Antimo. It would have amused Rowena. This decrepit railway bar had nothing more to offer. The time had come to telephone for a taxi. I could enjoy putting my limited Italian to the test.

It proved more complex than I anticipated. At my second attempt for a line I turned in the confined space of the booth to encounter the strained face of the stranger at disconcertingly close quarters. There was anxiety written all over it. And what I took to be hostility to a fumbling bald head of fifty something occupying a space he urgently needed. Before I could speak to him he had marched out of the bar. My linguistic talents secured a taxi from Montalcino. I vacated the booth and retired to my corner to observe his efforts from a discreet distance. They ended in embarrassment. He had insufficient ready cash to pay for his calls at the counter. The female attendant looked stern and unyielding.

I had no desire to impose or intrude. Rowena used to rebuke me for being too eager to please. She said I trotted around like a dog with his tongue hanging out waiting to have his head patted. This stricture was still capable of restraining my unconsidered impulses. *Don't be so ingratiating,* she said. *When you're being nice to people. Don't stand there, hunching your shoulders. You're not ten feet tall.*

'Can I help?'

We were the same height as it happened, and for some odd reason it struck me his face was as long as mine and part of our predicament was that we belonged to the same species. We were both somewhere we did not want to be. And he was caught in a situation that was an affront to his human dignity. There has to be fellow feeling between victims. His humiliation had begun the previous day. In a gravelly voice with an unexpected Yorkshire accent he declared that his pocket had been picked on the number seven trolley bus from the Duomo to San Miniato. By the time he felt for his wallet on the Piazzale Michelangelo the trolley bus had sailed on its way. There was no way he could catch the thief and the best part of his cash and all his credit cards were gone.

'My wife always said Florence was a tourist trap.'

He took little notice of my comment. It did nothing to alleviate the appalling nature of his predicament. All I could do was share his dismay. In order to keep a vital appointment, this very afternoon on this miserable station he had sold his watch and to cap everything the bloody woman hadn't turned up.

'Can you believe it?'

He was looking me straight in the eye and daring me not to. He was a plain blunt Yorkshire man and I was embarrassed with my own uncertainty how to react. I paid his bill as if it were my fault he had no money. Indignation watered his eyes and made them bloodshot. He was ready to hit back at a hostile world.

'Look,' I said. 'I've managed to order a taxi. From Montalcino. No more trains today and one of those lightning strikes tomorrow. If it's any help I can drop you off wherever you like.'

I half expected to hear him say it was very good of me. He didn't. I assumed he was still in the grip of bewildered indignation. He marched back on to the platform as though he still expected a female figure to materialise out of the gathering mist, burnished with the remains of sunlight, murmuring explanations and apologies. He returned to me because there was nothing else to return to.

'There's no point in feeling suicidal,' he said. 'Do you think we could have something to drink?'

What was on offer was little to his taste. He muttered a longing for Guinness but drank like a man in a hurry. He extracted a small note book bent from frequent use. He pointed a stub of pencil at me.

'It's what I owe you,' he said. 'I like to keep a record. It will all be paid back. I like to be strict about these things.'

I waved my hands and said it didn't matter. He insisted and I suspected it relieved him of the burden of repeated gratitude. The intake of alcohol failed to warm us towards each other. He went on at some length about his mother. She was a proud woman. An example of working class nobility. He hadn't a clue who his father was and she'd managed on nothing which was little short of miraculous and had sent him to university although she had no idea about art and the demands of art.

Never mind. He didn't respect her any the less for that. In his own case he had been compelled to put art first and it cost him a hell of a lot. As of this moment. But he had no real choice. To get anywhere in this business you had to fight and you had to make sacrifices. I paid him close attention which, along with a rapid intake of a disturbing mixture of Pastis and Punt e Mes, loosened his tongue.

'What line of business would you be in?'

The measured politeness of my question made him snort a great laugh. With his mouth open I detected a certain wolfish configuration in the teeth of his upper jaw: fangs at each end of his mouth. It was the 'line of business' phrase that amused him; like an exchange between two commercial travellers waiting for a train connection.

'I'm Simon Huff,' he said. 'You won't have heard of me. Although I'm a published poet. I make films as well. Arty films with words and music. And that, if you want to know, is why I'm here.'

He seemed to be waiting for me to treat him with a new degree of respect. He was a poet. I was just a face in the crowd with the crowd missing.

'Business,' he said. 'Sterling word. You could say it was business. Otherwise I wouldn't be seen dead in this god-forsaken hole. Or in Italy if it comes to that. I can't bear the bloody place. I've been lured here. That's what it amounts to. And left high and dry. Left swinging in the breeze.'

His indignation rose in his face like red dye in a thermometer. He was fired with intensity and frustration. I had to steady my ground as the only available target.

'Bloody women,' he said. 'You have to watch out for them all the time. They simper and smile and twitch their heads like polly parrots on a perch, and all the while they're after something. They make a bee-line for poets because they know the poor buggers are suckers for feminine charm. You can never tell what they're up to.'

Of course I thought of Rowena. To be honest I never quite knew what she was up to unless she happened to tell me herself. But it would never have crossed my mind to call her a bloody woman. She was much too wonderful. When I look back I can see that for me she was on a pedestal from the very start. Brisk and robust and curly haired she was in those days. A figure to admire. She would bring the first Lady Pascant into the garden and decide how long she would be allowed to smell the roses. Nurse Rowena was in charge supervising every detail from the kitchen to the bedroom and from the drawing room to the garden. And since I was the head gardener with two young lads to assist me, that included me. Happy innocent days. Nothing to worry about except the weather. When Lady Pascant faded away Nurse Rowena became the second Lady Pascant. To everyone on the staff and in the village it seemed a natural progression. As time went by it became my job to take Lord Pascant out in the old Daimler he was so fond of. Not to mention long walks pushing his wheel chair. I would charge his pipe with the shag he wasn't allowed to smoke in the house. Rowena used to say I was such a help taking him off her hands when there was so much to do. It was an idyllic existence and I was allowed to engage extra help in the garden to make up for the time I had to spend looking after Lord Pascant, and when he died in the end, Rowena said I may as well carry on looking after her. And to do that, Gwion bach, she said, best we get married. After the first shock I was more than happy to oblige, but I have to admit it caused more than a bit of a who-ha and the whole affair is at least as interesting as the trouble Simon Huff wants to unload on me. The difficulty is to decide whether I want to take him into my confidence. They say it brings some relief and even comfort to talk about things. I am not so sure. There are moments, even when I'm travelling, when I feel the tightness of my fate still closing around me. So much has happened there must be more to come. What else does Fate mean? Where do you find a sympathetic listener? I don't think this one qualifies, even if he is a poet.

'They play on their looks you see. You never know where you are with them. You can't help being suspicious. It's the way they do it. Damn it I've only got to think of my mother. She could stitch anybody up if she put her mind to it. Respectable. Chapel-going. Busy Martha. Butter wouldn't melt in her mouth.'

He said he was a poet but none of this sounded very poetic to me. I thought poets looked up to women. On a professional basis you could say. Practiced to sing their praises. I only wish I could have practiced a bit to praise Rowena. All I could do was to grow flowers for her.

'And a fool like me falls for it. She stares into my eyes as if I were the greatest multi-media man since Michelangelo and where do I land up? Here drinking sweet piss with... what's your name? I've got to put it down in my notebook. And your address. I like to be strict about these things.'

'Gwion Roberts,' I said.

I left out the Lloyd that belongs in front of the Roberts. It sounded fine on my grandfather: had a nice ring to it. *The Reverend Griffith Lloyd Roberts M.A.* But Lloyd Roberts never sounded right on me somehow. I didn't even pass the Eleven Plus. I'm quite willing to listen to sermons but I wouldn't have the first idea how to make one. He asked me to spell it.

'Is that Welsh?' he said.

I said I was afraid so.

'That's O.K.,' he said. 'Won't hold it against you.'

His mouth opened wide in one of his loud laughs and I saw his fangs again.

'And some bloody unpronounceable address, I expect,' he said. 'You'll have to spell it for me you know.'

He was taking humorous cognizance of my existence. I would not have been averse to doing the same myself, so that we could join together in jolly saloon-bar laughter. I hesitated because of the latent hostility in his mood. His disappointment was so intense, he was capable of destroying something within easy reach as a more convenient alternative to destroying himself.

'Of no fixed abode,' I said.

The word 'abode' brought our white bungalow above the dunes in south Pembrokeshire floating before my eyes. To avoid scandal and the distant relatives of the Pascant family, Rowena leased the house and the park to the County Council as a residential home for disturbed and unruly children. You could say we emigrated rather than fled to south Pembrokeshire. Ardwyn, our white bungalow in sight of the sea became the cherished base from which we travelled in assiduous pursuit of culture. This tended to revolve around opera houses since Rowena had a notable voice and in her youth had once contemplated a singing career. This also gave direction to her natural benevolence. She paid tuition fees for more than one aspiring singer of Welsh origin. Not that they knew it every time. I remember '*Do good as well as bad by stealth*' as one of her sly, dry jokes.

'I trusted the bitch, and look what's happened!'

I stepped back because the poet was becoming indignant again.

'For all I know she's gone off with that bloody Swede. He was sniffing around her, and he's got money. For all I know she may have found out he was a millionaire. Just the man to put up the money. No need for me. Cut me out.'

## II

Rowena taught me about hotels. How to sit around and wait to be waited on. I got used to them but even when she was there I was never really at ease. I couldn't wait to get back to Ardwyn. I didn't mind at all that we were stuck there for all those months that she was ill. To the very last it was a privilege to look after her. Her smile was the last thing to waste away. Once she had gone I couldn't bear the place. It was where she wasn't. So hotels of one sort of another have now become my natural habitat. The Bellavista is not a place I would have chosen for a prolonged stay: my definition of a prolonged stay is anything over a week. In Brittany I stayed in a sixteenth century manor house for over a month because they were converting a three acre park into a garden and I was interested in the way they worked. An educational programme can't last for ever. It's got to lead somewhere I feel. Waiting for something to happen can't be allowed to become a way of life. Soon now it will be the anniversary of her death. Some new process will have to start. Somehow or other I shall start working again.

Huff had nowhere else to go. The least I could do was put him up for the night at the Bellavista. He was drunk anyway as he fumbled with his little notebook. In the taxi he was mumbling away about a woman I thought he called Delilah. It appeared she was not really Italian. Just a Swiss Jewess from the Finchley Road who fancied making the same noises and gestures. She was a failed actress and semi-academic who couldn't sing and couldn't dance and had the nerve to take up directing. I should have heard of her.

Lilian Trenovo. I got him to enunciate the name clearly without spitting it out.

> In the room the bitches come and go
> Talking of Lilian Tre-no-vo...

He repeated the doggerel and stuck his elbow in my ribs to make me share his amusement. I wondered if he was trying to prove he was a poet.

This Lilian Trenovo. It seems she was an angel and a devil at one and the same time. She had accused him of being full of anarchy and aggression and I have to admit I was forming the same impression myself. He worked himself up and everything was fuck this and fuck that and he didn't seem a bit my idea of a poet. He wanted to make this film-poem about his grandmother being abused in West Yorkshire in the 1920's. She was committed to it. Ready to abandon her part-time university post. This Lilian Trenovo. Together they were leading a crusade against a film business dominated by effing Cockneys longing to be Americans. That's why they were here. To plug into sources of European finance, and the effing bitch had let him down and that's what you got in this world when you tried to mix business with pleasure. He was a poet after all. He wasn't hard enough. And having said that he subsided into an uneasy sleep and left me uneasily awake.

Things would have been so much easier if the poet had been a more congenial companion. He had staggered up to bed in the most boorish fashion leaving me to apologise and explain in basic Italian. It didn't matter really whether he liked me or not. My problem was to know what to do with him. One decision would lead inexorably to another. Rowena's voice had become too faint and distant to tell me what to do. If we got stuck together, how would we get unstuck? Impassivity alone was not enough. I had to maintain a reasonable distance. The only way I could do that would be to disclose a planned itinerary and a sequence of obligations: which was precisely what I did not have. I was not required to be at such and such a place by such and such a time. To have said so would have rung hollow and a gardener may live in a sheltered environment but in practice he acquires little skill in concocting lies.

He was late coming down to breakfast. I had almost finished when he stood blinking in the doorway of the breakfast room taking some time to recognise a man he had only met in a mist. There were two or three balding men breakfasting in the room. From the corner table I was obliged to raise a hand to solve his dilemma. As he joined me he seemed to be smiling upwards into his own eyes.

'It's a funny business feeling guilty,' he said.

At first I took this to be an oblique form of apology. His approach was more philosophical and I listened respectfully.

'We shouldn't need to apologise for existing. I don't think so. My mother didn't, so why should I? You can imagine it, can't you? All that chapel pressure to ask for forgiveness. My grandfather was big chapel in Bigsley. I'm here because I'm here and that means the world is a better place for me being in it.'

That wasn't a conclusion I had ever been able to come to. Not even with Rowena's help. I'd been around for fifty three years stumbling towards the future and never without a certain sense of being superfluous. I was some use looking after Rowena but now she had ceased to exist I was condemned to inquire daily into the purpose of my being.

The poet wasn't much pleased with the food on the table. He mumbled a longing for an English breakfast. If he turned up at home, no matter how unexpectedly his mother would always add black puddings and sausages to the bacon and eggs. That was a definition of home. He had written a poem about it. Very well received too. It was vitally important to keep poetry in touch with everyday life. And the same with film too, if only the bastards would see it. Rooted Regionalism in the end was all. All they could see was an urban mirage of American power and themselves at the centre like sticky spiders in penthouses gloating over an horizon of glittering skyscrapers. He had a great capacity for being disgusted.

He extracted his crumpled notebook from his pocket and laid it on the table, like a talisman on the damask cloth. He seemed to have more faith in the little book than he had in me. His mouth was crammed with the comfort of a bread roll thickly spread with butter and apricot jam.

'I tell you what,' he said. 'Can I ask you a favour?'

I would have loved to say of course he could. There was too much unknown about him for me to say it. It didn't seem to matter anyway. He was already setting out his case.

'There's this wealthy widow, Sylvia Hoffman-Eagle. She owns a bank would you believe it? The plan was to put it all in front of her. Our project. She likes Lilian. Lilian's been to stay with her and they get on, shall we say. But she's never seen me. Now my idea is it's time she did. Lilian or no Lilian. If the project's good, she'll buy it.

And I know it's good. I believe in it. So why shouldn't I be the one to tackle her?'

He was staring at me across the table demanding encouragement. I would like to have given it. I didn't have much else to do. And had the minimum qualification for being a good Samaritan. Enough pennies in my purse to pay for his night's lodging. With an effort I put my benevolence on hold.

'There are some things I have to see about,' I said.

This was true. In the roadside garage Angelo was seeing to the repairs on my motor car. He was someone I had no difficulty in liking. We managed to communicate. His bit of English, my bit of Italian. We enjoyed the process. I told him there was no great hurry and he showed me his little vineyard and the patch of maize and the kiwis and the figs and the olives and the tomatoes and his wife and three little children. The longer he took the more excuse I had to call on them. I told him I was a gardener but he didn't believe me.

'What do you think I am?' I said.

This took a bit of time but we both enjoyed the pantomime.

'A banker,' he said.

I passed my hand over my bald head and we fell about laughing.

There was no need to tell the poet what it was I had to attend to. Is a man a poet because he says so? Little use my feeling he didn't look like one or sound like one. What did I know about the appearance of poets outside an eisteddfod, or the sound of poetry outside the beguiling alliterative click of the strict metres? I was just a gardener with more money than sensibility or sense. If I gave him a lift to visit this wealthy widow where would that take me? I would rather stay around here and get to know Angelo better: lean on a gate like any old countryman taking an interest in his neighbours.

At the garage I found Angelo in a bad mood. There was more work than he could cope with. People were pestering him. My car was ready. He had no time to chat and was in a hurry to be paid. Standing alone in the morning sunlight squinting up at the view of Pienza in the distance I was surprised to discover myself overcome with a sudden desolation. If there was nowhere in particular to go, one place was just as good as another.

## III

I found him on the hotel terrace, scribbling on the back of a menu. He seemed unaware of my presence while he scribbled. When he looked up at me his lips were trembling.

'It's no bloody good,' he said. 'I would be better off making a wax lump and sticking pins into it. The bitch has turned me into a vacuum. That's what it amounts to.'

I sat opposite him and poured myself a cup of coffee. He pushed the menu across inviting me to read what he had written. His writing was awful. Something about the white church that lives in order to embrace fallen women, swallowing the menopause and casting aside cut flowers into a compost heap in the corner of the cemetery... I couldn't help shaking my head.

'I can't make it out,' I said.

'Neither can I,' he said. 'Is it Lilian or my mother? In any case it doesn't bloody well matter because it's no bloody good.'

He held his head in his hands and stared wild-eyed into the middle distance.

'I could have written tum-ti-tums about thrusting a knife into her faithless heart. But what good would that have done me?'

He looked at me, making a stiff effort to take me into account.

'I can just see why she dumped me,' he said. 'I'm such a tactless bugger. I never know how to play my cards right. Those were her very words. At the party in the B.B.C. Club. She was getting on like a house on fire with the Head of Features and Art Films. A big fat sweaty bugger who knew everything about everything. He had a trick of wriggling his fat fingers like a third rate actor playing the Emperor Nero. Twitching at the puppet strings. And he fancied her. And I said so. And that was the end of that. "At least I'm honest" I said to her. And what I got back was "Huff you are nothing but a piss artist absorbed in himself." And that's what I can hear now buzzing in my ear. And she was right to. And there's your reason why she's dumped me. "If you've got more ambition than talent," she said, "You've got a weak hand. And that means you've got to learn to play your cards right." And the fact is I haven't even thanked you. So it all goes to show...'

He looked despondently at the menu card and I felt sorry for him. In a sense we were in the same boat and he was worse off than I was. In which case it would not be inappropriate if we were in the same car.

'I'll take you,' I said. 'We can go now if you like.'

I stretched myself to enjoy being in command of the situation and to enjoy being generous. I was happy to bring him a crumb of comfort. It was good to have a goal in view, however transient. The Villa Hoffman. Was it Argentario or Ansedonia? Both names were scribbled in the little notebook on which his existence seemed to depend.

At the last minute, before we left, he asked to borrow some cash to buy cigarettes. He took out his little book to register the loan even when I told him not to bother. He said he needed some enchanted cigarettes. As we drove towards the Via Cassia I was surprised to see how little interest he took in the Tuscan countryside. He was a poet and there were all sorts of things to look at that could have inspired him. It was plain that he lived well outside my educational mode. He was subdued. He just smoked and sometimes I caught him smiling to himself. He could have been listening to the incomplete poem fermenting in his mind. I became sympathetically inclined to be concerned about what he was thinking instead of the usual treadmill of my own thoughts. I pointed out Radiocofani and Monte Amiata and he nodded out of politeness rather than interest.

'Just a puff of smoke.' he said.

He found the ashtray on the dashboard to stub out his cigarette.

'It was the old girl I must have been thinking about. Not Lilian. You don't get over it all that easily do you? At the crematorium. Seeing your mother going up in a puff of smoke. The question is did she exist to bring me into the world? Of course she did. In which case I exist to bring her back. So why the hell am I moving heaven and earth to make a film about my grandmother?'

I wanted to demonstrate a degree of understanding although I could see he wasn't expecting any answers from me. I assumed it was enough for me to listen.

'On the run, are you?'

His question and his teasing grin bewildered me. Who on earth did he think I was? How did I fit into the fantasies under his hair? Some kind of fugitive – an embezzling bank manager? And in that case how much should I tell him? I had not realised that being a Samaritan would have involved unrolling selections from my past like lengths of cloth being offered for sale in a street market. Since losing Rowena I had become an increasingly private person using money she left me to keep the world at a comfortable arm's length.

' "No fixed abode",' he said. 'I liked that I must say.'

I needed to set a limit to his galloping imagination. Did he think I was some kind of a thief moving from hotel to hotel across a continent and living under a pseudonym?

'My wife died last year,' I said. 'It's taking me a long time to get over it. Not a day passes that I don't miss her.'

In that sense I was on the run. He was taking his time to think about my explanation. Our relationship, if you could call it such, seemed to proceed in fits and starts. I had to wonder why. Were we so totally different? It wouldn't be fair to call him hard and cynical any more than describe me as soft and sentimental. We were just two random specimens from distinct cultural molds and we needed to make an extra effort to begin to understand each other: more than that, to start believing it was worth the effort.

'Was she cremated?' he said.

He didn't seem to consider the question insensitive.

'It was what she wanted,' I said. 'I followed her instructions.'

I could have added I was a man who'd spent most of his life following instructions and tended to be pleased with the fact, if not glory in it, when it referred to my seven years as Rowena's husband. And Lord Pascant was a decent employer too. He used to talk to me as though I were a valued friend. He had a great interest in Hindu religion. He told me about Shiva with a necklace of skulls on his chest and the lingam hanging down. He said as a gardener I should know all about it: the cycle of death and regeneration and nature running its show its own merry way. I used to chauffeur him around and then I used to chauffeur Rowena around and now I seem to be driving this stranger to wherever it was he wanted to go. Still awaiting instructions.

'Here we are,' the poet was saying. 'Two lonely buggers on the road to anywhere. We've got a lot in common.'

This was humorous enough to make him laugh and give me a view of those funny little fangs again. They made me laugh this time. He began to sing in a deliberately harsh voice, 'Two lonely buggers on the road to anywhere' to a tune that was familiar enough for me to join in. His voice grew more rude and raucous and I was alarmed to make out the words he was singing. 'The only good woman is a dead woman.' I don't know about poets but for me as a gardener words are things weighted. They don't just blow away.

It took him some time to realise how disturbed I was by the taste-less words. He went so far as to slap me on the arm.

'It's the way you mean it,' he said. 'My Mum. Your Missus.

That's what I mean.'

We passed a cemetery surrounded by cypresses and a high wall.
For once he took some notice of the landscape.

'There you are, mate,' he said. 'All in their alabaster chambers.
We'll be there soon enough. Nice and peaceful. Meanwhile the
struggle. This is a savage world and there is nowhere more savage
than show business. A poet in show business is a butterfly on a
wheel. That's Lilian for you. Knows it all. A bloody marvellous
woman. Such a combination. Looks like a model still at thirty seven
and a brain like a razor. Looks, brains, knowledge. She's got the lot.
Speaks four languages. What did she see in me? I hear you ask.'

I didn't ask at all. I just listened. Rowena used to say I was a good
listener and I always took it as a compliment.

'A genuine bloody Englishman. That's what she saw in me. A
rough north country diamond, not one of your effete metropolitan
smoothies. Yorkshire through and through. She loved that. All
bones and rocks and skylines. Mill-towns and dark streets and dead
canals and men carved out of the landscape. She loved it all. What
the hell am I going to do without her?'

We subsided into the silence of the bereft. A longing for Rowena
flooded my mind and made it incapable of anything else: a strange
numbing pain that took over my existence. It seemed related to the
noise of the engine, an extra fuel. A strange exercise to be in pursuit
of an unknown quarry. The only comfort was to keep going.

'Mind you, Welshy, a poet should be a poet wherever he is.'

This 'Welshy' meant that he had established his own degree of
relationship with me; cheerful, offhand, involving no obligation
because of the entries in his little book. If it made him feel more
comfortable, I didn't mind.

'With a poet you see, it's what is inside him that counts. The
trick is how to fish it all out. Do you see what I mean?'

As we drove along the narrow tongue of land to Orbetello the
sight of the salt water lagoon gave a fresh impetus to his fishing
theory. I gave him part of my attention as I drove around looking
for somewhere to park while we found somewhere decent for a bite
of lunch. He was still intent on his thesis when I led the way to a
fish restaurant with a view of the sea and the coast and Monte
Argentario filling its share of the horizon.

'The point is, you can't catch a big fish with a stick and a piece
of string. Bits and pieces of poems like flotsam and jetsam you can
pick up on the shore. Very nice. *Objets trouvés* and all that. Deco-

rative. Revealing. Little jewels five words long. But trinkets all the same when you get down to it. What I'm looking for is a structure. A dynamic dramatic shape, an architecture, and that's what I expect film to give me. A net, a frame, to trawl the depths of this ocean in my mind. It's an engine really. And I've got to capture it – take it by storm. There is no other way.'

I felt obliged to give him closer attention. The longer we were together the more insistent his demand for encouragement and support. The Villa Hoffman was on the road to Cosa and we had to retrace our steps across the causeway. Only at the last minute did the poet halt our progress while he entered the price of our meal in his little notebook.

His confidence ebbed visibly as we approached the gates of the imposing Villa Hoffman. I walked eagerly forward ready to study the range of exotic shrubs and flowers that sheltered beyond the walls. The gate for some reason had been left ajar. Had it been closed we would have needed to ring a bell and state our business into a metal speaker before it swung open automatically. I half expected to see and hear great German shepherd dogs bounding forward. Simon Huff hung back overtaken with uncharacteristic hesitancy.

'Lilian,' he said more than once. 'That's the truth of it. It's Lilian that should be here.'

Presuming the degree of intimacy attributable to 'Welshy', I suggested that he went back to the car to pick up his flute. He could play it at the gates and entice the banker's widow out to give us a chatelaine's welcome. This made him cross and more hesitant than ever as he brushed his black hair out of his eyes. I said if he wasn't prepared to be cheerful it would be more appropriate for me to back out of the proceedings and wait for him in the car. He came near to apologising and begged me to stand by him. So much hung on the outcome of this interview.

'Hang on,' he said. 'In case I shit myself.'

He made a stiff attempt at a smile. We advanced along the wide gravel drive until it forked on either side of a squat palm tree. Beyond this we were confronted by a wizened woman leaning on two sticks as though she had planted herself to stand in our way. Under a red headscarf her thin face was distorted with the kind of nervous fury an animal displays in order to frighten off a larger predator. She spat out in Italian.

'Where do you think you're going? How did you get in here?'

42

Simon Huff looked ready to turn tail. I offered an explanation in an innocent voice.

'The gate was open,' I said in my own slow English.

'You have no business to be in here.'

Our apologetic hesitations intensified her fury. Her thin body shook and seemed to twist around the two black sticks that kept it in balance.

'Threatening a defenceless woman.' she said. 'Blackguards. The pair of you. Now get out of here before I call the dogs. Go on. Get out.'

We were ready to obey when a pair of sleek sausage dogs trotted forward, their tongues out and their tails wagging waiting to be petted. They were followed by a large statuesque woman in a flowered dress with yellow hair and a majestic condescending manner.

'Thérèse, my dear. What on earth's the matter?'

'I caught these men wandering around. Intruders...'

At some risk to her balance she raised one black stick to point at us. She was anxious to be commended for her vigilance. She was rewarded with a measure of regal concern expressed in a modulated American accent. Here was a lady of great wealth and assurance.

'Now Thérèse, my dear. Why don't you go and rest. I'm sure it's what you need.'

She gave a deep sigh and transferred her attention to us. The moment she appeared Simon recovered his confidence.

'Mrs. Sylvia Hoffman-Eagle,' he said. 'You know about me. I'm Simon Huff. Lilian Trenovo told you about me. We were coming to see you.'

'Sylvia Hoffman.'

The great lady spoke with effortless calm.

'You can forget the Eagle. You must tell me. Where is dear Lilian? I'm quite longing to see her.'

I became aware of the distance between the warmth of her words and the coolness of their delivery. In the setting of this discreetly sumptuous villa she was a source of power and wealth in excess of anything I had encountered before. This woman could have owned several Pascant Halls without ever being obliged to live in any of them. The structure of this palace incorporated a classical Mediterranean dream. It was the shape of a world of wealth that dwarfed my own. What I owned shrank before my eyes into a modest competence, and this in itself was a pleasant relief. I could carry on being grateful without worrying so much about the responsibility.

We were conducted through a loggia to an inner court yard where a small fountain played sufficiently to catch rays of sunlight. Somebody had trained the bushes of little pink roses that were supposed to flower in every month of the year. Gardening in this climate involved a routine of tasks that I would find unfamiliar. The great lady was taking in my presence like that of a potential employee: bald but healthy in early middle age. I thought she assumed that I was the poet's chauffeur or some other form of loyal retainer. The disabled Thérèse was sent in search of a servant to provide us with English tea. Sylvia Hoffman pondered her departure in order to consider how to proceed.

'Thérèse reads so beautifully,' she said. 'I love to listen to her reading Proust in the evening. And I have a little lamp nearby. In case I need my English crib. I wouldn't want to miss a meaning while listening to the music.'

She had decided to receive us kindly.

'Lilian tells me you are a genius,' Sylvia Hoffman said. 'And I suppose more importantly, she tells me that you are new and different. Now the danger for an aging aesthete like myself is to allow things to go cold. Art I believe should always be infused with the will to live. The desire to take possession of each new generation as it arises. Do you see what I mean?'

From the first I was not included in the conversation. This allowed me to be quietly critical. Sylvia Hoffman's fastidious plea for a reverent revival of artistic endeavour seemed to me no more than an appetite for change in fashion: analogous to the length of skirt in haut couture, up one year down the next. But then who was I, a mere gardener, to judge?

'I have to confess to being exposed to too much art and culture too soon in my life. I was brought up by my grandmother in Fiesole. All those wonderful villas on the hillside and aesthetes peeping out of every hole. And of course I was over-protected. I suppose I still am. I suppose one can stray too far away from nature red in tooth and claw. Are you red in tooth and claw, Mr. Huff? Are you ready to tear your lungs and heart apart?'

His response surprised me. He had become all taste and sensitivity. In a drawing room he showed an abnormal interest in eighteenth century chinese wallpaper. In the large saloon there was a set of white and gold armchairs which Sylvia Hoffman believed had belonged to Napoleon's brother. On the inner wall hung paintings by Italian Futurists that she professed to dislike, but refrained from selling because Boccioni had been a friend of her grandfather. The relationship of artist and patron could be so close and so creative. Simon Huff was delighted to agree with her. He hopped about with the same eager lack of inhibition of a child who brings flowers to curry flavour with a benevolent class teacher. I was surprised that she didn't see through him. Instead she seemed to flourish and grow in the warmth of his admiration. It appeared they could become kindred souls, so acute were his responses to her considered insights. So much devotion to art was something that demanded to be shared. For my own part I lingered in the doorway at my most self-effacing with one foot well apart from the other, as Rowena used to say "ready to run off with the silver". Sylvia Hoffman paused to reappraise my presence. The poet was quick with his explanation.

'My good Samaritan,' he said. 'Gw-something. Welshy. We only met yesterday. I was robbed in Florence and this fellow traveller took me under his wing.'

It was a possible version of events, designed to place the victim of a robbery in the best possible light. No mention of the desolate railway junction or the Lilian that never turned up. It was his affair, and not for me to add anything. I was more than content to appear a benevolent stranger.

Over tea Simon Huff became voluble. He had a thesis and was determined to elaborate it. It was to do with the relationship of film and poetry and initially the great lady was prepared to give him close attention.

'It's the close fit between form and expression. Film moves in the light and poetry moves in the dark. In a dynamic construction they complement each other to such an extent that they raise perception to a new and altogether higher level. Stocks and stones and mill ruins become something greater. A unique combination of architecture, poetry and music. And the ordinary life of a mill girl can be made into a new reality of art...'

Carried away by his enthusiasm he failed to notice that the volume of his harsh voice was bringing a slight crease to the still perfection of Sylvia Hoffman's forehead. He had plans and synopses and preliminary budgets in his haversack in my car that he would love to show her. She brought the torrent of his eloquence to a halt by raising a plump but delicate hand in a restraining gesture.

'Let me out-Samaritan the Samaritan,' she said. 'I am dining with an exiled princess at Porto Ercole so I must take a rest before the ordeal. Why don't you two gentlemen occupy the little guest house at the end of the garden cloister? My staff will see you looked after. And then we can meet at breakfast on the terrace and work out how to contact dear Lilian with the least trouble and the greatest speed. As I told you, I love her very much and I simply can't wait to see her.'

IV

The poet was ready to believe that Sylvia Hoffman-Eagle with all her vast wealth had taken a fancy to him. He was restless with excitement and there was no one else to confide in except me. I had committed myself to taking an interest in his affairs and I was still wondering why. Perhaps because he was all future and it saved me from churning around the stagnant pond of my own past. We were trapped in the guest house like prisoners obliged to share the same cell. The books at the bedside and on the shelves were in at least four languages. I wondered about the value of the paintings and engravings on the pale grey walls. This was of little consequence to Simon Huff. He explored the marble elegance of the rooms, and decanters on a sideboard led him to the hospitality cupboard. He helped himself to a generous whisky in a cut glass tumbler while I was still wondering whether we were intended to.

'I'll tell you something. Hard to believe I know, but I've never seen a woman that reminded me so much of my mother.'

This resemblance was a source of such wonder to him that the glass trembled in his right hand. It could have been some frenzy of poetic licence I had never encountered before.

'A certain nobility,' he said. 'A sort of cold glitter in the eye that defies the world. I remember the look on her face when she hit the insurance man over the head with a scrubbing brush. The calmness of it. It's the same look. There's a sequence there you know I want to capture on film. The mill girl and the red soldier. I can just see it. I can make her understand you know. How you capture the depth in the myth of the region. The way the wind comes in from the stars. The misty hills where the meteorites of the imagination strike and burn.'

I had no idea to what extent he took account of my existence. There were moments when I thought I was a mirror in which he was talking to himself. I had been of use. More actively than any mirror. I had brought him here so that together we had crossed the threshold of his dreams.

'She belongs to that category of woman who have a proper pride in their own natural selves. They don't need the props and supports of social approval. An apparatus of false morals. And they want men who know how to act. Full of vital power. Unafraid and driving forward. Driven by visions. Not afraid to make sacrifices. Women like this claim the right to be adored. And they should have it.'

I adored Rowena. It was a way of putting it. In words everything boils down to ways of putting it and with this strange companion I feel a sudden urge to join in the liturgy. I am just as much a living substance as he is. As my grandfather would have put it our souls are of equal value. I don't know how much notice he would take if I said it was true that I was on the run. He was too absorbed in his own projects to want to hear about my wife and my life. During the night in the quiet of the guest house I could hear his steady snore as I lay awake thinking all over again about Rowena, like a man in a granary sifting through a a great heap of grain to find a missing jewel. This amazing girl from Merthyr who brought mystery and beauty into my life.

She should have been a doctor but she lived at home to look after her widowed father and trained as a nurse in the local hospital. Everything she ever did involved incredible effort. There was a consultant surgeon who tried to take advantage of her and in the end drove her into private nursing. There were dangerous adventures with rich and ancient Arabs and an unhappy time in London, until she arrived like a breath of spring in Pascant Hall. I have the impression sometimes that we blow around like seeds of dandelion clocks until we settle and take root in one favoured place and an accident is transformed into a destiny. This is an idea I could willingly pass on to the sleeping poet. The fact is when he is awake he will be even less inclined to listen.

I am still breathing the breath of scandal. Enough to keep me awake at night still torn between indignation at false accusation and aspects of reality that remain hidden. Hidden where? Deep inside me. In this sense he could well accuse me of being on the run. An army colonel cousin twice removed made a muffled demand for an exhumation. With a calmness that unnerved me Rowena pointed to the item of the will in which Lord Pascant directed his body should be cremated. For me as a gardener the life of the household revolved in a warm atmosphere of affection and I would have wished it to go on for ever. I said as much to Rowena long before we were married and she told me the life of the body like the life of the garden was based on a rhythm of growth and decay. I listened to her like an acolyte at the altar of a goddess of wisdom. I can see her now standing above the steps under the portico of Pascant Hall like a high priestess in front of her temple.

I think the village would have accepted his death and our marriage if Mrs. Ceri Pritchard at the Post Office had not worked so hard at the rumour mill. Ceri Post had the gift of making scandal circulate like a bad smell. Rowena and I had been secret lovers and she had taken steps to hasten his end. Such rubbish. While he was alive I wasn't certain she even liked me. Rowena was determined we should stand our ground and not be driven out. Given time, she said, she could have brought the village to heel. It was the relatives who made it imperative we should get away. The army colonel claimed he was gathering evidence of rich Arabs who had died in her care: which was ridiculous. As Rowena said, being rich never stopped anybody dying. A consultation with Jacob George the solicitor and Dr. Price the Chairman of the County Council, and she outwitted the distant Pascants and we were able to leave with the bulk of Lord Pascant's fortune intact. I'll never forget the way she laughed as we drove down to the white bungalow in south Pembrokeshire. '*You're a man of means, Gwion Roberts, whether you like it or not.*'

I was slow to come to like it. It was the price to pay for the joy of being with Rowena. Her affection for me was a fuel that gave me the power to work twice as hard. What better aim in life than to please her. And she loved being pleased and pleasured. *It's no sin to be happy Gwion,* she would say. *No sin at all.* Even now I can feel the touch of her hand on my bald head as she patted it. It was more than a reward. And she was still doing it on her death bed. She taught me how to inject her arm with the comfort of morphine and tapped my head as I did it. She smiled at me from her pillow as I massaged her feet with white cream. It seemed ironic to her, and yet just, that I should be nursing her with the same devotion that she had nursed others, especially the first Lady Pascant and Lord Pascant himself. It was all a process she seemed to be saying and I had to learn to accept it like the falling of the leaves.

## V

Simon Huff was quite radiant as we took breakfast on the terrace:
croissants, cheese, fruit, coffee and rolls served by a uniformed
servant wearing white gloves. We had a view of the blue Mediter-
ranean through the pine trees and a small island lying south of
Monte Argentario. He waved his hands about and said the hills
were all olives and vines and pines as though it was all a hymn to
his poetic powers. I supposed a man is a poet if he claims to be
one, but the most he could utter apart from waving his hands, was
to repeat 'It is lovely. You have to admit it,' as though I had dared
to assert anything to the contrary. He had slept so well and I had
slept so badly. I had begun to consider again how and when I could
decently detach myself from his company. I wanted to bring back
to mind some of the things Lord Pascant had told me when we
went out on our drives. Somewhere above the bay at Porthdinllaen
he had tried to explain the eastern idea of the transmigration of
souls. The suffering inflicted in one life must have its expiation in
another. He had a light tenor voice that was easily carried away on
the breezy headland and I had to strain my ears to catch the words
that I only partially understood.

Could it be that Rowena's soul had drifted as easily as a breath
of warm Mediterranean air into another body? Would that body be
near or far? As near as the poet tucking into his breakfast across the
table? How easily we are misled and deceived in our condition of
imperfect knowledge. I asked Lord Pascant if he really believed this
theory and he said it wasn't a theory: it was a very nice myth that
reflected a useful notion of eternal justice. Rowena used to say he
was a great one for teasing in that light voice of his. Even at the
very end when he ordered her to put him to sleep. Just as she
ordered me to do the same for her. The beauty of this place saddens
me with the notion of sequences of sin and suffering and I wish
Simon Huff would not chuckle so much and rub his hands together.

The tapping of Thérèse's two sticks made me turn around in my
seat. The previous afternoon at tea, Sylvia Hoffman-Eagle had told
us more about her.

Thérèse had been a prima ballerina until she was struck down
with osteoporosis after a calamitous fall, dancing at a festival. She
had borne her misfortune with extraordinary fortitude and expressed
herself now by a form of disciplined devotion to the Villa Hoffman
and its owner. She stood before us to command our attention.

'Gentlemen,' she said. 'Dona Sylvia wishes you to forgive her but she is unable to bid you goodbye before you leave.'

She was enjoying the consternation on Simon Huff's face as she delivered the message. It meant very little to me. This visit was an accident that had happened and come to an end. For the poet it looked like a dream shattered. The crippled ballerina with a wave of the letter in her hand had brought down a cloud capped tower of expectations.

'She wishes you to deliver this letter to Lilian Trenovo. You are to understand that it is urgent and should be delivered as soon as possible.'

Simon screwed up his face as he looked at the sealed envelope in his hand.

There was a coat of arms involving an eagle embellishing the left hand corner.

'You see the address – International D.H. Lawrence Conference, Ameglia. Not so very far away. Very nice for English poets.'

She turned away before he could ask any more questions. He was as helpless as a hero in a legend, dismissed from the court of the Lady of the Fountain with yet another impossible task to perform. He was cursing to himself.

'How the hell do I get there? And where the hell is it?'

They were questions I was no longer interested in answering. It was time for me to make plans of my own. I could return to the Bellavista and resume the vague plan I had of touring the gardens of Italy. It would be interesting to cross to the Adriatic via Chiusi and Assisi and visit those two spectacular Renaissance gardens at Pesaro. I had two guide books in the car and it would be pleasant to find some shady spot where I could park and take my time to consult them. Melancholy thoughts were easier kept at bay by motoring alone through a landscape embellished with vineyards and olive groves and cypress trees like graceful sentinels in the golden light.

'Welshy.'

My pleasant thoughts of freedom were interrupted by a cry of desperation in a Yorkshire accent.

'I don't know about you, Welshy, but I'm bloody stumped and that's for sure. I'd thought we'd got it on a plate.'

The tone of voice suggested that I was supposed to be as disappointed as he was. If I could have compelled myself to be as forthright as he was proud to be, I could have said, 'Mate,' or 'Brother,' or 'Pride of Bigsby,' 'all this has got bugger all to do with me.' Thoughts were one thing. Speech taking shape was another. All I did was raise my shoulders in the manner that was so common in this part of the world. It went with a phrase that I was quite accustomed to hearing '*Ma...Come si fa?*'

'Oh hell,' the poet said. 'Do I have to go on my knees?'

I made no response except in a preliminary way to harden my heart.

'Look,' he said. 'I'm sorry. I know I haven't taken you sufficiently into account. I've been absorbed in my own troubles. All I can do is appeal. Beg, I suppose. The fact is I'm an artist. Maybe a great artist. You have to take that on trust. Just as I have to myself, for God's sake. But you can't have art on any other terms. It's either an act of faith or a great big con. Is this going to be my punishment for my pride or a reward for my persistence? Take me as far as this place – this Ameglia. Just help me that far. Help me'

I softened faster than I could harden. Within less than an hour we were driving north.

## VI

A strange business being a poet. I wanted to ask him about it, frankly without being hostile. Did it mean for example that nothing on earth could make him be as interested in me as he was in himself? All this business of fishing into the depths of his subconscious: did that require a degree of concentration that blotted out the external world? Here we were bowling along the Via Aurelia and there really wasn't all that much to look at. It all only meant something if you swallowed the centuries that went with it. If there was a plot for an opera lurking somewhere in the ruins then Rowena would absorb the whole package from the Rape of Lucrece to the Second World War. I never intruded too closely on the territory of her dreams but I knew she could still feel it possible to learn great dramatic roles and appear on a brightly lit stage.

'So you were a gardener then?'

He was making an effort to interest himself in my existence.

'Aye.'

It was a fact that did not inspire much curiosity. He didn't wonder how the gardener came to be driving around Italy all by himself and I didn't feel inclined to enlighten him.

'My Uncle Tom was a gardener.'

He had achieved a connection by relating the occupation to himself. I inclined an ear towards him as a reward for the effort he had made.

'He worked in the gardens at Huffton Hall for thirty years. Bloody good gardener. Everyone said so. And do you know, when he retired they wouldn't let him keep his spade. He had to check it in. The mean buggers. The blade of that spade shone like Excalibur. I wrote a poem about it. He used to spend hours in his allotment. My mother used to send me there for carrots and onions. His hut was so tidy. They found him dead in there a week before Christmas. There was hoar frost all over him like a shroud.'

At least the poem meant he had some sympathy for the old gardener. The unpleasant alternative would be that the gardener's misery existed to provide him with a poem. Rowena used to say that most artists were egotists and only if their work was good could the price be worth paying. At the moment, in the case of Simon Huff, I was the one paying the price: but since it was small, I had nothing else to spend it on. I might as well do the spending with a measure of good will.

He opened the glove compartment to extract the letter addressed to Lilian Trenovo. The crest and the length of the envelope made it look important.

'I'll have to open this, you know,' he said. 'It's the only way I'll find out what they're up to.'

He smelt the envelope.

'Bloody women.' he said. 'You can never tell what they're up to.'

This was a theme he seemed to turn to whenever things didn't turn out to his liking.

'They can be kind, of course, and generous. But they haven't a clue about right and wrong.'

I couldn't help thinking about Rowena. She was kindness and generosity itself. If she had it in such abundance, right and wrong were no more than dust in the balance. In any case it didn't seem to me right and proper for him to open a letter addressed to someone else.

'That awful sister of hers is moving about somewhere in the shadows. I can just feel it.'

He could see me frowning and decided to take me further into his confidence. I had to appreciate that this was no small privilege.

'Joyce the agent crouching in that nasty little office of hers off Soho Square. Lilian listens to her. I can't think why. A dyke if I ever saw one. Joyce I mean. Lilian listens to her big sister who knows everybody and everything and smokes cigarettes all day and tries to look wiser than an owl in those ridiculous monster specs. You see that's Lilian's trouble.'

He raised the envelope to draw my attention to the address.

'She wants the best of both worlds. To put it crudely, show business and academia. She wants to keep a feet in both camps. I keep telling her she's got to get out of it. Drag her feet out of the academic slime before it turns into concrete. She agrees of course, in one breath. Then what does she do? Attends this creepy conference. And why? Because her Swedish millionaire has written a footling book called *The European Lawrence*. She's there with him simpering away at professors and research students from Vladivostok to Valparaiso telling them how important Erik-with-a-k's bloody book is.'

He had worked himself into a sufficient state of indignation to allow him to open the envelope. As he unfolded the letter a cheque fell into his lap. He gazed at it in wonder.

'Bloody hell,' he said. 'Look at this. A cheque for twenty thousand dollars made out to Lilian Trenovo. Bloody hell.'

It took him a little while to transfer his attention from the cheque to the letter. Its contents gave him no pleasure. He groaned aloud.

'Oh God, I should have guessed it. Sylvia on her hill of gold. She's a dyke too. Listen to this... "...interesting your Yorkshire rough diamond, but he does need some cosmopolitan polish doesn't he, my dearest... If you think it wise you can tell Joyce that any project you are fully committed to I would be prepared to back..." My God I can see through it all. It's a dyke's conspiracy! You can see what's happening can't you? I'm a working class boy being victimised by these rich dilettantes.'

He was desperately in need of sympathy but the volume of traffic between Livorno and Pisa demanded my closest attention. It did occur to me at intervals that I was being put to considerable trouble and inconvenience by a stranger of less that three days acquaintance. He had taken to muttering as he took off his socks to massage his feet with what I considered was exaggerated concern. They looked in perfect condition to me.

'I thought she was something substantial. A big woman in every sense of the word. Like my mother. Essentially genuine and generous. And she turns out to be a bloody dyke. I should have guessed it. She had that way of looking at men as if they were made of papier maché.'

In order to concentrate on my driving I made an effort to shut out the grinding of his voice. He resented my not listening to him with full attention.

'You're a working class boy,' he said. 'You must be if you were a gardener. You're Welsh aren't you? All the Welsh are supposed to be working class.'

He spoke as though he had the whole world scanned and summed up and it irritated me.

'As it happens', I said. 'My wife was the second Lady Pascant before I married her. Not that I've got anything against the working class, for goodness sake.'

In contrast to his white feet his face was flushed and his eyes were bloodshot with his repressed anger. He had no one to hit out against except me.

'What happened to the first Lady Pascant? Did she poison her?'

He thought this was funny and his mouth opened wide as he laughed. Everything to do with anybody else was a subject for mirth: it was only himself and his poetic ambitions that he was prepared to take seriously. There was little point in talking to him.

'There were evil tongues that tried to say as much.'

I made an effort to sound detached. What I inferred was that his silly remarks belonged with a compost of gossip any decent person would know was beneath serious notice.

'Probably true then.'

He was massaging his feet again as he spoke. I was outraged. I took the first turning off the Via Aurelia and pulled up under a row of pine trees.

'Get out,' I said. 'Get out. I'm not having you in my car any longer.'

Huff's mouth hung open in astonishment.

'What the hell's the matter?' he said. 'What's got into you?'

I couldn't be bothered to think of anything to say. I leaned over him to open the passenger door and pushed him out. There was no resistance. His body was soft and relaxed and my attack was so unexpected. I slammed the door shut and drove off laughing and chuckling to myself like a football fan whose team had just won a notable victory.

## VII

If it was a victory. Like all victories it was shortlived. I would injure myself before thinking badly of Rowena. The way of a servant is never to inquire too closely into the conduct of a mistress; only to hover at a respectful distance ever ready with service. And now by taking action to defend her honour I have committed a crime myself: attacking a defenceless man and leaving him barefoot on the roadside. I had attacked him for disturbing my peace of mind. And what did that consist of? A numbness of forgetting that I conveniently called boredom, to be alleviated by wandering around Italy looking at gardens, churches, palaces and museums and feeling soothingly sorry for my solitude.

On the floor in front of the passenger seat the envelope, the letter and the cheque lay like separate pieces of evidence. It looked as though I had robbed him and left him to perish. I picked up the envelope and looked at the name and the address in case they offered some solution. This was the girl/woman who should have met him at the desolate junction below San Antimo. It was her cheque, her letter, her property, and I had no business to be in possession of her things. No business at all. To dispose of these effects in the way I had disposed of him would be to commit yet another crime. I was conscious of the basic morality that had been drummed into me from my earliest childhood. The structure we understood to be at the basis of the life of a civilised community. There were other sins that could be committed but caused less disturbance if they were well hidden. There was a curious ticking in my head. It took me some time to recognise it was the sound of my conscience more than ready to undermine my resolve from within.

I found him nursing his knees under a pine tree. Had we been on better terms and if I could have managed the verse in English I would have told him he looked like Jonah sulking under his castor-oil plant. He was studying his bare feet with stiff resignation.

'I wasn't going to move,' he said. 'Whether I died on the spot or the police came to get me it didn't bloody matter. I'm pretty well finished anyway.'

I determined not to feel sorry for him. I explained I had only come back because his property was in my car. In any case I needed petrol and there was an Aggip a few kilometres down the road. As I filled the tank he came out of the car to read the meter and enter the sum in his battered notebook. It was so futile and unnecessary: a piece of pathetic pride. In spite of myself I felt a twinge of sympathy for the awkward creature.

It seemed as we continued our journey that we were strangers again, as we had been in the railway bar. We sat side by side, but the distance between us was as great as it could be between two wandering creatures on either side of an empty planet.

My own thoughts placed me petrified outside the French windows of the room where the first Lady Pascant slept to avoid the fatigue of climbing the stairs. Lord Pascant called her 'Jeanie' and treated her like precious porcelain. Her pacemaker made a noise in the night so they had long slept in separate rooms: but her illness had the effect of preserving a strange semblance of her youthful beauty. I had brought her a bunch of red carnations from the greenhouse. She smiled at me, polite and distant as ever.

'I don't want to die, Roberts,' she said. 'I really don't.'

She didn't expect me to say anything. All I had to do was put the flowers in a vase where she could see them while her cheek rested on the soft pillow. I tried and failed to calculate how many days passed between that cold moment and the day she died.

It was part of my job to listen to Lord Pascant talking calmly about death. Not that he could talk in any other way. He was always calm and even tempered and I could hear his thin tenor at some distance in the quiet of the garden. Did he really order her to put him to sleep or did he just acquiesce in the process? I hear him say he disapproved of suicide. He said it would never do because it meant exerting the will, not doing away with it. *Peace and Tranquillity, Roberts*, he used to say, *come from a denial of the will*. I was quite ready to accept that. As a servant trained to obey it was easy for me. But he was more or less saying that salvation came in one way or another from the suppression of the will and I was not so sure about that. And here I am now free to do more or less as I like and what I am driven to is going over and over the past in search of a needle of knowledge that would somehow stitch it all together with a thread of meaning. I seem to have too much will at my disposal and a negative equity of knowledge.

At the first opportunity I would dump Simon Huff at the door of the D.H. Lawrence International Conference, and go on my way. If only I could dump my unworthy suspicion with him. Lord Pascant may have submitted: but Jeanie didn't want to die. Ill as she was she wanted to linger inside life as long as she could: so who was entitled to terminate what feeble life she had left? And what had that nasty Colonel hinted about Arabs in Rowena's care? The wealth at my disposal was of the exact back-breaking weight as the torment of suspicion. How else could a casual remark, a spiteful joke, so easily prick my skin? I gripped the steering wheel and looked around at the landscape like a man searching for a means of escape.

Our road led through chestnut woods turning colour. The beauty of the scene left little impression on Huff, and I made no comment. Out of sight of the sea we were moving from tourism and what was left of fishing, through the vineyards and farms of the inland villages. We drove into the piazza at Ameglia and almost the first thing that caught my eye was a yellow sign stuck on a pillar of the town hall with black print in English, and an arrow pointing the way to the International Conference in the castle on the hill. Huff begged me to stop when he saw it. I pulled up outside the Town Hall. He was shaking his head.

'You were quite right to shove me out,' he said.

He lowered his head and screwed up his eyes and I knew it was an awkward confession to make.

'I was always too demanding.'

He was finding fault with himself. I listened, transfixed.

'I did a bit of thinking under those pine trees. More than a bit. I won't say my whole life flashed in front of my eyes, but some things stood out crystal clear. Number one. I don't wield any thunderbolts. I thought I did, but I don't. I'm a bloody sight smaller than I thought. It's complicated really. We were in love, whatever that means. There was a dream there. For those few days in Haworth we lived for each other inside each other. And then the power-game took over. Some bugger had put it in my head that you had to subdue a woman. Because power was the ultimate aphrodisiac and power in the end has got to mean the power of life and death. I wanted her to give up everything for me. Bloody rubbish. And that's why she didn't turn up. She was in flight from my attempt to overpower her. It's all so bloody simple and I didn't see it until I sat bare-footed under those pine trees. I've got a lot more thinking to do. So I have to ask you to take pity on me. Just this last time. Will you take that woman's letter to her? I don't think I could bear to let her see me in this condition.'

I looked at him closely and he didn't seem changed in any way; the same boyish gesture pushing his hair out of his eyes. We have to be grateful that we have no means of viewing inside each other: the display of inner turmoil would drive the entire species mad.

From below, the castle on its bluff of rock looked dark and forbidding. I knew from my guide books that this area had been frontier territory between the Genoese and the Pisans in the middle ages, not to mention the Florentines, and this accounted for so many fortifications. Rowena would have been thrilled with this aspect, approaching from the west and the dark tower on the hill. It was like a backdrop for one of her operas, all about love and power struggles, jealousy killings and suicides. I remembered how tense she could become in her seat when some tormented heroine belted out her aria. It always meant so much more to her than it meant to me and that was why she spent so much time trying to educate me. This place would turn out to be a college rather than a castle and I was filled with more nervousness than curiosity.

*Knowledge is power Gwion bach* she used to say, squeezing my hand as we came down the steps from yet another opera house. I was just happy to have her in that exultant state.

## VIII

The brooding aspect of the castle had been misleading. Once the road wound around the hill, a new approach revealed an eighteenth century facade. Wealth stood back to back with medieval security. In front of the steps that led to the entrance hall an elderly gardener was on his knees scraping out weeds between the paving stones. His smile showed most of his teeth were missing. With his trowel he pointed to an area where I could park my car. I was cross with myself for being so nervous. I had a legitimate errand. I was doing everyone concerned a favour.

The interior was yet another surprise. The castle was an international centre for European studies owned by a consortium of Mid-Western American Universities. Courses came and went, lasting anything from a week-end to a month. The reception area glittered with geometrical precision in chrome and glass inside the stately expanse of the baroque hall. There seemed to be no one about. Somewhere in the interior a piano was being played with dramatic urgency as if the notes were cascading from a high ceiling. The music said there was action here, of a kind, and sooner or later I would be part of it. This was a palace of many rooms. Near the deserted reception desk an electronic indicator announced the lectures on D.H. Lawrence were in the Scorzini room on the second floor. A course on music and the arts as instruments of social change had finished; and another on the function and future of Museums was due to start the following week. I could only shuffle about looking at paintings and isolated statues feeling ignorant and inadequate and waiting to be taken notice of. I was too timid to penetrate into the interior without permission and specific directions.

'Hi!'

A welcoming female voice with an unmistakable American intonation ended on an inquiring note.

'Can I help you?'

I was uncertain of the direction from which the greeting might have come. There was an echo on it and I traced it to a small neat woman standing on the wide staircase. When I moved closer I saw I was being greeted by a Japanese-American.

'Hi. I'm Susan Nimoto. I'm the deputy programme director. How can I help you?'

Her manner was so gracious it allowed me to relax. I was better able to take in the complexity of my surroundings. This was a gentle form of cultural colonisation. I was glad to see it for myself. When we left Ansedonia, Huff fulminated against what he called the American cultural take-over. He tapped Sylvia Hoffman-Eagle's letter and ranted on about the international distribution of crystalised cultural fruits wrapped in sanitised American cellophane. What the hell has it got to do with Nottingham? Since he wasn't here, galloping up and down the stairs, perhaps I could see for myself. Rowena had presented me with the means and the time to understand how the meaning of a place like this could stretch from Pisa to Omaha, Nebraska.

With a confidence that surprised myself I explained that I was looking for Lilian Trenovo. I could have handed over the letter and escaped, but I had a mounting curiosity to satisfy.

'Well now,' the deputy director said with unmistakably polite concern. 'The Lawrence Conference wound up this morning. But Lilian has stayed on to finish an essay for the *North Western Review*. I think you'll find her in the library. But you don't know where the library is do you?'

I said I was afraid I didn't.

'Let me show you the way.'

I said I was sorry to put her to so much trouble and she said it was no trouble at all. Our politenesses echoed down a complex of dark corridors until we were confronted with an ornate door flanked by bookshelves from floor to ceiling. With a grace that was both Oriental and American, Miss Nomoto pointed briefly at the door and invited me to enter. She even bowed before she withdrew, perfectly prepared to trust me to my own devices.

At the far end of a curved polished table a young woman sat in a pool of golden light. She was absorbed in writing. In the brightness I could see how smartly dressed she was, beautiful and as ornate in her own way as the gleaming two tiered library of which she was the sole studious occupant. She could herself have been the subject of a painting that a man could be content to stand and gaze at. She was startled when she raised her head to see a stranger watching her from the end of the long table. Instinctively her hand reached out for a book and I recognized the gesture of someone attempting to conceal the true nature of her work. As I came closer I realised how heavily made-up she was. Dark lipstick accentuated the circle of surprise her mouth made. The nails of the fingers dragging the fat volume close enough to conceal her work, were long and painted mother-of-pearl. Her agitation broke up the tranquil painting I had been looking at.

'Miss Trenovo. I have a letter for you from Sylvia Hoffman-Eagle.'

'Good Lord!'

I had to appreciate that my presence was a shock. I wasn't sure whether it was my message or my accent that surprised her most. Among the pillars and the chandeliers and the rows of books on the beautifully carved shelving, she was confronted by a clumsy bald-headed countryman of some obsolete variety: and yet he brought her a missive from a notable source of wealth and sophistication. There was much to be accounted for. In the silence of the library I could almost hear the speed of her mental adjustments. The letter, when she opened it, did not explain the situation. When she saw the cheque she replaced it quickly and gave the envelope a small push as if to distance herself from the contents.

'Who are you then?'

The question in an upper-class English voice was put in a cool but friendly manner. Lilian Trenovo had a winning smile. She seemed well aware of her own charms. She widened her large lustrous eyes and raised a hand to touch her dark abundant hair. She wasn't a type Rowena would ever approve of: too much make-up and concern for jewellery and fashionable clothes. All the same

I found myself liking the clear treble of her way of talking. She appeared ready to see the amusing side of all the explaining that had to be done. I couldn't really claim to be a friend of Simon Huff's. The nature of our relationship might be accidental; but it was too complex to encapsulate in a couple of sentences. As I stood in front of her, our encounter seemed fleetingly as complex a web as life itself. All I could offer was that I was with Simon Huff.

'Oh God,' she said. 'I feel so guilty about him.'

As well she might. At this moment he was crouched over a capuccino in La Baraccia on the piazza, too demoralised to move. And this was the woman he had hoped to subdue.

'Poor Simon. I really do feel guilty. Are you Welsh?'

'Of course I am.'

'Well there you are,' she said. 'You know all about it, don't you?'

She laughed, totally unaware of the raw spot she had touched. How could she be? She was still smiling so that I shouldn't take offence. There was a trace of lipstick on her teeth. But she meant well. A woman so girlishly positive and playful. How could she know what 'guilty' really meant?

'I'm only an East End Jewess pretending to be an Italian. So you can just imagine. I'm twitching with guilt of one sort or another from morning till night!'

She was resolutely jolly in an upper class English mode that had little to do with the East End or Italy: too perfect to be guilty of anything. The mode was theatrical and it went with extravagant gestures and high pitched laughter and nothing much that Rowena would approve of. She was all make-up and performance: I could see that. The things she said came out like recitations spoken at one remove from reality: but the noise was pleasant. She was a more agreeable person to be with than Simon Huff. She assumed I was his friend and hurried to take me into her confidence.

'I'm going to get my excuses in first whatever happens;' she said. 'Why don't you sit down and let me let you into a deep dark secret.'

We were quite alone in the library but she lowered her voice to give it a further degree of dramatic intensity.

'I'm not writing an essay at all. I'm writing a script. A film script.'

She was smiling at me acknowledging her naughtiness. I was to understand the innocence of the deception.

'And this of course is the ideal place to do it. I'm sure they won't mind in the end.'

The Conference Centre would forgive her because she was innocent and charming and imbued with the best creative intentions.

'Just look at this.'

I had to reach right down the table to pick up the old postcard she had thrust towards me.

'It's such a lovely story really.'

Her voice reverberated with sincerity and wonder. Anyone with the slightest glimmer of imagination would have to agree with her. The card was an old panoramic view marked Golfo de la Spezia.

'My poor old dad was potty about D.H. Lawrence. Can't think why, unless it was an inadequate sex life. He was no great reader. A little Swiss Jew in the silk business. But he spent one momentous holiday in Lerici when he should have been in Lucca on business, buying a consignment of fezes for the Egyptian market. One day he tramped over the rocks to Fiascherino and started talking to an old fisherman. This was way back in the fifties. It turned out that Lawrence had been the witness of the old boy's wedding all those long years ago. In 1914. Before the Great War. So my dear old dad got him to write it all down on the back of that postcard. The whole story of the wedding and how Frieda baked him a cake.'

I tried to take an intelligent interest. In truth it all meant very little to me. She was demonstrating enthusiasm and out of politeness I did my best to respond.

'My sister Joyce nabbed the card with the rest of his Lawrence memorabilia when Daddy died. When I came across it, it was like a flash of inspiration. What a film to make. About the run-aways making their first home in this pink cottage right on the edge of the sea. But it's the way I treat it!'

Her concept filled her with triumph.

'You won't pinch my idea, will you, if I tell you about it?'

As if I would or could. All I was doing was trying to show polite interest.

'They are ghosts. The English poet and the German woman. In my film. And so are their families. The Lawrences and the Richthofens. And so is my old dad. The little silk merchant clambering over the rocks in his patent-leather shoes and getting lost among the myrtles and the wild olives.'

I studied the old fisherman's childlike handwriting and I was pleased that I could understand the Italian. It was in its way a fragment of history and I could at least sympathise with her enthusiasm. It had belonged to her father and therefore it was a part of her past. Lord Pascant said the world inside our heads we share with ghosts.

*And it belongs as much to them, Roberts, as it does to us.* I listened but
I don't think I ever believed it. Now it felt like an uncomfortable
truth emanating from a disquieting source.

'So we've got to make him understand, haven't we?'

She was being charming again and appealing for my support.
When I had no idea why she should need it.

'How could I give this up for a piece of Simon's Yorkshire
pudding?'

She began to giggle and then disapproved of herself by clapping
a hand over her mouth. Without knowing why I was beginning to
lose my sympathy for her. She should have remained that intrigu-
ing seated figure in the painting I saw from the door of the library.

'Now that's unfair,' she was saying. 'Really unfair. Simon is a real
poet and there's nothing really wrong with his project. Except that
it just isn't as good as mine. Do you think we'll be able to make him
see that?'

Why should it matter to me? What had I got to do with film
scripts or film projects on or off the ground? The woman was
under the impression that I was Simon Huff's friend and she was
making an effort to win me to her side before their silly little power
struggle began in earnest.

'I hardly know him,' I said. 'I only gave him a lift here. He asked
me to drive up to the Castle and deliver the letter.'

She took hold of Sylvia Hoffman's letter to examine it again in
case it contained some explanation she could have overlooked. She
looked mystified and cross. I could see her again through Rowena's
eyes: a pretty girl abruptly transformed into a disappointed woman.

'Where is he then? Is he somewhere sulking?'

Neither of them were really my business and I couldn't think of
a polite way of saying it. They both needed putting in their place
but I was the last person capable of doing it. There used to be occa-
sions when Rowena would rebuke me for being too amiable. At the
moment I was gripped by silence and it was as much as I could do
to stand still on my feet.

Lilian had recovered her self-possession and was being jolly and
laughing again.

'You won't believe this,' she said. 'I got here by train and taxi. I
absolutely hate aeroplanes. Never use them unless I really have to.
If you know where he is Mr. Roberts, could you possibly be so kind
as to take me to him?'

What else could I do? At least if I got them together it would greatly improve my chances of escape – if escape was the word. Return to my world of brooding suspicion, no longer soothed by alternate intervals of interest and boredom.

'The poor lamb.'

I would never have described Simon Huff as a lamb.

'I do feel guilty. I never wanted to let him down. He is a genuine poet after all. A nugget of pure Yorkshire.'

## IX

I could hear Rowena's voice as Lilian Trenovo fussed her way into the passenger seat. She had so much in need of arrangement from the elegant shoes in the footwell to the scarf on her shoulders and the coiffured disorder of her hair. This was done to the rattle of bracelets and the glitter of jewels and a sequence of pouts and sighs. The way Rowena dressed, even for a night at the opera, was never far removed from a practical uniform. It was some kind of uniform she wore when she first started coming down to the gardens for flowers or vegetables and stopped on the path to watch me working.

*Lord Pascant says Roberts is a deep thinker.* Rowena was wearing some kind of uniform when she said that, I am sure of it. It was autumn and I was digging up tubers and rhyzomes for storage and there was still the pleasant smell of ripeness in the air. A neat precise figure. She liked to talk with her heels together and her hands clasped behind her back. She worried about the state of her hands and was always inclined to hide them. She came to the gardens like a commander who takes a brief break in a continuing campaign. With everything under control she could afford a few minutes to relax. I could never be sure when she was teasing me. *He says you are proof that it is possible to think without using words. Do you think that's true?* She didn't wait for an answer. Possibly because I was so slow in making it. Did the spaces between words have as much meaning as the words themselves? How often did she come down to the gardens? Was it every day or every other day? I had so little resource left to help me disentangle my past. Facts in my head were more elusive than fish in a clouded ocean. I took a firmer grip on myself. You have to give the closest attention to the present moment to have the slightest hope of making sense out of experience. I concentrated on finding a parking space in the piazza. The afternoon was still warm but there were no habitués sitting at the tables outside La Barcaccia. And in the gloomy interior there was no sign of Simon Huff.

At first Lilian Trenovo was amused.

'He's playing hard to get,' she said. 'Let's just sit down. We can have a coffee and wait for him to turn up.'

It occurred to me that whatever happened Lilian Trenovo would take immediate steps to make herself comfortable. Where had the poet gone, without any money in his pocket apart from the lire that I gave him; and that he persisted in entering laboriously into his grubby notebook. With her coffee, she surprised me by lighting a cheroot. She said it helped her to think.

'Mind you, he has got talent. There's no mistaking that. My fear is that he will turn out to be a miniaturist, ready to sink back and bury himself in his provincial obsessions. I've seen it happen before.'

She gave a throaty laugh as she noted the expression on my face.

'I'm not as young as I look you know. And he can be so wilful. I think it must have been his mother's fault. Only child and no husband to restrain her. The question is has he got it in him for large scale structures and ambitious enterprises? He thinks so and of course I hope so. After all in a sense he is mine, bless him. A poor thing, but mine own! No. That's not fair. I freely admit I love having him moon about me. And I never minded playing what my sister Joyce calls the electric rabbit that makes the greyhound run. She's a tough old professional, dear Joyce. Success, she says. That's what we're all about. And there are times when I have to believe her. Success for what? That is the question. Worth nothing unless it is driven by vision and inspiration. That's what I tell her. Why am I telling you all this?'

She had caught my attention wandering. I seemed to be more worried than she was about the poet's whereabouts. I had last seen him tinged with the kind of despair that could have led to something worse.

'I suppose it's obvious.'

She waved her cheroot in the still air.

'I'm making excuses. Painting myself in the most favourable light. Most women do that, you know. Male ambition is something quite different. You'll never find a woman artist waking up in the night screaming she's being ignored. Not a bit of it. The woman gets on with it. Struggle with the dust and the dark and dig out as much as you can get, and hold on to it. And get on with it!'

I could not prevent myself from sifting through this painted

65

lady's outbursts on feminine psychology in the hope of discovering hints that would help me to get closer to understanding my Rowena. Was it too simple and obvious that everything she did was for my sake? Whether or not that was the case, it was the end result. Was I supposed to suffer for it? Did this have to be the reason why I sat here in the Italian afternoon sunlight listening to this chattering woman. I could do with some reasons.

'Tell me,' I said. 'Why didn't you turn up at the junction near San Antimo?'

Her immediate response was another throaty laugh and a wave of the cheroot.

'My goodness,' she said. 'Male solidarity.'

It was so far from the case I did not bother to correct her.

'What would you say if I told you his wife wouldn't let me?'

Her voice was low and roguish. She was ready to laugh again. I maintained a stone face.

'You didn't know he was married, did you?'

How could I know, unless he told me? And why should it matter to me? I was no more than another stranger in a foreign land.

'With three children. And a live-in-mother-in-law. In a semi in Hounslow. No place for a poet really. The poor lamb was being smothered.'

'How did she stop you?'

She might call herself an artist but she wasn't sensitive enough to realise how much I was out of sympathy with her. She seemed to me just another person prepared to move through life in a chariot of cherished illusions.

'Dear Alice Hoff, let me tell you, is a bit of an avenging angel. She is at my throat for letting down the feminist cause. Poet or no poet, a male animal should not be allowed to escape from the confines of his responsibilities. Lilian Trenovo was nothing better than a traitor-bitch luring him away from his duties. Giving the enemy succour.'

'Did he have a job?'

'They both had jobs. Simon taught Music and English to the lower forms in a Hounslow Comprehensive. The fierce Alice ruled her Primary School with a rod of iron.'

'How could she stop you? Turning up at San Antimo?'

'Great one for facts, aren't you Mr. Roberts? Maintenance. There's the simple answer. Alice Huff rang up my sister Joyce threatening poor Simon with blue murder. A maintenance bill as long as your arm. And she had an army of union lawyers on to it. Joyce thought the poor lamb didn't stand a chance. So she advised me to keep well out of it.'

I couldn't resist making my closest attempt so far at a worldy comment.

'Maintenance,' I said. 'So that's what romance boils down to.'

In 'romance' lovers were supposed to overcome all obstacle, if possible to the accompaniment of string music, and perhaps flutes, on deserted railway stations. Underneath her make-up I could see she was blushing.

'We were in love,' she said. 'It was one of the most transforming experiences of my whole life. You can't describe it. The experience I mean. It's on the very edge of the inexplicable.'

I longed to question her more about what she was saying. I longed to hear something, like news from a distant frontier, about what women really felt and how it governed their behaviour. I had so much to learn: mysteries of my own to solve. Her eyes were half closed as she attempted to explain the inexplicable.

'There's a flow of communication. Those days together away from the world. You never stop talking. Two minds so close you double the powers of perception. The stars shine twice as brightly.'

She was smiling eagerly across the table and I could see the poet again, alone and disconsolate, waiting for her, on that deserted railway station, changing his socks to pass the time. The way she was smiling suggested to me that what it all meant for her was an enlargement of herself. To be adored was a small taste of immortality. What pained me was my inability to grasp what love meant to Rowena. She married me out of an odd affection for innocence and stupidity. She liked patting my bald head. She liked watching me work in the garden. I was her private pet. The object of her undemonstrative devotion.

'Where is he?'

Lilian Trenovo was getting worried about her poet.

'He should have turned up by now. I'll go and ask the bartender if he saw which way Simon went.'

Lord Pascant used to say we clutch at each other for comfort in this world. And the reason for this, he said, was because we knew in our heart of hearts that we were lost. We just feel that much less lost when we cling to each other. And he used to say anything was beautiful if it made us feel less lost. I learnt a lot from him, but clearly not enough.

She came back trembling with excitement.

'It's amazing,' she said. 'It's an omen. He took the local bus to Fiascherino. Can you imagine it. Oh Mr. Roberts!'

She clasped her hands together in girlish appeal.

'Could we go there right away? Do you mind? It's only eight or so miles over the top road.'

X

The road was steeper than I expected. If I was to become chauffeur to the world in general, doomed to wander for ever over the face of the earth, I would be well advised to buy a bigger and better car at the earliest opportunity. In this modest vehicle the passenger was placed too near me. Lilian Trenovo's scent was not to my liking. She chatted away with gay abandon.

'I can't tell you Mr. Roberts, your coming has been absolutely providential.'

I hadn't vouchsafed my christian name for fear of the fuss she would make about how to say it. In any case I was satisfied that the formal address placed a comforting distance between us. And it showed a little more respect for my bald head than 'Welshy'.

'Sylvia Hoffman is such a wonderful person. Such a rare combination of wealth and sensibility. And she'll do anything for me. She's more or less said so. Once I put the idea to her in proper detail. I mean it's got everything. Humour. Intelligence. Honesty. Not just the story of the patron saint of sex. So much more than that. There will be sex scenes of course. Done with discretion and good taste. After all, ghosts don't smell, do they?'

Her laughter rang both coarse and hollow in the confines of my vehicle.

'There are cheap directors who go head-on for outrage. Plenty of those around. But that never was my style. My mission as I see it, is to reconcile Sylvia's backing with Simon's poetic gift. That's my job. It sounds simple but I've got an uneasy feeling it's going to be hellishly difficult. Never mind. Rise to the challenge, Lilian, my girl!'

From the highest point of the road we had a fine view of the gulf of Lerici and across the water the medieval towers of Portovenere.

'Of course this place will never do as a location. It was ruined years ago. Hotels and villas, and restaurants and marinas all over the place. Not a rock left for poor dear Lawrence's ghost to lie on like a lizard and bake in the sun. My dear old dad was just in time to catch a glimpse of the place and realise how it had been in its pristine glory. He thought he saw it as Lawrence had seen it. An hour's walk from Shelley's house, hidden among the vines and the olives. And the moonlight turning the sea silver and the rocks jet black and the little pink house within a stone's throw of the waves. And this time of the year fat figs ripening in the garden. I think I've got the answer. Near Dubrovnik. A gulf not unlike this one, but not so appallingly developed.'

She insisted that there were at least half a dozen hotels where once her father had scrambled through the olive groves above the rocky little bay in search of the ghosts of Lawrence and Frieda and the fishermen. Now there were more pine cones than vines between the trim hotel gardens. She was convinced we would come across the poet somewhere among the rocks on the water's edge. He would be gazing out to sea, communing with nature. The Mediterranean was still warm and blue and inviting. Down below on the smoother beach there were people bathing close to the shore. Very fat most of them, elderly and scantily clad and determined to have their skins absorb the last dab of sunlight before returning north to face the winter.

'Fat Germans,' Lilian Trenovo said, with a sniff of disapproval.

It was her idea that we should separate. She sent me into the more inaccessible rocky inlets. She herself took the smoother path towards Lerici. She took it for granted that I was there to help her. This was a pleasant enough place for me to wander and become absorbed in my own thoughts. It seemed to me that the woman was far too intent on the business of living to have any hope at all of seeing ghosts. What she saw were the golden palaces of Sylvia Hoffman and the money to be found inside and latched on to. She would have me understand that film was enormously expensive. You couldn't build an adequate dream world without huge financial resources. She was among the elite, the chosen few, who could cope with the dangerous balance between art and business. You were engaged in building an alternative reality and this in itself was equivalent to building a great city where ghosts could live instead of people.

I must have been dreaming myself when I looked down and saw Simon Huff's blue haversack leaning against a rock. The flute was peeping out of the side-pocket at the same angle that I had first seen on the deserted railway platform. I raised my head to call Lilian Trenovo, but she had passed out of sight.

I had to consider whether there could be any cause for concern. When I left him he was in a low mood. It might have been remorse or the depth of despair or just bad temper. I knew so little about him. I didn't know then that he was the father of three and deeply in arrears on child maintenance. How deep? Hundreds or thousands? Enough to drive him into exile. I had taken him to be a poet who had been robbed rather than a father on the run. All that bravado about his poetic project – in reality he was a vulnerable creature weighed down with disappointment, and from what I had seen of Lilian Trenovo I couldn't be sure she was any kind of cinematic goddess capable of resuscitating his muse.

There was no sign of a swimmer in the expanse of calm sea that stretched from this rocky shore to the horizon. The water's edge had the presence of a dormant monster licking its wide lips. An empty sea was as fascinating as death. It existed to swallow people. For the time being my best plan was to stay close to the haversack in the expectation that he would return to it. As I lowered my head I noticed a spider's thread stretching from the mouthpiece of the flute to a cistus plant growing between the rocks. In the last hours of her life Rowena stroked her cheek with weak fingers and muttered that her face was being covered by a spider's web. It frightened her. She begged me to give her a double dose of morphia to ease her pain. The guilt I still carried was being responsible for her death. Would I ever find release?

I brushed away the spider's thread and drew the haversack closer. There was a label on the inside that gave the poet's name and address: S.H. Huff, 23a Albert Grove. Maybe in happier days he had used it to carry a family picnic. It never crossed my mind to want children since it never appeared to be part of Rowena's plan. For some reason now I had a vision of a family making a small fire on the shore and children dashing back and fore from the water's edge to the fire. It seemed incredibly simple and pleasant. Like a tune on the flute.

He appeared behind me wet and shivering.

'Pass me a towel out of that, won't you? These rocks are killing my bloody feet.'

I was so pleased to see him I hastened to do his bidding and smiled at him like a long lost friend.

'The water's lovely and warm. I stayed in too long though. Thought I'd go and see where Shelley got drowned. Pay my respects. As one poet to another. Mind you, that's the last thing the buggers do when they're alive. Talk about backbiting and cut-throat competition. The only thing they'll ever get drowned in is their own eloquence. Why don't you take a dip? I'll lend you my trunks.'

I was too embarrassed to tell him I couldn't swim.

'I've been thinking of writing a poem about you.'

He rubbed himself vigorously with his towel. The action clearly stimulated his ideas.

'About me?'

'The Wandering Welshman,' he said. 'How's that for a title? Looking for lame dogs to help over crooked stiles. Don't look so worried. I shan't mention you by name.'

I was disconcerted by the unexpected interest he was showing in me. It was a form of exposure and I didn't like it. It was absurd to suggest I was wandering around looking for people to help. Our encounter was an accident. One I would never have chosen to happen. He had enough troubles of his own to attend to. I regretted ever having so much as mentioned my bereavement. Why should he presume to play about with my distress and expect me to look pleased about it?

'She's searching everywhere for you,' I said. 'Miss Trenovo.'

This made him laugh as he pulled his clothes on.

'Let her search,' he said. 'She kept me waiting long enough. I don't know what would have happened if you hadn't come along, Welshy.'

It was a pet name that relegated me to a bit part in the great drama of the life of Simon Huff. I resented it. Everything about the man's behaviour was manic depressive. When I left him in the bar on the piazza he looked suicidal. Now he was behaving as though he had the world at his feet. Bursting with rude health after his swim: full of confidence and resolution.

'She knows she'll never get very far without me,' he said.

He hoisted his haversack on his back and looked ready for battle.

'I'll tell you one thing, Welshy,' he said. 'I won't be going cap in hand to that Lesbian queen bee. Not me. We'll get the show on the road on my terms. What did that old Hollywood maniac used to say?... "Total creative control!" '

This was a great joke. As we moved away he looked set to laugh and sing.

## XI

In spite of my reservations I was strangely warmed to witness their reunion. There was a moment's hesitation as they stared at each other and seemed to be deciding whether it would be peace or war. Then their feelings overcame them and they ran towards each other between the flower beds and embraced under an exotic palm tree. There were elderly people sitting out to watch the fierce colours of the evening slowly taking over the horizon. The lovers began to sway and dance under the tree and the old people started clapping. Against the sunset they could have been bats or butterflies: whatever they looked like, it was briefly beautiful. They looked young and they behaved with the spontaneity of youth and the old people approved. They moved off with their arms around each other's waists and they could have been acting out the happy ending of a play.

It was time for me to leave. Some kind of cycle had been completed. The meeting that should have graced the misty platform at San Antimo had now taken place in the full glare of the setting sun. For my part I was condemned to wander on alone and it was a sad fact that any direction would do. However far I travelled and however sorry for myself I felt, I would not meet Rowena again. In any case there had never been such glad reunions in our relationship. I was always shy and uncertain and Rowena was ruled by a passion for discretion. I adopted the same attitude to please her. I did most things to please her. Compared to this colourful encounter our meetings were furtive. It was possible that Simon Huff and Lilian Trenovo had access to secret joys of living that we had never come across. Perhaps this accounted for Rowena's deep interest in opera; apart from her love of singing. Sometimes, when I waited in the car outside the opera house for the performance to finish, I had a sense of being excluded. There was a world and a life in progress inside that building that I knew nothing about.

The woman recovered her rational faculties far more rapidly than the poet. She took charge and in her best Italian manner she completed her arrangements. They stood in front of me, hand in hand, to tell me they would spend the night at the Shelley e Delle Palme and if I wished there was a single room available for me at the Europa. But what they would like more than anything, she simpered girlishly as she said it, would be for us to meet up at the restaurant Conchiglia and enjoy a late dinner together. She had cast me in the role of benefactor and it was up to me to live up to it. In this fresh vision of romance they were busy constructing together, it had become important that the reunion had been brought about by a mysterious stranger.

I arrived too soon at the Conchiglia; or, I was too promptly on time, having nothing else to do: and the happy pair, of course were elsewhere more pleasurably occupied. I took my seat at the table that had been reserved for three and lapsed once more, as I waited, into the mode of the anonymous man. I could look around me and observe in the manner Rowena used to say was best suited to my further education. I know that, in some way I cannot define, this state reflects the passivity she adopted when she realised that she only had a limited time left. Her tranquillity amazed me. And a new patience that she had never shown before. We had visitors I couldn't wait to get rid of. Mrs. Watkins, a retired civil servant, who seemed burdened with her own rude health and kept bringing Rowena jellies and jams that she believed would do her the world of good. And there was Madame Clara Bowen, the widow of the famous tenor, who loved to sit in Rowena's bedroom and reminisce about the days of her husband's glory. It was as though she were listening to some pleasant sounds in the distance. If she spoke there would be a gnomic power to her utterance. *We have to accept what happens, Gwion, and not think of it as a punishment or a reward.*

At a nearby table, five elderly gentlemen were enjoying their meal. I realised they were or had been high-ranking army officers. Two waiters were paying them close attention and I could hear the lavish use of ranks and titles as the waiters bowed themselves in and out of service. I could see discreet decorations in lapels and there were exploits being recalled in light-hearted tones with a wave of a cigar. Death was a joke at a safe distance. Could these be Fascists who felt it was safe now to creep out of the woodwork and display their medals.

I could feel myself become dangerously detached. I sat so still the wheel of time stopped turning and the waiters froze in their obsequious attitudes. People outside time were marionettes drained of any sympathy or significance. The wheel had to turn or I would be left in a cold space where I cared for no one or nothing and therefore no better than a marionette myself. As much as the general's medals, we are all entitled to our wafer of history. Death takes us at his leisure unless generals decide to help him out.

Everything was restored to time and motion when the lovers appeared glowing with a satisfaction close to a cloud of glory. They had well-being and goodwill in abundance and were now ready to share them. They were hungry and said so and smiled at each other and scanned the menu with intense interest. There were reminders of old jokes about octopi and monkfish and oblique references to other shared occasions before she laid both manicured hands on the table and leaned forward to give me her concentrated attention.

'Mr. Roberts. You are wonderful. You've brought us a happy issue out of all our afflictions. You really have. And we are longing to know all about you. Aren't we, Si?'

'I have to, don't I,' Simon Huff said. 'I'm going to write a poem about him.'

Hearing her call him 'Si' was being let into a secret I would have preferred not to share. And this business of a poem about me was assuming threatening proportions. They were both smiling at me and I was being invited to relax and unbutton. Any moment now she would want to know my christian name. This is the way they are and therefore this is the way the world should be: open and frank and nicely laid out for their convenience.

'I'm just a gardener,' I said.

'He's more than that,' Simon Huff said. 'He was married to the lady of the manor!'

Lilian Trenovo clapped her hands with girlish delight.

'What a wonderful story,' she said. 'I really must hear it. Chapter and verse.'

She kept an eye on me while she engaged the waiter in a knowledgeable discussion on the wines of the Cinque Terre.

'Where was this?' she said resuming her interrogation. 'Where? In Wales of course.''

'Helygen Foel,' I said.

I warned myself not to mention Pascant Hall. Once aroused there would be no limit to their curiosity.

'What's that? The name of a village?'

I nodded.

'Full of gossiping neighbours,' Simon Huff said. 'This is going to spoil my poem. Not another *Under Milk Wood*.'

I was painstakingly truthful. I was the slow and backward younger son. I had a clever older brother who was now a Professor of Organic Chemistry at Vancouver. I had been sent to an agricultural college. Then I made a joke I had made many times before. I preferred plants to animals because they didn't answer back. In the garden I found sufficient reason for existing.

Having given away as much, I was relieved to watch them concentrate on satisfying their hunger. Once their stomachs were full their minds would be unable to resist returning to the projects that were so close to their hearts. I had every hope that my dull recitals had sabotaged whatever enthusiasm Simon Huff might have had for writing a poem about his accidental benefactor. I would be quite content for them to assume I was even more naive than I appeared as a bald benevolent presence the other side of the table.

'Simon has seen the light.'

Once again Lilian Trenovo was taking me into her confidence and I felt the necessity of being on my guard.

'Once I put it to her, I'm sure Sylvia will back this all the way. I'm sure of it. What do you think of *Ghosts and Lovers* as a title?'

'Bloody awful.'

It wasn't so much the title that embarrassed him. It was watching me and knowing that I would be recalling his bold remarks about a lesbian queen bee. He needed to make more noises to demonstrate his masculine independence.

'And get this. My collaboration depends on a firm agreement to push on with my Bigsby epic when your flirtation with your bearded ghost is over.'

She touched his cheek and murmured.

'Maybe you you should grow a beard.'

They were plainly in tune with each other. They raised their glasses like singers in the first act of *La Traviata* and I sat and watched them as though Rowena was at my side. Perhaps I had a knack of basking quietly in reflected pleasure. I had to admire their ability to thrive in a world of illusions. It was difficult to imagine either enterprise reaching fruition. The poet gave me a brief wink when he thought Lilian wasn't looking. He wanted me to understand that all he had done was make a tactical move and that his idea was still much the better. When I made a sceptical remark at the opera Rowena would say all plots were absurd. *It's the passion with which they are pursued that matters.* She said it more than once with a quiet conviction that disturbed me still as I remembered it. Plots are only lurid reflections of plans and purposes. Did she have everything in mind from the beginning, when she saw that Jeannie Pascant would never recover?'

'Let's be quite clear about this.'

The poet had been frivolous and Lilian Trenovo was asserting her authority.

'The story is from Frieda's point of view. You have to under-stand this. She has given up her three children as a sacrifice on the altar of Lawrence's genius. Talk about Abraham and Isaac. She had walked out on the three of them. Now you should know all about that, Simon Huff!'

He didn't even look guilty. All this imagination he was supposed to have, couldn't he apply it to the condition of his children? How could his desertion be anything but a tragedy for them? I was dining with a pair of repulsive purveyors of unnatural fantasies: a pair of candy-floss manufacturers in pursuit of some sickly new formula that would make them a fortune and allow them to go on feeding themselves on magic mushrooms until they dropped dead from excess eating. The alarming possibility was that their celluloid illu-sions could coincide with some irrational surge in the collective consciousness and become a resounding success in the cinemas and networks of the western world.

'Listen here, Welshy. Why don't you give up your wanderings for a bit and come in with us on this one?'

The poet was smiling at me in the friendliest way possible. He pushed the hair out of his eyes and leaned over the table.

'It's been an adventure, hasn't it? Now you could follow it up with a little venture capital. Not much. Just a tiny piece of the action. You could come back with us tomorrow and we could have an exciting war council at the Villa Hoffman.'

Before he had finished I was shaking my head and declining the offer. It was possible he wished to keep me under observation in the interest of that dubious poem; and certain that I had no wish to be observed. Call it escape or retreat: what I needed to decide was where to. The place I came from was haunted. I had a momentary vision of Helygen Foel and my grandfather's grave in the wet grass at the bottom end of the churchyard. I could visit it again and read the inscription on the stone that I already knew by heart. I could loiter on the drive to Pascant Hall and find some satisfaction in the sound of the disadvantaged children playing in the park. I wouldn't want to see the gardens. That was a past to which you could never return.

The grubby notebook had appeared suddenly on the table. I was tempted to enquire whether it also kept a record of his maintenance arrears. It was not the kind of humorous remark a stranger could make. And yet it was in that moment it occurred to me that this was something I could see to myself. Lilian Trenovo was sparing me a glance between smiling at him fondly as he made his ridiculous calculations. She wanted to make certain I appreciated his integrity. He may have shown wayward qualities common to poets, but he kept a close record of his debts, large and small.

'Look,' I said. 'It's very good of you but please don't bother. Please. Just believe me. It's much more fun to give than to receive.'

## XII

My heart began to pump furiously as I stood outside the gate of No. 23a. It was a suburban semi just like any other. Quietly proud and private. Already I had walked the length of the avenue for no other reason than to postpone the encounter. I had no telephone number. In any case there were no effective statements I could assemble until I saw Alice Huff face to face. This was a damp country. In the light of the setting sun you could see the earth breathing. That powerful low light picked out every dry leaf and every blade of grass as well as the delicate formation of clouds in the sky. Compared with the brown certainties of Italy, this was a pale water colour world. In this light even the rows of houses seemed as unsubstantial as the clouds. Places to dream in.

This was a strange journey's end. I left the Europa in the early morning. Over in the Shelley e delle Palme they would have been still asleep. Whether or not in each other's arms, they deserved each other. They could still be discussing whether the ghost of Frieda should obtain access to those three children. They were caught up in the project, so their relationship revolved inside it like lumps of butter in a churn. At La Spezia I bought a new car and headed north. My scheme seemed all the more satisfying the more thought I gave it. I heard Lord Pascant telling me again how he believed we were on earth in order to expiate suffering. It didn't seem all that different from my grandfather's talk about penance. *It may seem the same to you, Roberts, and I suppose it will do. The greatest truths are inaccessible to the crude human intellect. Not just yours, Roberts. Mine as well.* Strange impractical things my grandfather said had sunk into my bones as well as my subconscious. *Never mind worldly goods! Accumulate a deeper knowledge of peace and love. The more you possess the more there will be to share with others.* Rowena never had much to say to preachers but I had known my grandfather long before I ever met her. She had given me the wealth. I could use a whisper of his wisdom to distribute it.

I stood inside the arched porch. It was a confined space and I had to avoid a hanging basket containing a withered geranium. I pressed the door-bell. It felt a momentous act. Inside the house I could hear the faint screech of children quarrelling.

There was a rhythm to it. The protest of a small child against some huge injustice. The clash of offence and punishment. A large female shape materialised beyond the coloured glass. It paused before deciding to open the door. The grim faced woman placed herself as a barrier between me and the warmth and noise of the interior. It had to be the mother-in-law. She had no smile to waste on a stranger. She stared at me as though I was a door-to-door salesman and kept one hand on the door ready to shut it in my face.

'You don't know me,' I said. 'My name is Roberts. I wonder if I could speak to Mrs Alice Huff?'

She took more time to study my appearance. When a stranger stands on the doorstep there is always preliminary intelligence to be gathered. My cap was in my hand and she could see my bald head. Her stance made it clear that she was resolute in defence. It was unlikely that I would be allowed to speak to Alice Huff without giving her mother some indication of the nature of my business.

'I came across Simon Huff in Italy,' I said. 'I was able to help him.'

It wasn't what I had rehearsed, but I hadn't anticipated it could be this formidable lady that would answer the door.

'That one.'

Her grey anaemic features began to turn red with indignation. Anyone who helped Simon Huff was guilty by association.

'It's in prison that one should be, not in Italy. She did everything for him and this is the thanks she gets.'

The mother-in-law let go of the front door so that she could advance a step in my direction. I retreated politely until I felt my back against the wall of the porch. As a male and self-confessed companion of a villain I was also culpable.

'Do you know that creature had a sound-proofed study upstairs that Alice had specially made for him! And this is the way he treats her!'

She had so many reproaches to make it was all she could do to hold herself back from pouring them over my defenceless head. I could feel myself shrinking away from her attack. It was a relief to have a younger woman appear in the doorway and place a restraining hand on her fleshy arm.

'Mother. What is it?'

The daughter was a smaller prettier version. And much prettier, it struck me at first glance, than Lilian Trenovo. But stern and unsmiling like her mother: and already worn with the responsibilities of motherhood and the headship of a large primary school. I was conscious of a depth of sympathy towards her. My first instinct to come to her aid had been correct. They could both see me smiling for no apparent reason.

'I have the means,' I said. 'I would like to help.'

I wished the mother would move to one side so that I could address Alice Huff more directly. I had a package of good intentions to make clear. It had to be done with an emphasis on the disinterested nature of my interest and this on the surface could appear to be a contradiction in terms. I wished the older woman was not so intent on protecting her daughter.

'It sounds as though I'm interfering. That is the last thing I want to do. But I know he is in arrears with his maintenance payments. What I would like to do is make them up. And whatever else I could do to help.'

'He should be in prison. That's where he should be.'

The mother-in-law was bent on retribution.

'And I'll tell you more, Mr....'

'Roberts,' I said hastily.

'Mother. Will you please leave this to me.'

The headmistress was asserting her authority. It was quiet but firm and based on the practice of rational discourse among assemblies of young children.

'Lucy wants some more toast. Let her do it herself, but you supervise. Please.'

The mother withdrew reluctantly. At last Alice Huff and I stood face to face. I was hoping she would ask me in. It would be so much easier to discuss delicate matters inside: anywhere indeed rather than the doorstep.

'I don't really want to hear from him.'

Now her hand was on the door. Once more there was a threat it might close in my face.

'We can manage perfectly well. To be honest with you, he was always more of a burden than a help. Did he send you?'

'No,' I said. 'Goodness me no. I hardly know him really. It's just that I felt this need to help.'

She was in control and I was the supplicant. It wasn't at all like this that I imagined it. All she saw was a bald stranger who kept shifting his weight awkwardly from one foot to the other.

'We don't need help,' she said. 'Thank you all the same. I'm sorry that he's troubled you.'

Then she did close the door quietly but firmly in my face.

I was tempted to ring the bell and start a new approach. They should know how much I knew. They should know how well equipped I was to help them. It took me time to realise that it would be useless. They were more than sufficient unto themselves, beyond my reach. For a moment I felt the strength ebbing from my legs and I was tempted to sit on the porch step to recover. I remained sensible enough to realise this would only embarrass them. The most important thing was to get away and start again. There were journeys that had to be made. I could not allow guilt and failure to destroy me.

# MENNA

## I

Arnot Stephens woke up from a deep and nourishing sleep and immediately began to worry about his wife. It was vital that her Sabbatical leave be put to the best possible use. He sprawled alone in their large bed blinking uneasily in the morning sunlight. She was already working in her study. Nothing wrong with that *per se*. She had a focused industrious nature. He was as much in awe of it as of her physical beauty. It was a miraculous combination and he was still given to trembling slightly when he thought about it and about his privileged position as her husband and guardian angel. It was she, Lisa, that called him 'angel' and merely to hear her say it increased his confidence in himself. Not that he lacked confidence in his professional capacities as a lawyer: his higher and in many ways more difficult role was nourishing, safeguarding, encouraging the flickering flame of her genius in a cold and indifferent world.

Even after reaching the haven of their marriage Lisa still had much to contend with. She had escaped from the predatory world of television to the comparative calm of her academic post. But her energies were still precariously divided between scholarship and creative ambitions. Her academic publications were signed R.L. Pugh: the literary work they both prized more highly were by Lisa Puw. For the last week she had been wrestling with a project with an intensity that disturbed him. There were moments when she would look up from her desk and he would see the small face of a pretty, frightened child. He knew this was misleading and stemmed from his own feeling of helplessness, his inability to enter the throbbing world of her imagination. He was driven to castigate his own lack of sensitivity. He knew as well as she did that her implacable drive towards an excellence she believed almost within her reach could bring on psychosomatic storms over which she had little control. Her only recourse was to lie speechless for hours on end in a darkened room: and he would be reduced to wandering about the empty house and

81

the garden as if there had been a bereavement in the family.

He was too devoted to chide her for attempting too much. In any case it was assumed between them, from the beginning, that his belief in her talent was even greater than hers. It was, he said, as she tried to warn him, written into their marriage contract. They were dining in an expensive restaurant when they took the decision and every word and movement Lisa made in the subdued light remained etched on his mind.

'You are taking a bit of a chance, you know,' she said.

Of course he was. From the beginning her hidden depths intrigued him just as much as her surface beauty.

'I'm horrid really,' she said. 'Deep down. I'd rather be a bitch and write well, than a sweetie-pie who writes badly.'

Of course she would. He leaned over to reassure her that they were of one mind on that score, more perhaps than any other. An inch or two taller, he said, as a joke and a tribute, and he could have lived comfortably on her immoral earnings as a fashion model. This did amuse her momentarily. She took care of her appearance. She answered there was no place on the catwalk for dry academics over thirty.

'You can see the risk can't you, Arnot? I might develop into a first class bitch and still write badly.'

She bent forward in the flattering light to sip her cool glass of Chablis. It was all he could do to stop himself bursting into song. She was wonderful to look at and even more wonderful to know. Over and above that they had a world of causes and intellectual attachment in common. Arnot was a lawyer with a social conscience. He admitted to a bundle of awkward allegiances that were obstacles to preferment and Lisa said they gave him dignity and substance. She loved his integrity. It was far more than the *basso ostinato* of her own drive towards excellence. In the days before the Assembly he had stood as a Plaid Cymru candidate without losing his deposit. Lisa liked to refer to his staunchness as her pre-Cambrian rock.

Arnot stretched himself in their double bed and with the same muscular reflex assured himself for the umpteenth time that Lisa was really something. She was hurrying out of the college library with books under her arm when Arnot fell off his bicycle at her feet. It was a miraculous moment. He had no business to be there: training in the gym by courtesy of a friendly acquaintance with a P.T. instructor. He was late for the office. The weight of his untidy saddle-bag and, he was bound to insist, the vision of Lisa's dark good looks and those mesmeric startled eyes, threw him off his balance into a state, he also insisted, of suspended animation in which he had continued to exist happily ever since.

The risk she had talked about turned out to be no risk at all. A couple who could take on the world in their talk were twice as able to confront it. In the marriage of true minds the element of risk was no more than a speck of dust in the balance. There had been other men in her life. How could there not have been for heaven's sake? And in his own case a limping affair with an older married woman that he kept secret from the world in general and from his mother in particular. Lisa had tried television and travel journalism until they became what she described as 'blocked outlets'. And he knew exactly what she meant. In television there had been jealousy and a damning with faint praise. Upstairs, attention had been drawn to a discrepancy between the svelte appearance and a voice that wobbled uncertainly between a whisper and a squeak. From pillow to pillow Arnot assured her that her dulcet tones were music to his ears and Lisa giggled appreciatively in his muscular embrace. Travel journalism was too exhausting and was complicated by an affair with an English poet who lived in a mill on the Brecon Beacons in a state of complete squalor. It was burgeoning literary ambition, Lisa said, that drove her to take the risk. By upbringing and inclination, the daughter of a prosperous Cowbridge wholesaler, she was uncompromisingly bourgeois. She had never decided whether it was the dirt or the competition for literary attention that put an end to the affair with the poet. She beat a strategic retreat to the Department of Romance languages in the belief that a more hum-drum existence would give her more time to write. This, she said, was what she was still around to prove: how to transform an ambition into a vocation without dying in the attempt. Hence the sense of unease, and even danger. He had to take care of her by leaving her alone. And that was something more easily said than done.

He would not disturb. Merely get dressed, prepare breakfast and take a patient walk in the garden. Love and good fortune were indefinable uncovenanted blessings that prevailed in delicate balance. Arnot and Lisa lived in a modern house which had been given to them by his mother. A reward, Lisa said for agreeing to be married in chapel, instead of living in sin.

The new 'Craig-y-Don' gave a commanding view of the Channel. Across the water the Mendips or the Quantocks, he was never quite sure which, hovered at the correct distance to give promise of a dreamy land of summer and a different world to visit and still keep at arm's length. The original 'Craig-y-Don' had been built by a Cardiff shipping magnate in the eighteen nineties. In the nineteen sixties it had been bought by Arnot's enterprising father Reg, who immediately pulled it down, ballroom, billiard room and all, to build half a dozen executive dwellings on the site, reserving the best corner to build a Dutch-style modern two storey house for himself. This was the house that Arnot and Lisa now occupied. The domestic interior the scene of crises Arnot could choose to forget, since it had all been refurbished by a feminist interior decorator who was a friend of Lisa. This, Lisa said, would deprive the walls of their ears. His parents did not get on. Menna, his mother, consoled herself with the garden and its design remained unchanged. The space was marked out by grass and granite paths into the shape of a Celtic Cross not easy to manage. Arnot and Lisa were too pressed for time to spend it gardening. With his mother's approval they engaged a cheerful pensioner to come once a week to save the cross from disappearing in a wilderness of weeds.

Arnot carried a pair of binoculars to pick out any interesting details at sea. This was holiday weather. In a few days time they were due to set out for France. There were sites that Lisa needed to visit both for her academic and creative projects. She liked to insist there was no essential conflict of interest. She did not include herself among the ranks of subjective writers ready to analyse themselves to bits. She would make her academic field serve also as her creative quarry. Obstacles existed to strengthen intellectual muscle. And over and above all that lay their abiding problem: how to reconcile their misgivings about the prevailing Anglo-American cultural hegemony with the bitter-sweet temptation of writing in English. Being bilingual they agreed, could be the very devil. Two languages were not necessarily better than one any more than schizophrenia was a guarantee of brighter visions. Unsympathetic colleagues hinted that if she had something of importance to say she should say it in a language everyone could understand. This deepened her agony. It was to Arnot particularly she confided the myriad insights that came and went in the older language like motes in a beam of indoor sunlight. He was always there to understand and sympathise. There was no end to the degrees and distinctions that lay between creative dualism and double vision.

From the top of the garden he saw Lisa giving a weak wave as she stood in the conservatory doorway. She was wearing dark glasses. He hurried down to console her. Even before he could take her in his arms he heard her whisper.

'I've bitten off more than I can chew. I'm hopeless.'

Her body was limp and soft inside her padded dressing gown. He cradled her tenderly in his arms, kissed the crown of her untidy hair, and crooned an assurance that there was no need for her to speak until she had something to eat.

## II

At the breakfast table Lisa drank coffee while Arnot made her toast. Her difficulties were so complex it seemed better to remain silent or talk of something else. When he was sure Lisa was warm enough Arnot placed a saucer of milk for the cat in the open doorway so that Lisa could watch the speed of the little red tongue lapping the milk.

'I've got a confession to make,' she said.

He stood smiling by the grill prepared to be amused. In the spacious well equipped kitchen he was a large reassuring figure: not quite big enough to be called a gentle giant but powerfully built and in excellent condition. His fair curly hair was thinning out and this made his forehead bigger. He was accustomed to holding his peace at length as he paid close attention to what a client was trying to explain. The intensity of his stare made him appear stern so that when a smile eventually broke across his face it was a source of relief as well as pleasure, as though the sun had broken unexpectedly through the clouds on a particularly dull day.

'I can't think what came over me,' she said. 'But I do of course.'

She crumbled a piece of toast between her fingers.

'Confession is good for the soul.'

He was prepared to take the matter lightly to ease her tension.

'We were talking about something quite different. Your mother and I. About this man Yoreth. With his private press. She's rather taken him under her wing. One of her causes. Wanting to print something I haven't even written. Then out of the blue I said, "Menna, why don't you come with us?" I was amazed at the sound of my own voice.'

'And what did she say?'

Arnot's jaw hung open while he prepared to digest unpalatable news.

'She would love to come. See medieval France through my eyes. Nothing she would like better.'

He could not hide his disappointment.

'If it's what you want,' he said.

'It isn't at all what I want. It's just a stupid confusion of imagination and reality. I'm ashamed to tell you how confused. For the last three days I have been trying to transpose your mother into the shape and form of a twelfth century heretic.'

She stared at him to make sure he wasn't laughing at her.

'Last night I thought if I could see her in those sort of surroundings it would do the trick. Study the subject at close quarters. A lazy pseudo-academic way of sparing my feeble imagination the trouble. I should have talked to you about it first. But you know what I'm like. I was afraid to break the spell.'

'Eat,' Arnot said. 'It will make you feel better.'

His quiet encouragement made her realise how hungry she was. She crammed toast and marmalade into her mouth and held out a hand for a piece of kitchen roll to wipe her fingers.

'I don't deserve you,' she said. 'You are so damn good. You spoil me. You ought to beat me sometimes. Make me suffer.'

Arnot stood behind her chair to massage her neck and shoulders. If she felt so inclined he was strong enough to pick her up and carry her back to bed. He could soothe her and calm her fears by stroking her quivering body as he had done so many times before. He was alive to the burden of exposed sensitivity she carried. His strength was at her command and the beauty of her naked body was his unfailing consolation. Lisa raised a hand so that he could hold it.

'The plain fact is your mother is a more intriguing figure than any heretic maiden resisting clerical rape in a twelfth century French orchard. And now more infuriating.'

'Well there you are,' Arnot said. 'You can study her instead. Fuse your fiction with incontrovertible fact.'

Lisa rubbed the back of his hand against her cheek.

'Who is the most dangerous person you know?' she said. 'Yourself, who else? What does it all amount to in the end except self-indulgent stratagems to indulge in exercises of self-regard.'

'Rubbish,' Arnot said. 'You don't belong to the subjective school. You say so yourself.'

'I am an impossible woman, And your mother knew it. I make shameless use of you. I hinder your progress. Hobble your career. She knows it but she never says it. I hate to admit it but she is a hundred times more interesting than me. Her life has been nothing but a sequence of trials. Of torments really. Torn between a tyrannical father and a brutal husband. Blamed for the death of your twin... giving us her house! At sixty two a model saint. She's so good, I can't stand her. And we are going to take her with us.'

Arnot sat down so that they looked at each other despairingly across the table. It was some time before he pulled a face to make her laugh. He waved his hands over the surface of the table as if he were fighting his way through a dense undergrowth of difficulties and complications. Lisa began to giggle.

'Think of those interminable polite tussles,' she said. 'All the way through France. There'll be a daily pantomime of me insisting that Menna sits in the front. And Menna nobly resisting. And of course there will be nothing she won't pay for if given half the chance.'

'I tell you what...'

Arnot sat up straight to show he had an inspiration.

'You drive. I'll sit in the back.'

She smiled at him fondly.

'There wouldn't be enough room for those long legs of yours. In any case your mother can't bear women drivers.'

'How on earth do you know that?'

'I think it's to do with your father. A subliminal remnant of bullying. Let's blame the great Reg. The great manly man. How did you put up with it all? When you were a boy?'

She could see the distaste on his face but she persisted.

'I'm horrible,' she said. 'Dabbling in the murky parts of your past. It's a compulsion. I have to do it at regular intervals. Perhaps it's you I should write about, my love. How do you fancy becoming a Cathar Perfect? Not that you aren't perfect already.'

She offered him her hand across the table and he clasped it eagerly: it seemed childlike and vulnerable inside his large and tender grip. The contact alone was a spur to confession.

'He was a great hero when I was a boy. A force of nature from the valleys. Implacably forthright. Every word he said had to be the gospel truth. "I'm a socialist" he would say on any suitable occasion. "What's money got to do with it?" Can you imagine George Thomas and Harold Wilson having beer and sandwiches in this very kitchen at election time? I can remember George Thomas asking for orange juice and my father giving him a large whisky. It was a huge joke.'

'Where was your mother?'

'Nowhere to be seen that I can recall. He had his debentures for rugby internationals. I used to sit next to him and shout whatever he shouted. Basking in his reflected glory. Cigars, red face, sheepskin coat and all. But then when I grew up I changed sides. And that happened without me noticing. I must have come to realise how badly my mother was treated. From then on he saw his son a frivolous failure. Wishing it had been the other twin who'd survived. I know that. Anybody who drops the ball instead of using all his strength to push over the line has to be some kind of traitor.'

Arnot smiled and poured himself another cup of coffee.

'So there you are. That's where my sense of guilt and inadequacy comes from.'

'What about your grandfather? The tyrant of Pen-yr-Orsedd.'

'What about him?'

'I was thinking about Menna.'

'You'll be able to think about her all the way through France.'

'...Torn between a tyrannical father and a brutal husband.'

'That's what you say. You are probably right of course. But I've never heard her say that.'

'Exactly. She never whinges and never complains. It's most annoying. Sometimes I see her as one of the last of a long line of Welsh idealists. Like the Albigensians and the Cathars. Scheduled for extinction. Too perfect to exist in an imperfect world. Stop me. I'm starting again. For three days I have poured over heaps of cold facts and they absolutely refuse to come to life. I thought your mother might turn a key or something. if only she would complain a bit sometimes. Moan about things.'

'Well...'

Arnot shrugged his shoulders regretfully.

'Perhaps that's the way she wants them. Dead and buried.'

'You think I'm a grave robber. A necro-something or other.'

'Of course I don't.'

'I'm looking for meaning.'

'Of course you are. I know that.'

'All those years of not speaking. Cut off from her father and more or less not talking to her husband. Can you remember all that?'

'I prefer not to.'

'You saw him anyway, didn't you? In the end. Your grand-dad. Taid Pen-yr-Orsedd. What was he like?'

'He was ill and old. His mouth twisted after a stroke. It frightened me the way he looked at me.'

'What way?'

'As if he could eat me. Like a wolf. I was petrified.'

'You poor darling. You poor darling.'

Lisa was suddenly moved to console him as though he were still a ten year old boy confronted with an inexplicable terror.

'It was probably nothing more than clotted love turned sour,' she said. 'Let's go into the garden. What's sunlight good for except to dispel the fears of the dark.'

He opened his arms and they were prepared to take comfort in each other. He was tender and careful and they responded to each other consciously as if two halves were predestined to make a satisfying whole. Whatever they chose to murmur was a private music never meant to be overheard. They were absorbed in each other when they heard his mother's voice calling gently from the other side of the house.


## III


Arnot's mother came into the world on the fourteenth day of October at Pen-yr-Orsedd farm in the county of Caernarfon. She was baptised Menna Mair Cyffin not without difficulty since her father David Cyffin insisted on registering the birth in Welsh. Menna was always aware of the irony and said she had been born into the thick of the language battle. Her father had failed to obtain that Welsh Birth Certificate after coming to blows with the part time Registrar. Menna enjoyed her monoglot Welsh childhood. It revolved around home, school and chapel and all the animals on the farm spoke Welsh. The high points of her existence were competing in Eisteddfodau where she sang and recited and wrote essays and joined choirs to her heart's content. English came more or less with adolescence and was equally disturbing.

Her father's difficulties were part of her growing up as if they had been inscribed on tablets of stone on the farmhouse wall. Dafydd Cyffin lost his older brother in the first war and the younger, irony of ironies, in the second. It had been his melancholy duty to keep the home fire burning on the hearth of Pen-yr-Orsedd. He used to mutter things like '*Myfi yn unig a adawyd*' – *I alone am left...* (self-pity with a biblical overtone) and was always conscious of a special responsibility for an inheritance that weighed like a cape of lead over his shoulders as he trudged around his fields. Menna was seven years old when that second great blow fell and she could still remember it. Green blinds were drawn all around the farm house although there was no one about to observe the signs of mourning, and only herself and her brother Geraint to listen to the sobs in a darkened house. History was against Dafydd and had been as he saw it more or less since the fifteenth century. He had a special hatred for the Tudors. He wasn't much of a farmer, too fond of reading until his convictions made him give up buying English books. He had one skill that stood the family in good stead. Castrating. At certain times of the year he was much in demand. Sheep. Cattle. Horses. Cats and dogs even. This not only gave her brother Geraint his first introduction to surgery. It also helped to pay his fees at medical school.

Dafydd was a man that needed constant understanding: her mother Annie needed nothing more than the occasion to love. When Menna brought Reg Stephens of Pontypridd home for the first time Annie's welcoming smile lit up the kitchen doorway. She used her pinafore to conceal her rough red hands. The tea table was laden with scones and cakes and the air was fragrant with the smell of home baked bread. Annie saw the young man as a hero from the South and she was eager to entertain him with worshipful affection. Dafydd may have been jealous. He decided Reg was an uncouth barbarian who couldn't speak Welsh and wouldn't try.

Menna could have gone to Oxford but it was her father who had insisted on Cardiff. It seemed that the vagaries of some historical necessity were at the source of all her troubles. At Cardiff her fair fresh beauty caught the attention of Reg Stephens, the brave and brawny captain of the first fifteen. Nothing could more clearly demonstrate that physical attraction with all its power was never enough. Over eager to please Reg and his boisterous family Annie had the wedding invitations printed in English. Dafydd Cyffin on the lame excuse of fading health, did not attend the wedding.

Having disappointed her father, Menna went on to disappoint her husband even more. She was insufficiently appreciative of his growing network of business and rugby connections: and he was impatient with her quiet adherence to idealistic Welsh causes. There was a brief interval of happiness and mutual tolerance when the twins Arnot and Idris were born. But this was shattered for ever when Menna took the little boys, aged barely three to stay with her brother Geraint near the orthopaedic hospital where he worked in Staffordshire. Reg said the visit was totally unnecessary. An obscure north Wales tribal ritual related to obstinate language devotions. Menna insisted on going. Geraint's impressive house was on the outskirts of a quiet village but this did not save little Idris from being run over by a heavy lorry, when for a fatal moment Menna was not looking. Nothing could roll the seconds or the minutes back, or restore the original love between husband and wife. Reg grew wealthier, became more fervently socialist, glaring at the world straight in the eye and insisting that problems be sorted out.

Menna became thin and other-worldly. They stayed together for Arnot's sake and because they had no clear idea what else they could do.

Her father died, Menna thought, because he was too angry with the world to go on living in it. What was the point of a congregation bawling out hymns about great Jesus taking possession of every continent, when it was so manifest that exactly the opposite was the case. Dafydd's causes were all failed causes and he was continually tempted to sulk in his tent. There was a fatal anger in her husband too. When the last Labour government fell, Reg announced he was giving up socialism for psycho-analysis. He also took to drink and to womanising, and spending more and more time away from home pursuing a bizarre mixture of business ventures with even more bizarre success. A wealthy widow with whom he had a financial and sexual liaison found him dead in a hotel bedroom in Malaga. He left a note for her saying he had had enough. This woman appropriated a good part of his fortune. Menna made no attempt to get it back. She had her home and her son and an adequate income and the tensile strength of her quiet convictions.

IV

Menna tapped the kitchen door with her knuckle although it was already open.

Arnot and Lisa stood apart, disengaged from their embrace but held in their web of affection.

'My dears,' Menna said. 'What a beautiful morning. I bring you good news. My disappointment but your relief.'

She stood with her thin hands clasped together like a benevolent infants teacher about to make an announcement to the class. Her blue eyes were enlarged by the lens of her spectacles and her small mouth was curved in a characteristic sweet smile. She was neat but she had little concern for her appearance. Her face was etched with lines and her faded hair was in need of attention.

'I can't come.'

'Oh no...'

Lisa gave a prolonged cry that could have signalled relief or disappointment. She and Arnot were transfixed by Menna's beatific smile.

'Have you done your meditation?'

It was all that Arnot seemed capable of saying. His mother would have penetrated immediately any pretence on his part. She responded now as if her mental regime were an appropriate subject for polite jokes. Her observances and duties divided her day with such regularity, Arnot could tease her by urging her to look around for some suitable nonconformist monastic order.

'I'll stay home and feed the cat,' Menna said. 'Isn't it odd the way things all happen at once? It's the bouncing bishop again. I was already in bed when he rang. "We've got to make a concentrated attack," he says, "all guns blazing." That's the way he talks. Like most pacifists he is obsessed with military metaphors. He does tend to chatter. I tell him quite frankly, "Bishop Bob, when words come to an end, life begins." '

Arnot and Lisa tried to smile. In spite of her consistent affability Menna's remarks often had a way of turning into a disturbing query. Whether they responded or not never seemed to concern her. Menna's ship of life, Lisa said, sailed on an even keel of unimpeded benevolence.

'What does the bouncing bishop want this time?' Arnot said.

'Money. What else? We've got to advance on the citadels of capital to capture new water grants for our centres in Southern India and Kenya. We may even have to go there. But the first step is to attack the Brussels-Strasbourg eleemosynary axis! And behind that of course the multinational citadels. My goodness! I'm getting to sound just like him.'

'Will you have a cup of coffee?'

Arnot raised the coffee pot to show that he was ready to pour. Menna shook her head to show she couldn't spare the time.

'Anyway my dears, you will be able to enjoy your holiday in peace. Except that it's not a holiday, is it? It's work really. Books to be written. I am full of admiration.'

Her speech was measured as if she were making a public statement by which she was prepared to take a stand. She took little

notice of Lisa's vague fluttering gestures to suggest her own inade-
quacy.

'I couldn't go to sleep last night thinking about your obstinate
heretics, Lisa. I just had to come to a conclusion. I mean the world
is wicked, no question about it. Do you know what I think the
mistake they made? Poor old things. They forgot the spirit could be
more wicked than the flesh. Simplistic of course. But it brought me
some comfort.'

'Ah well...'

Lisa seemed eager to be as open and frank as her mother-in-law.
Only the complexity of her thesis held her back as she groped for
an equally forthright and simple mode of expression. Menna could
not wait to draw attention to the proof of her preposition. She
laughed delightedly at her son.

'There he is,' she said. 'The evidence. Flesh must be more good
than bad. There's Arnot to prove it. Flesh of my flesh and my pride
and joy. Could there be a better reason for carrying on breathing?'

Menna clapped her hands she was so pleased with the line of
reasoning.

'Why else do we sing *Unto us a child is born*... And that's not blas-
phemy. It's sound theology. It accounts for continuing worthwhile
existence. And I'm rambling on when I've got a hundred and one
things to do. I'm off. You two take care of each other.'

It seemed a brief blessing. She disappeared and left them stand-
ing under the spell of her visitation.

'You see what I mean,' Lisa said. 'She's quite unbearable.'

Arnot was uneasy at the thought of joining an attack on his
mother.

'Oh, I don't know.' he said.

'Unbearably good of course. In perfect contrast to me. What is
my concentrated hysteria to compare with all she has suffered? A
life time of misfortune. An awful father. An awful husband. A lost
child. But she doesn't brood. She rises above it.'

'Well,' Arnot said. 'That's pretty good.'

'Of course it is. But could you hear what she was really saying?'

'She always says what she means.'

'You need a woman's ear to hear it. It's not even a hidden
agenda. *Flesh of my flesh...unto us a child is born.* More than anything
in the world, including fresh water in those orphanages in southern
India. She wants me pregnant.'

V

Lisa drifted between the bedroom and her study. Her attention was unequally divided between the slips and notes on her desk and the business of making lists and packing. Arnot had many last minute problems to attend to in the office and Lisa had said the least she could do was the final preparations for their trip. They had agreed to take as few clothes as possible. It was early June and they would be travelling south. A slow circuit in search of the essential atmosphere. Not just the obvious places in the Languedoc but lesser known pockets in the Jura and Savoy and even the Ardennes. Arnot had been planning an epic expedition for his own pleasure but also to relieve her intensity: the awkward struggle between research and imaginative freedom, the search for the magic formula that would resolve the contradictions that tormented her. She was surveying the paper chaos on her desk as though deciding whether or not to take the whole lot along with them in a green suitcase in the boot of their car, when the customary polite tap on the door announced her mother-in-law's approach. When she came in the room her smile was as cherubic as ever.

'There are always people who interrupt at the last moment. And I seem to be one of them. There was just something I wanted to tell you.'

Her attempt to hide something behind her back looked like a child's innocent exercise in mischief.

'What you were saying about your French heretics. It's been on my mind ever since. Was I one of them?'

The question was so direct Lisa began to blush instead of providing a satisfactory answer.

'You're too busy now,' Menna said. 'I shouldn't be disturbing you.'

'Of course you're not disturbing me. I need a distraction. All I'm doing is going over in my mind all the items I'm sure to forget. Keys are a particular nightmare. And money. And credit cards.'

'I've been burning diaries,' Menna said.

She was releasing news she could no longer contain. She sat herself neatly on the window seat cradling a discoloured quarto volume in her lap. She was dressed in a brown tweed suit that fitted her so loosely it made her appear thinner than ever. Her spectacles enlarged her eyes in the evening light and added to the intensity of her smile.

'Quite an unpleasant experience,' she said. 'Looking through them. All those years of mistakes and misery. Why did I keep it? An adolescent habit. I suppose it was a way of talking to myself and I had to keep it up. If there's no one to talk to except yourself what you put down becomes so bloated and distorted. They're all old anyway. I gave up the habit when we lost Idris. So many unspeakable things. I began to appreciate the blessings of silence.'

She stopped speaking to think more intently.

'Buried alive in an avalanche of soul searching. I remember how I used to feel. Until you long for the great calm of death. Is that what your heretics were doing?'

'Well they certainly thought the world was wicked.'

Lisa frowned with the effort of formulating a rapid response to the challenge.

'They had to escape from the vileness of their bodies to make themselves spirit as far as they could.'

Menna gave a slow sequence of nods to show understanding both of how the heretics had felt and of Lisa's purpose.

'And you think our native idealists have much in common with them? People like me for instance?'

Lisa was blushing again. Her mother-in-law could so easily exert a capacity to make her uncomfortable.

'Not you for heaven's sake.'

The denial deepened her discomfort.

'I was thinking in general terms. Idealistic nonconformist pacifism and so on, combined with the doom-laden atmosphere that goes with a language and culture in decline. That is the trouble really. General terms are so bloody pedestrian. Lacking in life and colour.'

Menna raised the old diary in her hand.

'I kept this one back,' she said. 'The brand rescued from the fire. Just in case you could use it. 1969. Another fatal year. That's what I thought when I was burning them. One fatal year after another. And yet they couldn't have been all that bad. Not when you look at me now.'

She sat on the window seat modestly inviting inspection. A thin ageing creature so much at ease with herself that nothing in the world around her could offer her any terrors.

'Storms in teacups and turning points. Which is which? There you are. Make what use of it you like. All I ask is that you burn it when you've finished. They were real turning points at the time.

95

We were invited to be presented to the Prince of Wales before the Investiture. I refused to go. Reg was furious. That was when we began to stop talking unless there was somebody else present. And that was the year my father began to go blind. Poor old Dafydd also decided to start preaching. Emptying chapels even faster than the telly, my brother Geraint called it. A few years later he had his colostomy. That's when he became disgusted with his own body. He didn't die, Geraint said, he imploded in a fever of indignation. I didn't get there in time to find out whether he recognised the incredible loving care of his wife before he died. She'd nourished him for forty years so that he could go on complaining. That was a way of looking at it.'

Lisa held the old diary in both hands as though she were afraid of opening it and reading the lines of small cramped urgent handwriting.

'Guilty people always try to destroy the evidence,' Menna said.

'You are not guilty.'

In an impulse of unrestrained sympathy Lisa sat next to her mother-in-law so that she could take her cold hand in her own.

'Those diaries told me clearly enough I must have been responsible for at least three deaths. My son's. My husband's. My father's.'

'Now then.'

Lisa squeezed the cold hand and then shook it in disapproval.

'You mustn't say such things. They are not true. And you have no right to torment yourself or blame yourself in any way at all.'

'I might have it now. But I didn't have it then.'

'Have what?'

'Enough love to save even one person.'

Menna spoke with a calm certainty that was more disturbing than any quiver of remorse. She was summing up her own experience with the detachment of a scientist explaining a theory of infinite detraction to someone else and prepared to follow a tenuous thread of reason.

'I could see what Reg was from the very beginning. One of those raucous socialists from the valleys who spend a lot of energy proving they are not only as good as but better than anyone in sight. From the very beginning the pinnacle of proof for Reg was showing off in London because that was his top of the midden. I knew all that but I was so smitten with those angry good looks I was ready to make myself believe anything about him so long as it said he was wonderful. And I suppose in his own way he was wonderful. All that energy and animal power. And then of course when he really got going I couldn't keep up with him. He used to call me "Menna weak and milky." '

Even now, in spite of her calm, there was a residue of hurt in the way she uttered the nickname. Lisa opened her arms in a gesture that implied there had to be circumstances, sociological imperatives that could explain an unhappy conjunction of events. She restrained herself from speaking because she surmised there was little she could say that Menna did not already know.

'I left the gate open because I was in a desperate hurry to get into the house and stop Geraint from telephoning my father. About something so trivial, but it seemed desperately important at the time. My father wanted to speak with the young people at a protest meeting. The language of course. Geraint thought it was a mistake. I thought he was doing the right thing. And little Idris wandered into the road and got run over. It's so terrifyingly simple. The way things happen.'

Menna pointed at the diary.

'The facts are there. And all the excuses. Make what you can of it, my dear. It's no longer part of my progress. As you get older you have this curious sensation of the past falling away in order to make way for a different existence. This must be where I differ from your medieval heretics.'

They smiled at each other like two intelligent well-educated women ready to share their doubts and misgivings about life in a calm reflective mode.

'We need to go through it,' Menna said. 'We need to be in the here and now to exercise our share of free-will and not be terrified of being tested. That's the path I see, like a personal experience of evolutionary biology. It used to be called the progress of the soul. That's another snag, isn't it? Words and phrases fall away and we have to work out a new vocabulary. You'll write something for him. My Mr. Yoreth and his private press. Translate my miserable little misfortunes into a higher fiction. He says he wants to bury new treasures in our language that will make future generations want to dig them up. I think that's a noble ambition. I know he'd give anything to publish a story by you. His right arm, as they used to say.'

Menna's dry smile showed that no flattery was intended. Lisa was obliged to laugh to disguise how much she had been softened by the compliments.

'Poor Merfyn,' Menna said. 'He'll be Sir Merfyn Yoreth one day. He's made so much money in the mass media, he's longing to produce beautiful books in the old language. He's quite intelligent really. He says the trick is to wrap up the best secrets and bury them in their own beauty. Like the Sybilline books.'

Menna's sudden hoot of laughter was far in excess of the humour in what she was saying. Lisa was paying her such close attention she became solemn again. The 1969 diary lay on the window-seat between them.

"I was just about your age, Lisa when all that went on. But so immature and foolish. I offer you my suffering that was, so that you won't need to experiment on yourself, my dear.'

Her head turned in an owlish motion so that she could peer closely into Lisa's pretty face.

'It gives me so much pleasure to see the depth of understanding between you. I try to keep my distance but it's so wonderful to watch. You have so much to achieve. The future really is yours. That's the end of my pronouncements. I must leave you to get on with your packing.'

She stood up with the precision of a teacher who anticipates the reverberation of the bell that signals the end of a lesson. Lisa had one more question to ask.

'Menna,' she said. 'You don't see me as standing in his way?'

Menna stood in the doorway taking time to answer.

'My son of prophecy,' she said. 'I must have felt all the time he was the thing worth living for. My one success to justify all my failures. That's the kind of thing one has to believe I suppose, to keep going'

'You want him to stand for the Assembly?'

Menna took her time to answer this question too.

'Well he is the kind of person who would give the thing substance and meaning. And the kind of dignity it needs. Arnot always thinks before he speaks. Not like his father.'

'And what else? What else would you like to see us do?'

Menna's smile was mischievous.

'Just perpetuate yourselves. Not like those heretics of yours. You are too good not to inhabit the future. And above all, ignore me. These things must come from within. Please yourselves and forget about pleasing me. How does the saying go? Love and do what you like.'

## VI

The dominating sensation was floating towards an extended else-
where on a motorway as unsmirched as a stretched ribbon. The
index finger of Arnot's powerful right hand was in easy charge of
the steering wheel and from time to time his content expressed itself
in tuneful humming. It was still early in the morning and the sun
shone over the late spring countryside. These were the southern
English counties and everywhere there were glimpses of a romantic
past to be visited at some other time. Arnot was more aware of their
immediate surroundings than Lisa who was slumped in the passen-
ger seat as though to demonstrate how far she was also slumped in
her own thoughts.

'It's not a bit like her.'

Lisa could have been talking to herself. Arnot smiled with the
quiet pleasure he always enjoyed at being allowed to share her
thoughts.

'You mother's diary. So depressing. And bitter. You seem to
have been the only thing that made her life bearable. The fight for
this and the fight for that. The epic battle with your father to send
you to the Welsh school. And keep you there. He seems to have
thought it was a hotbed of Welsh Nats. Closet Fascists he called
them. Stuffing the language down freedom loving socialist throats.
Oh dear.'

Arnot was prepared to launch on a recitative.

'Look at lovely England. All around you. Turn left for Fairford
and all that gorgeous stained glass. This blessed plot. Long live the
English and their miraculous capacity not to be anybody or
anything but themselves. The best in the world. Look at it all
around you. The home of benevolent speculation. Lord and Lady
Unfettered-Whimsy. God save the Queen!'

Lisa's spirits lifted.

'Let's go somewhere where the world will never find us!'

Arnot was delighted and began singing again.

'Pack up your troubles in your B.M.W. and smile smile smile...'

It was his job to cheer her up and he undertook it with a will.
Gifted women were vulnerable. Just as vulnerable as medieval
maidens in distress. In need of his protection. It was part of the
purpose of his exceptional health and strength. He was there to look
after her and enjoy doing it.

'Is it possible to be as free as a bird?'

Lisa was squinting up at a sparrowhawk hovering above the motorway.

'We can but try,' Arnot said cheerfully. 'They're not free anyway. Chained to their appetites.'

They were bowling along so easily it became a fact that they were enjoying a release from their responsibilities that gave them greater freedom than any bird: the well tuned engine designed to carol the joys of escape. A vast enticing world was laid out to offer them the privilege of exploration.

'Like stale bread breaking under your fingers.'

Lisa's thoughts had slipped back to her mother-in-law's diary.

'The sadness of it. Those spiritual struggles. That's what they were. She'd be looking at you and thinking of your twin and her responsibility and guilt. He's a ghostly presence all the time. The life that was there and the life that wasn't there. So dispiriting. To read about it. And your impossible father. I don't know why she gave it to me. It's not really relevant to my research. And yet she obviously thought it was. Amazing how easy it is for people to misunderstand each other.'

'Except us,' Arnot said.

He held out a hand to grasp hers and squeeze it confidently.

'Were you aware of this ghost? When you were little?'

Arnot released her hand and leaned forward over the steering wheel to deliver a considered answer.

'I still am,' he said. 'Down at the very bottom of my dreams. A fissure that is there and not there. A good definition of a ghost.'

'She makes me feel mean and selfish just to have a duty to myself.'

'I don't follow.'

'She wants a substitute for that missing twin. And I am the one appointed to supply it.'

'Has she said that?'

'Not in so many words. But she thinks it. That's the real reason why she's given me the old diary. So that I can put two and two together. What she was like when she was my age and what she's like now. If I don't follow the correct course I shall prove myself to be a monster of selfishness.'

'Gosh.'

Arnot sounded so genuinely bewildered by such labyrinthine reasoning that Lisa burst out laughing and grabbed his arm affectionately.

'I do love you,' she said. 'Did you know that?'

They drove on contentedly enough until the traffic grew heavier and then progress was reduced by the red and white cones of contraflow. They had the car radio and a collection of cassettes at their disposal. Lisa folded her arms and lapsed into a pleasant melancholy as she listened to a soprano singing *Nacht und Traume* with sustained sensitivity and skill.

'You are not really in touch with the depth of my dilemma.' she said.

There was no reproach in her voice, only a continuation of the song's heartfelt regret. Arnot straightened in his seat to become fully alert to her change of mood.

'I don't blame you,' she said. 'How could I. It's not just the comprehensive curse of being a woman. That's just a feminist excuse. Mind you I'm not above using it when it suits me. I am a bird condemned to sing inside my biological cage and all that convenient crap. The truth about your wife, Arnot Stephens, is that she is not a professional story-teller. Good word that "professional." I am not a quick concoctor of plots. And at this moment in time that is exactly what I need to be. Then I wouldn't be driven into these absurdities. Turning your sainted mother into a twelfth century French heretic. I must have been desperate. And yet there is something lurking in there. If only I could get at it.'

Arnot was eager to make encouraging suggestions. Instead he continued to pay close attention since it was clear this was what she most required him to do.

'I haven't got words like whips and scorpions at my finger tips either. And yet, damn it, I do have something to say. All these perceptions, understanding, clamouring inside me to find an outlet. And I thought this was it. Two forms of heretical puritanism, a millennium apart. The human race, sliding up and down above the gulf of primeval chaos. The human condition and all that. It's a bloody thesis not a work of art. And it's all I'm good for. What's the good of a vision if it filters away like water between your fingers?'

She was so vehement. He was at a loss to provide the appropriate comfort. He murmured her name once or twice in an attempt to reassure her. It would have been no use telling her she was the brightest woman in the world at a time when she believed exactly the opposite. He was at her side to clear any obstacle out of her way if only the obstruction took on a physical dimension. Meanwhile he had to exercise an almost religious restraint and wait for her to compose herself.

'In some annoying way, your mother understands better than you do. Or I do, come to that. It's as if she were standing on a further shore and watching me struggle in a welter of watery wishing. She's been through it all. Every modern woman's dilemma. Career or motherhood, or make a mess of both. My unwritten books are my unborn children.'

The flow of traffic was reduced to a crawl. Lisa was still absorbed in her problem. With her small fist she struck Arnot on the arm.

'Be more selfish won't you Arnot Stephens. Stop being so perfect. Less of this natural Christian soul business.'

His response was an attempt to demonstrate a capacity for ill temper by swearing at the traffic. This ended with a laugh at the absurdity of any form of protest. They were in holiday clothes and they needed to maintain a holiday mode. Lisa was still muttering about writers being self-absorbed shits and what was he going to do about it. Arnot weighed the matter carefully.

'Writers take their own kind of risk... What did that French chap say? "Expose their nerve ends to the sharp knives of experience?"'

The traffic stopped and Lisa was constrained to take in their immediate surroundings. All they could do was sit in their metal capsule and wait to move forward by miniscule fits and starts. The arbitrary uniformity of humans caged in immobile motor cars took her fancy. She compared their situation with an army of terracotta soldiers in a Chinese emperor's tomb all pointing in the same direction beautifully disciplined and arriving nowhere.

'Do we drive or are we driven?'

Her attention was taken by the behaviour of children on the back seat of the car in front of them. The girl with wild fair hair and the round faced small boy were absorbed in attempts to devise new methods of behaving badly. The intermittent progress and prolonged stops established a relationship. Arnot was benevolent enough. He waved with his fingertips while both his hands rested on the steering wheel. The girl had a lollipop to wave about before she stuck it in her mouth. One suck was enough before she stuck it in her little brother's ear and he burst out crying. Urged by the father at the wheel the mother turned in her seat to aim a swipe at her daughter who dodged it with what appeared to be practised ease.

'Makes you long to have children, doesn't it?' Lisa said. 'Just look at that one. She's in training to become a witch.'

The car in front braked suddenly and listening to Lisa, Arnot drifted into it. The bump was inconsiderable but noisy. The children collapsed out of sight. Their father emerged from his car in a threatening manner. His bare arms were decorated with tattoos.

'What the hell do you think you're doing, mate?'

Arnot had lowered his window ready to apologise.

'Can't you see I've got children on board. And look at that! Look what you've bloody done.'

Arnot emerged to examine the damage. Lisa watched the practised manner with which her husband calmed the irate father. Arnot seemed to give him such close and sympathetic attention that when the plump wife joined in to claim she had suffered 'whiplash' and demand compensation, her husband told her to shut up. Arnot gave him his card. They agreed the damage was negligible and when other motorists began to hoot he turned what little wrath he had left against them.

'You were marvellous.'

Lisa stroked Arnot's thigh when he resumed his place behind the wheel.

'I'm so grateful for you. I can't tell you.'


VII


Arnot gazed fondly at his wife across the table. She was burbling on, inspired by the wine to give a mini-lecture on the re-emergence of the medieval in the new unity of modern Europe. It was a favourite theme of hers but when she was soberly intent on one of her creative compulsions, she kept it rigorously in check. She had to be aware of the dangers of over-simplification and yet she knew the foundation of an imaginative superstructure demanded a bedrock of unambiguous simplicity. Arnot for his part listened with unalloyed pleasure to the music of her voice weaving her arabesques of speculation.

'Perhaps this is what I should do!'

Lisa was enjoying the sensation of listening to herself through Arnot's admiring ears. Her eyes glittered in the candlelight with the joy of discovery.

'*Plus je voyageais loin, plus j'aimais ma patrie.* Take a line like that and extemporise. Variations on a theme. The style to be the substance fricassee. A gorgeous illusion of chips and splinters.

Transferred from canvas wood and stone to words. And you Arnot the Everready, with pencil poised and tape recorder switched on... Do you remember Daisy Winger? Of course you don't. She sat in the back and took notes at Winger's lectures. Just in case a pearl should fall from his lips and no one picked it up.'

Lisa stiffened in her chair and brought her hands together in imitation of the statuesque stillness with which those lectures were delivered.

'They came out of his little mouth like long strips of monotone ectoplasm. And dear old Daisy would scribble scribble away.'

It seemed that from the moment they drove on to French soil Lisa had resolved to elevate herself to a level of existence where uninhibited expression became the rule rather than the exception. She uttered loudly whatever came into her head and since it was in Welsh, wherever they were, she assumed that only Arnot would understand her. He was more than willing to respond to her whims and caprices. First they searched for medieval bits and pieces, stained glass, belfries, tombs: places that they knew about and wanted to re-visit, or new references noted for her researches. Lisa scanned the landscape with concentrated passion. Somewhere or other she would encounter an ancient orchard near a river where her heretic maiden was accosted by that lascivious cleric. Searching a countryside of orchards they would somehow discover the very spot where the sly fellow had observed her comeliness, and where she repulsed his advances with a simple gesture and sober words that would lead her to her doom. If she were once defiled and lost her virginity she would suffer eternal damnation beyond all help. Hearing this, the lustful cleric knew her for one of the heretic sect of Cathars and denounced her to the archbishop. The B.M.W. almost got stuck in the wet soil and when they reversed out of it Lisa declared that at least the river was the same even if the water was changed.

In her mood for medieval miraculism Lisa became convinced that there were dolmens moving in the landscape and cromlechs following them around. She found proof positive in the courtyard of the Musée des Beaux Arts de Troyes and insisted on photographing Arnot alongside the sombre stones in the shade of the spreading oak tree. In search for yet more passage graves in the gathering twilight they stumbled across the rambling rundown manor house hotel the proprietors chose to call, Chateau Marigny. Monsieur was of Italian origin and on the excuse of paying them obsequious attention pirouetted gallantly around Lisa, eyeing her shapely form and complimenting her on her excellent French; until Madame, a statuesque native whose stiff coiffure and heavy make-up failed to disguise her dour aspect, called her husband to attention.

When their lengthy meal was at an end it was Madame and not Monsieur who led them back to their bedroom which was a converted outhouse. In the dark corridor, once her husband was out of earshot, she launched herself into a practiced oration that gave them a potted history of the chateau. As though it might account for any existing shortcomings she intoned that the house had only been partially restored in 1830 after it had been destroyed in the Revolution. It was, she assured them redolent with history more than sufficient to make up for any deficiencies in its upkeep. Staff was hard to find and harder still to keep, and a socialist government seemed bent on driving the hardworking self-employed into an early grave. The room they were allocated had been termed the Bridal Suite in better days and she had once slept in it herself and it still combined a magnificent decor with the most modern conveniences. She took her leave with the deliberation of a public servant who has discharged her duty with decorous correctness and closed the heavy door behind her.

'My god!'

A fit of giggling made Lisa unsteady on her feet.

'It's a barn not a bedroom. There must be chickens here some-where!'

Anything they happened to say in their mildly inebriate condition could pass for being witty. She collapsed into an ancient green sofa disturbing the dust and her giggle was overtaken by a fit of cough-ing. Gasping for breath she pointed at a tattered tapestry stretched across the wall to conceal long cracks in the plaster.

'Just look at that!'

Faded Rubensesque naked ladies bathing in a forest pool were being spied on by overdressed cavaliers. Their commander, mounted on a rearing charger, was pointing in a different direction as though urging them to return to duty: to turn their fuddled minds from dalliance to the field of war.

'That's you up there, Arnot Stephens! All you need is a hat and a moustache and you'd be a grand duke!'

Arnot moved to the three windows that looked out on a moonlit lake.

'No one knows where we are,' he said. 'And we don't either. All we've got is each other.'

He was making an effort to be serious without growing maudlin. Lisa continued to explore their surroundings. In stark contrast to the big room and the old fashioned furniture that looked too heavy to move there was a bathroom attached that was all chrome and glass, gleaming and glittering in a rosy light. Set into the wall above the bath was a recently completed mosaic of a reclining odalisque scantily clad but still wearing a diaphanous yashmak. The mattress on the matrimonial bed was new while the drapes of the four poster were thin and even worn in places.

'I tell you something Arnot Stephens. This barn is a part time brothel. God knows what goes on here.'

Arnot smiled but he was finding it difficult to attend to her speculations about their surroundings. He was caught up in the contemplation of the uniqueness of their relationship. Being in strange surroundings only brought it into sharper relief.

'People have no idea.'

His intensity made him mumble hoarsely.

'Such a force,' he said. 'Such an overwhelming power.'

Lisa held her head to one side to concentrate her attention on the solitary figure standing in the middle of the room.

'It's what you do for me,' he said. 'That's what I'm talking about. A sort of awareness I never had before. Every day it's there. Here or wherever. I absorb so much more than I can put into words.'

Lisa took his arm and led him closer to the bed.

'You are my darling,' she said. 'That's all there is to it. Your strength is never wasted on me. We are beyond words. We can escape into each other wherever we are.'

'Good wine,' Arnot said. 'Very good. But there was no need for alcohol. I've got you!'

He lifted her and laid her out on the bed to undress her. She responded willingly, praising the relaxing power of the wine until she held back his hands and said she had things to attend to. Then, she smiled, he could be as barbaric as he liked. While Lisa was in the bathroom, Arnot indulged in a series of exercises as though to prove he was in proper control of his body. He tripped over a loose carpet, fell on his face and lay stretched out laughing like a boy who has let a wild bird escape from his clutches. As he struggled to his feet and tried to exercise again, Lisa opened the bathroom door. There was a look of dismay on her face.

'Disaster,' she said, 'Disaster Arnot. I've packed the wrong pills.'

She sat on the edge of her bed in her thin dressing gown. Naked, Arnot slipped under the blue sheets and then turned to put a hand over Lisa's shoulder to comfort her.

'I can't believe it,' she said. 'Packing the wrong pills. It's worse than a *lapsus linguae*. It's too ridiculous. Unless of course your saintly mother switched them!'

'My mother?'

Arnot sounded bewildered.

'My mother-in-law'.

Lisa made a sudden decision to treat the matter lightly. She jumped to her feet and began a pantomime of searching the room.

'She's here somewhere you know. Hiding. Like that heretic.'

'What heretic?'

'My heretic maiden. She carried a spool of thread and when the fire was kindling in the city square she threw up the thread and vanished like a bird through the cathedral window. That's your Menna for you. Or have I got this wrong?'

Lisa returned to sit on the edge of the bed as though to puzzle out an insoluble problem.

'Russian roulette! Life is a gamble.'

Lisa shook her fist and smiled.

'You lie there my pretty boy. I'll have a quick wash and powder and then we'll see what fate has in store for us.'

Arnot lay back with his hands behind his head.

'Are you sure?' he said. 'Do you want to take the risk?'

Lisa emerged from the bathroom and threw away her dressing gown with a gesture that showed she was throwing caution to the winds. Under the sheet she transformed herself into a small submissive suppliant and with the persistence of a child playing with fire passed her lips and the tips of her fingers over his outstretched body from his lips to his feet.

## VIII

At breakfast Monsieur le patron was much in evidence, conspicuously spruce and enjoying greater freedom in the absence of his wife. There was little for him to do except vaguely supervise, dry wash his hands and exchange cordial morning greetings with the guests as they arrived. A damp mist had enveloped the countryside so that the lake was no longer visible. Rain water was still gurgling sporadically in the drainpipes after an overnight downpour. None of this was Monsieur's fault, but he persisted in apologising for it. It pained him deeply that the clientele should be deprived of a view of the beauties of the countryside with the Parc Regional so enticingly in view on the western horizon.

Having guided Arnot and Lisa to a corner table he took personal responsibility for attending to their needs. All his actions conveyed that he regarded them as privileged guests. It was both a pleasure and an honour to serve them. They became a focal point to his peregrinations between the tables in the long room and there were morsels of tasty information to accompany ample supplies of Evian water, coffee, hot milk, and baskets of baguette and croissants. Their bridal chamber, they would have sensed was a room of historic interest. Even after the Revolution the custom persisted for local wet nurses to lurk in the dark corridor and throw corn in the bride's face. They would cry out *planté, planté,* and make clucking noises. It was no longer the case of course. Such strange rituals, though. Persisting from the dark ages and even before that. There was a broken statue in the church which would be worth a visit. Epona, he thought it was called, a pagan goddess of the horse.

While he spoke Lisa more than once pressed her finger tips to her forehead. Monsieur was quick to notice and express concern. Lisa assured him it had to be the weather: a sudden change in air pressure: an element of subliminal dazzle in the light. She rummaged in her handbag for a pair of sunshades and Monsieur retreated backwards as though leaving a royal presence.

'Well at least I got rid of him,' Lisa murmured across the table. 'In weather like this, La Belle France is worse that Ffestiniog on a wet Sunday.'

Arnot's response was guarded. He was reluctant to bear responsibility for Lisa's mood. She was obviously worried, but he had done all he could to exercise his physical strength to please her. She had abandoned herself and now she was regretting it. He had made his offer of restraint and she had thrown caution to the winds. What else could he do except maintain a dignified silence. To make love with so much abandon was a blind ecstasy, a revelation, a quivering towards an unknown identity, a transformation of his being succeeded by a slumber like a benediction. Now at the table, he was confronted with the cold congenital inability of a male to plumb the full depth of the female psyche.

This was getting to the point of agony since there was supposed to be such a perfect flow of understanding between them.

He spoke quietly of how they might continue their journey. The wet mist was not the weather for exploring orchards. Should they make for some city with Gallo-Roman remains like Autun or more east to Dijon and make their promised expedition to explore the Palais des Ducs? Lisa was unhelpful.

'I need the sun,' she said. 'This place is depressing beyond words.'

Arnot looked around as if in search of an element in their surroundings he had been unaware of before. Inadvertently he caught the benevolent proprietor's eye and was obliged to make a small negative gesture to indicate there was nothing they needed. The decor of the place was heavy and tasteless but last night all that had amused her. She had even said it was medieval which, in her present creative phase, was a most complimentary epithet.

'I want to see Albi again.'

Arnot was ready to respond with enthusiasm. This was a positive move. Perhaps movement was what they needed most. Even if it were no more than an illusion driving south was bound to instill the exhilaration of escape. This could be easily shared in spite of the weather or Lisa's temporary dejection.

'Before I die.'

He heard her say it without first understanding it.

'Or pay the price of your pleasure,' she said. 'Which is more or less the same thing.'

He was hurt and he had no way of concealing it. When she realised this Lisa was immediately contrite. She sought to cover his hand with hers and found it cold and motionless: not so much unresponsive as paralysed. She lowered her head to whisper urgently

'I'm sorry. Take no notice of me. I don't know why I said it.'

Arnot nodded and smiled bleakly but he could think of nothing to say. He was able to concentrate on the mechanics of departure. He explained to the proprietor that his wife was prone to migraine. Monsieur replied that his wife was also a sufferer. He had a range of homeopathic pills in their bathroom and it would be no trouble at all to fetch some if Arnot thought they could help. Arnot explained that Lisa had all she needed. At the reception desk the two men seemed to establish a certain rapport. Arnot paid their bill and he was explaining how they were Welsh not English when Lisa reappeared safe behind her defensive looking sunshades. Their departure was sealed with handshakes and bows.

Seated in the car Arnot studied maps and there were polite consultations about the best route to take. They were agreed on not using the autoroute. They would take their time, see what they could see, and wait for the weather to clear as it certainly would.

Both made an effort to be positive and cheerful: but this petered out as the clouds sank lower and nothing around them offered the comfort of diversion. Arnot gripped the steering wheel and wondered aloud whether the autoroute would have been better after all. Lisa muttered he should do as he pleased. Whatever lay ahead had to be better than what they were leaving behind. In her passenger seat she was the captive of a prolonged silence. The prospect was daunting. If communication between lovers broke down each was faced with the threat of the awesome isolation of a piece of debris hurtling towards the void of outer space.

The autoroute offered little comfort. Gusts of unseasonable rain from the north west scudded across the road and Arnot swore and cursed every time spray from overtaking lorries threatened to engulf them. He was caught up in an interminable chase as if being left behind was a life threatening disgrace. Lisa was jerked out of her mood of introspection by a spasm of nervousness that made her sit up and stare into the blurred image in the offside mirror. Under these conditions a car with a right hand drive was under a distinct disadvantage. Lisa cleared her throat and in a strangled voice begged her husband to restrain his aggression and turn off the autoroute at the next available exit.

Once on the Departmental road Arnot reduced his speed and the rain seemed to ease. They were offered brief but cheering glimpses of woodland and fruitfulness. Lisa became sufficiently relaxed to indulge in a bout of self-criticism.

'I'm a bitch,' she said. 'And now you know it.'

Arnot shook his head in vigorous denial.

'Nothing to hide my naked bitchery. No comforting rags of routine. Have you started missing the office yet?'

'Don't talk rubbish.'

He spoke so harshly she was driven back into silence. They could no more escape from this inability to communicate freely with each other than from the rain. Arnot developed an intense interest in road signs and the windscreen wiper sliced the silence between them with the relentless accuracy of a metronome.

'We should have brought her with us.'

Lisa muttered as if she were talking to herself.

'What are you talking about?'

Arnot peered angrily through the windscreen.

'I can just imagine the effort she would make to ease the tension. If she were sitting on the back seat now.'

She touched his arm gently and smiled. He had to give in. At least they were ready to laugh together.

'She has this saintly touch,' Lisa said. 'And saints can work miracles. No question about it. She might even transform me from a bitch into a loving wife.'

High walls and rows of houses replaced the countryside. The place name had a hyphen in the middle but they had driven past before it registered. Approaching the modest town square Lisa pointed to the luminous green cross above the pharmacy.

'There's a place to park,' she said. 'Opposite in front of the church.'

It had stopped raining but the leaves of a row of chestnut trees in front of the church were still dripping.

'Black catholic country.'

Lisa sounded knowledgeable.

'Stained with the counter-reformation. Give me pure medieval every time.'

'The church looks old enough,' Arnot said. 'Even for you.'

He was curious to hear more from Lisa about what she liked to call her version of the medieval world view, but she was already intent on visiting the pharmacy. The sombre beauty of the ancient church was surrounded by a meticulously well kept cemetery. Arnot walked around to look at the angled polished grave stones carrying family names in gold and silver lettering and dates and photographs of the more recently deceased taken at some frozen moment in their living prime. He followed the path to the rear of the church to study the older tombs and take note of the dates and the ages inscribed on them. There was a variety of grief stricken angels of discoloured marble mourning children dying within months rather than years. It became clear that at one period in the mid-nineteenth century this little town in its idyllic rural surroundings had been visited by cholera.

He returned to the comfort of the car and sat in the driving seat with his chin on his chest, waiting for Lisa. She emerged from the pharmacy looking cheerful and relaxed like a person resolved to turn over a new leaf. She opened the car door and waved a pair of toothbrushes in their plastic cases under his nose.

'Useful places, pharmacies,' she said. 'Attend to all your hygienic needs.'

His spirits rose with hers. The last traces of discord were dispersed as they were both eager to acknowledge how much easier it was to face the world together than alone. There were interesting ruins two kilometres outside the township, the chemist had told her. The remains of a monastery and further on the palace where worldly bishops had lived in sumptuous celibacy and hastened the end of the middle ages by over indulgence.

Lisa held up her packet of contraceptive pills.

'Each age seems to tackle its problems in its own predetermined way. To be civilised in any shape or form involves taming nature.'

'So there you are.'

Arnot smiled happily. His wife was the brilliant one designed to make great leaps forward in the light of dazzling perceptions. His role was to support her and supply as required a firm rational touch on the tiller.

'You've forgiven me?'

Her plea was childlike and on the verge of being coy as she held her head to one side. His admiration and devotion were restored to full power and he had to kiss her. She laid her head on his shoulder.

'It was worth it,' she said. 'To prove we're not too old to live by impulse. I mustn't become a control freak. All the same no more Russian roulette.'

He was content to stroke her head.

'And I'll tell you something else,' Lisa said. 'No more heretic maidens. From now on your mother is to be my one and only model. Whatever I manage to write will grow straight out of it.'


IX


The weather improved. The further south they drove the greater grew Lisa's resolve to enjoy a guide-book holiday. Arnot's tolerance and good humour were her source of strength, she said. For several days she was content to explore and marvel at a variety of gorges and Gothic churches. Arnot acquired a particular skill in discovering logis that were both interesting and comfortable. At Louhans they got into conversation with a Dutch couple: a professional singer and her husband, her accompanist. They were on their way to a festival at Aix. The four dined together on chicken gratine and drank Poligny-Montrachet. Fortified by the wine Lisa became so inquisitive about the singer's career and the couple's way of life that Arnot had to touch her arm and divert attention with the old story of Charlemagne's wife nagging the king for staining his lily-white beard with his favourite red wine.

At the abbey church at Brou, when he gave up a concentrated effort to photograph each of the life-like carvings surrounding the royal tombs, Arnot turned around to see his wife in the distance, sitting on a solitary bench in the deserted Gothic nave, absorbed in reading. In a book shop in Bourg-en-Bresse she had seized on an old copy of Etienne Gilson's *La Philosophie de Saint Bonaventure* and had insisted on reading it aloud in bed when he was longing to get to sleep. He knew how she enjoyed developing a speculative theory and he had no wish to discourage her. Each church they looked at supplied her with ammunition. She would be inclined to wave her arm at the light pouring down from a clerestory and detail the beauties of the Age of Faith.

'It's such a shame we are irreligious.'

She shook his arm and poked her elbow in his ribs.

'Give them their due. The church as organised through a thousand years of those middle ages. They had perfected a way of dealing with the nasty flaws in human nature. Something we can't manage... Alright it was a closed system, but it embraced philosophy and faith and art and reasonable behaviour... and look around you! This is the result.'

Arnot made efforts to argue back, chiefly to stimulate her enthusiasm. He described this as a variation on the joys of the chase. It lent an added spice to their tours of inspection. He raised his camera to frame a picture of a solitary young woman reading. The light poured in from the high windows in such a way that made her presence in the empty nave a dramatic focal point. Only when he reached her side did he realise it was his mother's diary she was reading.

'This was such a vital time for her.'

He was struck afresh by Lisa's beauty as she looked up at him. It seemed such a remarkable quality capable of infinite renewal: her eyes always so large and enquiring, her lips parted on the verge of a smile, her slim hands holding the diary with a balanced poise in itself sufficient to give him pleasure.

'It's all past of course. But so is this building. Past and still here. It must be the same for her. And in that case for us. We ought to give her a ring.'

There was a sepulchral reverberation in the nave which caught her low voice to give added solemnity to what she was saying.

'She had so much to put up with. It's all here. The loss of your brother. And taking the blame for it. Heaping the blame on herself. That tyrant of a father tugging at her conscience. And your impossible father and his ridiculous social climbing. A socialist besotted with royalty, longing to ride in a golden coach. And yet we know now she emerged from it all more than a conqueror. How did she do it? I could never do it. What is the secret?'

She took Arnot's outstretched hand and shifted so that he could sit on the bench alongside her.

'It wasn't just you. Though you were part of it of course. You were loveable. You are loveable. I can vouch for that. Every inch of the way. But was that enough? Is the world loveable? So why should she want us to love and want us to procreate? I'll tell you something Arnot Stephens. Those Middle Ages handled it better.'

He warmed her small cold hand in his. Her voice grew more confident. Arnot kissed her hand and called her his little Franciscan preacher.

'Handled what exactly?' he said. 'Hygiene? Mental health?'

'The flaw.' Lisa said. 'All those atomic particles and evolutionary biology and scientific technology can't disguise it. The basic defect of human nature. The fly in the ointment. Look around you. The calm built into these walls. The careful balance between art and philosophy and religion. And it flourished for a thousand years. Bring back Bonaventura!'

Arnot was about to accept her findings with an affectionate embrace when a discreet cough made them aware of a stranger approaching on polite tip-toe.

'*Cymraeg yw iaith yr aelwyd hon!*'

The words were pronounced with an accurate precision that was calculated to please. The speaker was dressed in a jacket and short trousers of the same blue serge material that suggested something of his own design, based on a Tyrolean model. His mouth was opened wide in an ingratiating smile below an untidy moustache. His scraggy neck was exposed by his white open-necked shirt. He wore boots and grey worsted stockings with tasselled garters. His razor had missed a plantation of grey bristle under the right side of his jaw.

'You must forgive me' he said.

He brought the palms of his hands together in an oddly oriental gesture.

'I could not help overhearing. Whispered words in the language of heaven. I am a philologist you see. Language is my passion. And I have pursued it as far as Bangor and Bala. And Harlech of course, Coleg Harlech. What a happy place! What a happy session.'

He offered his card. It read, *Count Guy Fronsiac de L'Epine. Specialist in linguistics.* Arnot and Lisa studied the card in turn. They smiled politely, but seemed at a loss to make an appropriate response. The Count Guy retrieved the card and prepared to withdraw with apologies for his intrusion. Arnot immediately jumped to his feet and struggled to express polite pleasure at such an unexpected encounter. The Count remained critical of his own impetuous behaviour as he studied his card before replacing it in the breast pocket of his blue serge jacket.

'I am a Count but it doesn't count.' he said. 'That's one of the jokes I make in my English classes. I have a chateau but it's falling around my ears. So I depend on my language classes. English mostly. What else. And I have a brother to support. Here he comes. We have to confess we've been watching you for some time. I heard your beautiful voices in the cloisters.'

The brother approached carrying a video camera on a tripod. The red light indicated that the battery was still on. Before he could be introduced he set the camera down and stood behind it as if it were some kind of defence.

'My brother Roland. We are twins as you may have noticed. Not identical. Roland wears his beard to prove it.'

Roland fingered his luxurious beard, smiled politely and laid one hand on top of his camera as if in a gesture of benediction.

'Do you know perhaps Professor Hughes?'

He was quick to detect Lisa suppressing her laughter. He pointed at each of them in turn and began to shake with laughter himself.

'That is like saying Professor Singh from the Punjab!'

His brother was nodding approvingly. Merriment was an acceptable demonstration of good will and understanding.

'But we all need a local habitation and a name.'

Count Guy was eager to expand the notion to a receptive and intelligent audience. He found the deconsecrated church a pleasing echo chamber and then lowered his voice with an apologetic gesture.

'Such warmth,' he said. 'Such hospitality. Such welcome. I was never so content. And then my parents died you see, so I had to give up my researches and come home to look after the estate and my brother. So you see how your voices attracted me. Like music to my ears.'

Lisa was easily drawn into animated conversation with their new acquaintance. Arnot was more cautious. He kept half an eye on the red light on the video camera and the strange figure behind it. The tripod was raised high enough for Roland to peer into the view finder with barely bending his head. The aura of greying hair surrounded the twin brother's head as if to underline its watchful stillness. He seemed a person who had decided to observe the human race rather than join it. It was Lisa who proposed they might cross the south forecourt for a cup of coffee in the cafe across the street. Count Guy rubbed his hands together to demonstrate boyish delight. The three sat together at a table under an awning, while Roland remained standing behind his camera.

'If you'll forgive him,' Count Guy said. 'Roland prefers to stand. That's how we are I'm afraid. What have we got left except to cultivate our eccentricities? At home you know he has a room fitted with electronic gadgets. He says to extend his sight and his hearing. He feels safe there. In his room in the tower. Keeping a check on the world. It's ironic in a way. He has no desire to speak. Only to watch and listen. A division of labour do you think? I do all the talking.'

Lisa leaned forward over her coffee to listen to the Count with beguiling intensity. As though to counteract this effect Arnot leaned back in an attitude of stern faced neutrality. He was uncomfortable with the unwavering scrutiny of the hairy twin and his video camera.

'Take no notice.'

The Count directed a brief parenthesis in Arnot's direction.

'Roland prefers to be ignored. I don't think he has any film left in his camera.'

He drew breath and resumed the argument he was elaborating for Lisa's benefit.

'One must no longer define just by nationality or even tribe, except on the most superficial level. But that of course is where the bulk of humanity live and breathe and have their being. A very thin envelope. We should define people by the contribution they have to make. I've had my dreams, I must confess. To convert Chateau de L'Epine into a conference centre for Philosophy and the Arts. In my view the study of Philosophy and the Arts are the most urgent need of the modern world.'

Lisa's close attention prompted him to dig deeper.

'There must be a mechanism that allows the good to flow freely out of Nazareth. And I'm not being blasphemous. That is why this encounter gives me such pleasure. What we all need in my opinion is a purpose in life. And that I suppose is precisely what I lack. Except of course for the business of looking after my brother. There is an irony there. This great expert on all forms of electronic communications is totally averse to communicating himself.'

The coffee was drunk. The Count was on the point of ordering more. He was ready to outline his concept of a Philosophy Centre in greater detail. His brother Roland suddenly began to stamp his right foot and clear his throat even as he maintained his fixed smile. The Count became apologetic and pushed back his chair.

'Oh dear,' he said. 'It looks as if we have to go. Treatments to attend to. Such a shame. I was so much enjoying your company.'

Once again he extracted the card from his breast pocket. This time he scribbled on the back with a stub of blue pencil.

'This is our address. Our overgrown fastness. You can still find us in the undergrowth. Roland doesn't like the grass cut. The tennis courts are a jungle. Quite delightful in their own way. Roland thinks so. And we have Fax and we have E-mail. If you called to see us on your way it would give us enormous pleasure. If you came to stay it would be an even greater honour. *Croeso mawr.*'

Lisa smiled and nodded and studied the card. It was only when the eccentric pair were well out of earshot that Arnot released a deep sigh of relief.

'What's the matter with you?'

Lisa put the card away safely in her handbag.

'I couldn't wait to see them go,' Arnot said. 'They gave me the creeps.'

'Arnot! Don't be so intolerant. He's a most interesting man. Do you know what I was thinking when he talked about turning his place into a conference centre?'

Lisa peered again more closely at the address the Count had written on the back of his professional card.

'He's just the kind of man your mother would like. A would-be philanthropist looking for a cause. A bit like that television chap Yoreth. It's very cheering to think that Europe must still have a decent sprinkling of them. Where was that place in the Bible that was spared just for the sake of one good man? I find that very cheering. Don't you?'

'How do you know he's good? We don't know them from Adam.

They don't mean anything to us.'

'Us? Us? The world shouldn't be just "us" and "them". You are an old cynic. Inside this impressive exterior there's a dry-as-dust lawyer hiding.'

She took his arm and shook it with affectionate reproach.

'It's my job to look after you,' Arnot said.

He made an effort to sound less solemn.

'Your official escort,' he said. 'Your right hand man. Your guide, philosopher and friend designed to keep you on the straight and narrow. What about Albi?'

Lisa pulled a face to demonstrate lack of enthusiasm. One plan of action had been superseded by other surprising possibilities.

'I'm here to stop you jumping on a horse and riding away in all directions.'

'I wish your mother were here.'

She pretended to sulk.

'She understands me better than you do,'

'We're booked. So we may as well pass on.'

'I tell you one thing,' Lisa said. 'And it's a disturbing thought. It's quite possible we need her more than she needs us. You've got to get her on the telephone. At least we must keep in touch.'


## X


In Languedoc, Lisa's interest in Catharism was briefly rekindled when between them they drew parallels between the brutal campaigns of Simon de Montfort and the so recent atrocities in the disintegrated Yugoslavia. What amazed Arnot was that a region of such spectacular tranquil beauty should have such a blood soaked violent past. Lisa said that this demonstrated what a good innocent soul her husband was: the landscape was a reflection of the way he looked at it. He was being perfect again in his own inimitable fashion and she, flawed and wretched as she was, was the residual legatee of his natural goodness. If she could find the place, she could quote Bonaventura to prove it. She had a vague recollection of a Bosnian ruler in the twelfth century who had resorted to encouraging a version of the Cathar heresy to counteract the sectarian power struggle between the ancestors of the impossible Croatian Catholics and the uncontrollable Orthodox Serbs. It seemed, momentarily, an exciting discovery; but for the life of her she could not remember the ruler's name and in any case it was no more than yet another instance of the ineradicability of the fatal flaw in human nature.

It was hot in the hotel at Albi and the rosy reflections of light through the open window did nothing to cool the atmosphere. They were tired from a day of exhausting sight-seeing and they both lay naked on the wide bed. Lisa drew her hands over her belly as she concentrated on it as an object of particular interest.

'I don't know why I go ferreting around in the remoter corners of history,' she said. 'It's the ordinariness of the ordinary that's the real mystery.'

'Does your friend Bonaventura say that?'

Arnot turned on his side to admire her and gently stroke her skin.

'I suppose he does in a way. The trouble is you have to make that leap of faith to really get at what he's go to say. It's all about a Vision. All I can cope with at present is the me-ness of me. If it was a nicer phenomenon I would call it a miracle. As it isn't, I have to be satisfied with calling it a mystery. And take all the comfort I can get in the you-ness of you. Now that is a genuine miracle. How about some iced water?'

She watched Arnot rummaging in the bedroom fridge. His athletic physique was something to admire.

'To think there could have been two of you,' she said. 'It's not so much how we exist as why we exist at all that's the mystery. That's where old Bonaventura scores you see. This remarkable assumption that everything is in the mind of God. Do you think your mother believes that?'

'I don't really know what she believes,' Arnot said.

'She used to take you to chapel...'

'Yes of course. I must have thought all that was just cultural. Respect for tradition and so on. Belief gets to be so personal. It gets to be on the verge of indecent to inquire too closely.'

Lisa sipped her glass of iced water.

'Everything is poised on the head of a pin,' she said. 'That's the miracle. Am I pregnant? Is there already the seed of being inside me in the process of becoming? Is there a soul already hovering around waiting for a new body? And what happened to your little twin's soul when he was killed? Is it indecent to think about that?'

The long mirror on the opposite wall reflected the nakedness of their bodies. When they moved, the gestures they made looked as primitive and exposed as though they were recent exiles from a

Garden of Eden. Lisa moved to the window to admire the massive strength of the cathedral. The vast rose-red building dominated the sky line.

'The soul is such a wonderful package,' she said. 'So why not pray for it? I like that. Mediaeval logic. Part of a way of life. And then of course they went and spoilt it all by saying why not pay for it.'

'There's something weird about that pair.'

Arnot sat up and looked resolute.

'I don't think we ought to call on them.'

Lisa drew her glass across his forehead to uncrease it.

'Why not?' she said. 'Are you scared of twins?'

He took hold of her by her narrow waist. His physical strength was no match for her persuasive wiles.

'Maybe I am. It struck me it was a complication I could do without. It disturbed me. Maybe I had been jealous of my brother. Maybe that's why I used to feel so guilty. Why I tried so hard to forget he had ever existed when I was young. Banish him from my mind. But of course he's been there all the time.'

'Maybe it's you I should write about...'

'I used to have a dream,' Arnot said. 'A recurring dream. I knew when it was coming and I used to dread it. It was Idris coming back. Not exactly him but a force that stood for him. Encroaching on my little piece of space. Wanting to be me. Or me to be him. And that meant in effect wanting to possess everything I had.'

Lisa pretended to shiver.

'Does that include me?'

Arnot took the question seriously.

'It was when I was a kid,' he said. 'I don't have it any more. Only the apprehension of having it again.'

'And you never told your mother about it?'

'Good lord, no. Wouldn't dream of telling her.'

Lisa rolled off the bed and made for the bathroom. It was time to get dressed and go down for their evening meal.

'I can't wait to see her.'

Lisa raised her voice as she made up carefully in the bathroom mirror.

'It's as if she were the solution to everything. Not that she can be of course, but that's the way I feel. She's got all the answers. Maybe for you, Arnot, as well as for me.'

She looked down at him affectionately as he lay stretched on the bed with his hands behind his head.

'It's one thing I can do,' she said. 'Arrange things. Everything that is except construct a decent plot. Do you know what Thomas Tinsel told me? Without a word of exaggeration.'

'Who?'

'You remember. I told you about him. Head of Programmes. Thomas the Telly. Or Thomas Tinsel. Never create a character who uses words of more than two syllables! Honestly. I heard him say it. With these very ears.'

Lisa laughed as she fixed her ear-rings. She was enjoying the unconcealed admiration in Arnot's eyes.

'It's not far out of our way,' she said. 'Menna will wait for us at Joinville. She likes it there. We'll just pop into Chateau de L'Epine. To satisfy my curiosity. And maybe find some inspiration. And exorcise your twin syndrome.'

Arnot spread out both his hands in a gesture of willing surrender.


# XI


Arnot's car was parked in the shade of a great beech tree on the edge of the forest. Lisa was sprawled in the back, with the door open scribbling notes on her pad. What was left of spring had expired in the grip of summer. The carpets of blue bells had died back and the birds had stopped singing. The heat seemed a prelude to a storm. The picnic was over and Arnot was tidying up deciding what food to throw away and what could be kept in the cool-bag in the boot. Lisa persisted in an intense attempt to imagine the relationship between Arnot's father and mother before they were married. Arnot was less intrigued with the subject as an adjunct to their holiday. He had even suggested pocket chess as an alternative. Lisa had narrowed her eyes to say she hoped they would never get to be that bored with each other. He held up his hands in surrender and swore he only existed in order to help and encourage and even take rides on her flights of fancy. They would grope around together in the dim past in order to allow her to recreate in the palpable present and bathe their findings in an understanding light. Lisa's voice, raised to gain his further attention, was an alien sound in the silence of the forest.

'Express the barrier between Reg and Menna even in those early days. The potential for misunderstanding. I mean the language of bodies is potent of course. But so primitive. Can anyone cross a language barrier without making a supreme effort? You can see poor old Reg confronted with an impenetrable thicket of unknown nouns and verbs. He was bound to resent it. There's always a power struggle involved in who speaks what. She could speak her Gog-English and that was that. He was too coarse-grained to begin to understand the importance of the poetry of language to a girl like Menna. Her nature, her background.'

'Oh I don't know...'

Arnot spoke like a lawyer making a case of fair play for all.

'He had a great devotion to the Rhondda. He never tired of trumpeting the virtues of the people of Ferndale. Such wonderful people. Neighbourliness on a scale the world had never seen before.'

'Hum. So that was why he lived in a mansion in Penarth.'

'For him it was halfway between a religion and a mythology. And when you come to think of it, not so very different from the world view of Dafydd Cyffin, Pen yr Orsedd. So what you've got, Lisa Puw, is a clash of loyalties. It's not just a language. The fragmentation factor built in to the sociology of mountain people.'

Lisa sank back into her seat to give a convincing imitation of sulky despair.

'Post-mortem dissection. That's what you are doing. I'm trying to create.'

She placed her hands over her eyes.

'That delicious spring before they got married. When they had bikes and used to go wandering around the Vale and she tickled his nose with a dry cow-parsley stalk...'

'That was us,' Arnot said. 'Not them.'

'But there must have been a season of first love. A kind of adamic innocence. Especially in her case. Deeply in love with this handsome rugby hero. Heart and soul infatuation. I can just see her with her hand clutching the back of his head as if it were more precious than a holy grail made of gold.'

'Steady on...'

'You can't expect me to tell my imagination to steady on!'

All the same she removed her hands from her eyes and sat up.

'And inside that precious skull printed circuits bright enough to win rugby matches and make money but totally incapable of sensing what made this adoring girl in his arms tick. I should get all that down before it runs into the sand. I shall have to ask her tonight. Press her really hard. I must work out a strategy. Get her to myself. You'll need to make an excuse and go for a long walk.'

Arnot sat in the driving seat to study the fax Count Guy had set them to help them find their way to the Chateau de L'Epine.

'I just wish I could make out the writing of your friend, the Count.'

'He's not my friend any more than he's yours.'

'I think he fancies you. Faxes and telephone calls.'

'It's not me. It's not us. It's the language of heaven and fond memories of Bala.'

Arnot turned the fax paper sideways to try and decipher a place name on the diagram.

'Is the word *abouter* or *aboutir*?'

Lisa could not decide.

'Never mind.' she said. 'We'll find out when we get there.'

'If we ever do. Our mistake was trying to follow your imagined footsteps of Bonaventura.'

'Well he must have come this way,' Lisa said. 'This would be the route surely from Narbonne to Paris. Or vice versa. Not by car of course. They could move about more than you think. How did he get out of Bagnioregio anyway? What a man. Some of his ideas are so beautiful. The *appetitus*. The desire the body and the soul have for each other. The soul existing to animate and perfect the body. I can't wait to talk to your mother about it. It's right up Menna's street.'

'Are you going to stay in the back?'

'Yes I am. I can lie down and hide from the sun. You are the camel driver and I am a female Magus.'

'Maggot more like,' Arnot said.

She thumped him gently on the shoulder. Once they moved out of the shade the heat made them sweat even after limited exertions. All the windows were open but Arnot could not travel fast enough to create a cooling breeze. He held the fax map between his teeth ready for consultation.

'I'd be quite excited if it weren't so hot,' Lisa said. 'These people he's invited to tea. The organist of St. Aiguan. And the old doctor who knows all about cromlechs. And Melle. Delorsy who has a cousin in Ludlow... Characters all from another world.'

Arnot was peering about from left to right.

'We've been through here before. I'm sure of it. Look at the fax-map won't you...?

He turned his head to invite her to take it from between his teeth.

'We're going into another forest.'

Arnot groaned.

'Babes in the wood.'

On the left side the woodland was better cared for. Trees, centuries old had been allowed space to flourish. The shade in the beech glades even more than the dappling of sunlight was deeply attractive. On the right there were dried out marshes and pines being choked by bramble. Arnot was forced to brake suddenly when a gang of naked children chased each other across the road and into the trees on the left. They seemed to be pursued and the noise they made suggested a quivering mixture of fear and hilarity. Arnot waited but there was no one apparently in pursuit.

'They hunt children around here instead of deer.'

Arnot leaned over the steering wheel to rub his eyes. Lisa waved the fax over his head.

'We're there!' Lisa said. 'Take the next turning on the right. Drive on until you come to the pillars with a missing gate. A drive and a dirt track run parallel with each other. I wouldn't be at all surprised to see them both waiting to meet us. Roland with his camera. Guy in his boy-scout shorts.'

Between the pillars, when they arrived, a gendarme sat on his motorcycle lighting a cigarette. He made no move to get out of their way. He was not the one obliged to account for his presence. Arnot raised a tentative hand in greeting. He had to explain they were visiting the Chateau de L'Epine as guests of the Count. The gendarme was unimpressed. He asked to see their papers and wanted to know their nationality and where they were staying. He seemed impervious to Lisa's charm and Arnot's friendly manner. He said an investigation was in progress and advised them to postpone their visit. Arnot might well have agreed to do so: but Lisa insisted their visit was of great importance. They had travelled all the way from Wales and it would be a cruel disappointment not to pay a call however brief. At last, the gendarme shrugged his shoulders and moved his bike. He gave some kind of warning but it was so mumbled and indistinct Lisa was still trying to decipher it as they crept cautiously forward.

'Overrun with riff-raff,' she said. 'Did he mean us? Keep off the dirt-track. The chalets at the *etang* are stuffed with refugees and displaced persons. Is that what he was saying?'

The drive narrowed as they penetrated further into the unkempt overgrown woodland. Somewhere beyond the shrubs and the brambles and the rotting pines there had to be a chateau. The

Count spoke of his home as though they lived in it under siege. A hotel chain had made them an offer. The consortium had local allies. There were conspiracies afoot. The twins hid themselves away in the depth of the wilderness in the hope that they would pass unnoticed. The Count had his own interests that did no harm to anyone and he had his responsibilities, the chief of which was his brother.

Lisa laid her hands on Arnot's shoulder and brought her face close to his. They were approaching a corner in the drive when a small police van roared past forcing Arnot into the shrubbery. Lisa fell back on the seat.

'Did you see that! The bastards! Did you see that?'

Arnot kept repeating his protests as they struggled out, his offside rear wheel spinning in the mud.


## XII

The Count sat at the head of the table nibbling pellets of bread to comfort himself. There were places laid for several guests but only Arnot and Lisa had arrived and they declared themselves too hot to eat. Wild vines slumped across the unwashed windows of the dining room creating a green gloom without cooling the stuffy atmosphere. The food on the sideboard had been covered with sheets of white paper but the flies were already manouvering above it. Lisa and Arnot gulped down iced lemon with muttered relief and gratitude.

'You have to understand our situation,' the Count said.

He thrust his neck forward as though to acknowledge their polite efforts to conceal their embarrassment.

'We are victims of history, my brother and I. Dear Mrs Stephens you could write volumes about it. The Decline and Fall of the Fronsiac de L'Epine. Our great ancestor rode to the Crusades as the Knight of the Holy thorn. *L'amorosa Spina*... What's the use? What chance have we got?'

'Where is Roland?'

Lisa ventured her polite enquiry. The count shook his head in morose despondency.

'He has locked himself in the Tower. Surrounded by his equipment. Driven into his corner. Poor fellow. He is so hurt. The good name of the family means everything to him. He knows everything about two things. Our pedigree and electronic equipment. The past and the future he calls it. Poor fellow. What a miserable present.'

The Count gestured towards all the empty chairs around the table.

' "Bidden to the feast",' he said. ' "And they would not come." How easily they are put off. The organist at St. Aigan smitten with an unexpected choir practice. The doctor called to attend a family funeral. Melle. Deloisy in bed with sunstroke. What a co-incidence of calamities.'

His long teeth glittered under the moustache as he extracted a trace of humour out of his situation.

'There was this Cerebus of a gendarme at the gate,' Lisa said. 'People could have been turned back!'

'But he didn't turn you back! My good friends from the country of goodness.'

Arnot felt bound to question such an exaggeration.

'Oh I don't know about that,' he said.

'My friends. I keep telling you. You are too modest. I know from first hand experience what precious human metal hides among those green hills.'

Arnot resolved not to allow the discussion to float away on a cloud of hyperbole. With practiced forensic ease he asked:

'What was he accused of?'

The Count responded by sinking his chin on his chest and looking wearily philosophical.

'Of being different. In this hidebound corner of France eccentricity is a capital offence. What crowd are we supposed to please? What they want is this chateau converted into an atmospheric hotel all cuisine and emasculated calm to benefit the local economy. It's all, all part of the plot. I tell you. It's a conspiracy to get rid of us.'

'What did he do?'

Arnot persisted quietly with his question.

'Take photographs, what else. It's a lifetime preoccupation. But in this instance, of naked children. A capital offence.'

He was so alert to their reaction, Lisa and Arnot took care not to be caught looking at each other. Lisa demonstrated sympathy and Arnot a willingness to understand. This seemed to bring the Count a substantial measure of relief.

'Was there ever a greater need for philosophy?' he said. 'Don't tell me it will never make any difference. That would shatter me. Finish me off. It really would.'

He was encouraged by Lisa's attentive nod.

'What else is this house for! What a happy issue from all its afflictions. To become an Academy in the Greek sense. And to be on the Internet! A new electronic route for ancient wisdom. In his own way Roland understands. You could say in a sense he suffers from a surfeit of understanding.'

He had to show them the house. Most of the rooms they passed through were empty and cool, the shutters excluding the sunlight except where it squeezed through to send thin bars of light across dusty floors. The library was impressive. Bits of plaster were falling from the ceiling and a film of dust dulled the surface of two handsome oak tables. Leather-bound books of great age fitted the shelves of the inner wall from floor to ceiling.

'You can see the place has great potential.'

The count's back stiffened with pride and then indignation.

'That's why those hotel villains are so interested. There's American money behind them you know. It would give me such enormous satisfaction to beat them off. Do you think your mother would be interested? Will she visit us, do you think? To see for herself ?'

'Oh I'm sure she will,' Lisa said.

Arnot kept his mouth firmly shut. It was not at all clear that the Count understood Menna was his mother, not Lisa's.

'There are things she should know. Apart from this hotel conspiracy. To account for a certain local hostility. My father was a Pétainist. He served Vichy. Ah, such a black mark. And so did Mitterand, for heaven's sake, but it did him no harm. A politician understands that in popular mythology life is a sequence of tableaux vivants. Nothing to do with day to day reality. That just goes plodding on.'

He insisted on showing them the kitchens. They were a museum of antiquities, he said, but they functioned. An old woman bent over a large lead sink washing vegetables. In a darker room her grand-daughter was skinning a rabbit. She barely raised her head to return the Count's greeting. He made an obscure joke about loyal retainers and looked around for the keys to the cellars. There was so much to see, he said. From the cellars to the attic. Why not stay the night?

Arnot was quick to decline the invitation.

'My mother,' he said. 'She will be at the hotel. Waiting for us.'

'*Your* mother!'

The Count paused at the foot of the staircase as though confronted with a fresh complication. Lisa reassured him.

'I call her mother too,' she said. 'We are very close.'

She stood back to admire the nobility of the curved stone stair-case. On the walls, as they ascended, oil portraits of ancestors alternated with heraldic carvings. Lisa was curious but refrained from asking too many questions when the Count made it clear more than once how much of a burden he found the family past. There was nothing he would like more, he said, in all seriousness than rent a cottage on the shores of Lake Bala and devote his life to the study of Celtic Philology. But he had a duty to his brother and Roland had an umbilical attachment to the place. He cultivated electronic devices and his illustrious ancestry with equal fervour.

All three stood together outside the closed door of Roland's room in the tower. Instead of knocking the Count tried turning the door knob without making a sound as if to demonstrate to the others that it was well and truly locked. He gnawed his moustache as he considered whether or not to call out Roland's name. He pulled a face and decided on retreat. An adjacent room was Roland's photo-graphic studio. There was a lighting stage, a backdrop and a wardrobe for costumes.

'We call this Roland's toy cupboard,' the Count said. 'He enjoys it so much. Hours of innocent pleasure. I can't claim he has over-taken the Lumière brothers!'

He beckoned Lisa and Arnot to follow him to a stone balcony where he could speak more freely. They stood in the shade of the tower to admire the wide vista of wooded countryside. Immediately below them the outlines of a tennis court, an empty swimming pool and a terrace were still visible in a confusion of unmown grass, brambles and overgrown shrubbery.

'Am I my brother's keeper?'

The Count drew their attention to a group of chalets just visible in the distance beneath a wooded hill. They had been set out on the edge of a sheet of water.

'What was he doing?' he said. 'Tossing coins into the lake and photographing children as they dived in after them. Naked of course but what is the harm in that? I can't spend every hour of my waking life keeping an eye on him.'

'My husband was a twin.'

Lisa smiled and nodded as she released a piece of interesting information. It could have been an attempt to relieve the Count's anxiety by shifting the conversation to a more generalised level. Behind her Arnot stiffened like a man unexpectedly called to account.

'His twin was killed in a road accident.'

The Count leaned against the stone balustrade with his head lowered as he breathed what could have been a sigh of relief. Before he spoke he sketched out a series of sympathetic gestures.

'So you will understand my difficulties,' he said. 'Responsibilities.'

He stared at the chalets with a deep loathing.

'There are refugees and there are locals,' he said. 'But you can't tell which is which when they are naked. Anyway it was that Communist mayor that insisted on stuffing those horrid chalets with Albanians and Rumanians and Slovak gypsies. Just a political gesture. Stuff them in there and forget about them. My brother isn't equipped to face such a confusing world.'

The balcony didn't offer enough room for the Count to shift and eddy about as he tried to find some kind of answer to a succession of insoluble problems. He had so much to say confronted with such a sympathetic audience. They should descend to the shade of the vine covered pergola on the north terrace where they could drink coffee and discuss social problems in the light of philosophy. Lisa seemed agreeable but Arnot insisted they had to leave. He emphasised his concern for his mother. The Count disciplined himself to demonstrate practiced politeness. He was infinitely grateful to them for making the effort to come and see them. In the hallway he paused to make a last appeal.

'You won't let all this photographic nonsense put you off?'

He looked at Arnot, ready to rely on a fresh understanding as well as cultivated tolerance.

'I think it is fair to say we share a Vision. We share a genuine interest.'

Lisa showed warm support while Arnot was still searching for a satisfactory form of words.

'And you will bring your mother to visit. We would be very honoured.'

'Of course we will,' Lisa said.


## XIII


For some time Lisa was so absorbed in her own speculative chatter she failed to notice the depth of silence of the man at the wheel. The sun was lower in the sky, he was wearing dark glasses and she must have assumed he was concentrating on the route. One forest looked much like another. He had to reach the sleepy village before finding the road to the new hotel that was close to the autoroute. It was his habit to encourage her to leave practicalities in his capable hands while she pursued her speculative arabesques.

'All that stuff in the tower,' she was saying. 'What exactly is he up to? There are paedophile rings on the Internet, aren't there? Of course we are all innocent until we are proved guilty. Or should it be the other way round? I know I shouldn't be excited but in a curious way I am. It wouldn't be my style to drag in lurid detail for stylish effect and use four letter words in every other line. Fuck this and fuck that. In the end there's nothing more boring. I was very intrigued by those family portraits. You can just feel Guy's dilemma in the air as well as see it all around you. There's a Henry James title for you, Guy's Dilemma. Burdened with a twin brother who suffers from a perverted libido. Just as well you lost your twin, Arnot Stephens. The fact is we belong to a very weird species.'

At last she sensed Arnot was upset. She saw the rigid set of his mouth.

'What's the matter?'

In silence Arnot drove off the road into a parking lot in the shade of the trees. There was clearly an argument to be conducted and a firm decision to be taken. He switched off the engine and tugged at the handbrake with excessive force.

'We can't possibly take my mother to that place,' he said. 'The whole notion is too ridiculous.'

Lisa was unprepared for the assault. Arnot was uncompromising.

'Your writing is very important. Of course it is. But it shouldn't be allowed to come before everything. I couldn't help seeing that very clearly this afternoon.'

'Dear me.'

This seemed the one response Lisa was capable of making. Her fist closed against her chest as if it was anticipating some difficulty she could be having in breathing.

'Of course it's important. Just as important for me in a way as it is for you. But it isn't the be all and end all of our existence. There are other values. And they can be even more important.'

'Are there really,' she said. 'You must tell me about them.'

She struggled to control her breathing. She stared at his profile as though she had suddenly found herself sitting alongside a stranger. There had to be elementary steps she could take to defend herself.

'Knowing what a self-absorbed bitch I am they could quite easily escape my notice.'

Arnot waved a hand as if he needed help to avoid the unpleasantness of a confrontation. He had taken a risk in being so direct and the danger now was they should take up entrenched positions. This would be so far removed from their normal practice: the comfortable free flow of loving understanding in which difficulties so easily dissolved.

'You say you welcome criticism,' he said.

'I should hope so.'

'You want me to say what I think.'

'Of course I do.'

'You just can't manipulate other people; exploit them in order to create a situation that will unblock your writer's block.'

'Oh so that's what's the matter with me...'

'God knows what would be the end of it. That Count of yours could be quite dangerous.'

'Dear me.'

'I don't mean dangerous in any mortal sense. There's nothing wrong with his own politics as far as I could gather. What I mean is, he's after something. He's manipulative.'

'Just like me?'

Lisa smiled to present herself at her prettiest; as if to remind him that this was the girl he liked to idealise and paint one sort or another of a halo around her head.

'No. Not like you. He's in all sorts of trouble and people in trouble always jump at the chance to drag down other people into it. I see it happening every other day of my working life. It's what lawyers spend their time having to deal with. Now you know what my mother is like. She collects lame dogs. You can't just push her into this mess just for the sake of having something to write about.'

Lisa opened the car door and walked away into the trees. Arnot seemed tempted to let her go. He locked the car and tapped the roof with his fist before following her. He kept his distance for some time, only keeping her in sight as she wandered further into the wood. When eventually he overtook her he was distressed to find there were tears on her cheeks. At once he wanted to comfort her. She shrugged his hand away.

'You are right,' she said. 'I've got to learn to look at myself and I hate what I see. But that's the way I am. What can I do about it?'

She looked up at him in her distress.

'You've seen right through me. Nothing pretty to look at there, is there?'

She wandered on and he shadowed her closer, until she turned to face him again.

'You know what frightens me. Things will never be the same between us again.'

She stumbled on through the trees as he tried to convince her of his unswerving devotion. She was the light of his life and until she forgave him he would be condemned to live in a mist of misery. She said everything was her fault and there was nothing to forgive. They persisted in trying to convince each other of the unconditional nature of their reconciliation. Suddenly tired Lisa slumped at the bole of a great beech tree. She was shaking her head.

'I just hope I'm not pregnant.' she said. 'I'm not fit to be a mother. I have all sorts of qualifications except that one. Not fit to be a mother.'

Arnot stood above her to emphasise how much he appreciated the purity of her motives. They were creative and above reproach. He was so fervent in the end she saw it as comic and gave way to a smile and even a charming giggle. She held out her hand so that he could pull her to her feet and embrace her. On their way back to the car they were able to calmly agree that his mother could quite easily decide for herself whether or not to visit the Chateau de L'Epine.


XIV


Menna arrived at the hotel in a burst of energy and brightness that took them both by surprise. After what they had assumed to be a difficult train journey she looked fresh and youthful in a pale blue dress neither of them had seen before. She had shared a compartment with a nun on her way back to a leper colony in the Pacific and a lorry driver on strike on his way home from a demonstration, and in halting French she had been able to chat with them both. She said it gave her quite a sense of achievement.

She was bubbling over with praise for Bishop Bob. He had invented this theory he called Strangers on a Train and it was much too complex and fascinating to discuss in the glossy reception area of a new hotel. Arnot carried her travelling bag and they crossed the floor of polished marble in the direction of the lifts with the special care of people walking on ice. The lift took them to the third floor where they would occupy adjacent rooms. There were some unfamiliar gadgets and conveniences to wonder at and manage.

Lisa sat on the edge of Menna's single bed to listen to her mother-in-law expound the Bishop's theory. It didn't seem sufficient to account for her excitement and frequent laughter. Lisa watched her with close attention as if she were able to discern the lineaments of that young girl in love about whom she had been trying to make so many notes.

'He's such a case,' Menna said. 'He comes out with the most outlandish things. There we were in the square at Strasbourg with this group of Lithuanian Lutherans so eager to practice their English. We were staring up at the Cathedral clock and he started going on at length about his congregation when he was a rector in Montgomeryshire. He said they had the gift of giving souls equal weight and that this was the only democracy that really mattered. He's a nonconformist at heart you see, and he admits it. He went on about Ann Griffiths to these poor Lithuanians until they were glassy eyed.'

'What about this stranger in a train business?' Lisa was ready to bide her time to bring up her own concerns. There were clearly adjustments to be made. It was best at this stage to encourage the flow of Menna's reminiscences and revelations.

'It boils down to something so simple. It's the way he puts it really. He's so enthusiastic. I don't know how he keeps it up. You are in a train and the person opposite is a total stranger. He's just another object like a hat or a coat or a newspaper. He's an object to you. And you are an object to him. The journey goes well and you never speak. And the objects melt away into nothing. Or something happens. Some contretemps. The two "its" start talking and become two "somebodies". And then the great mystery starts. He makes a big thing about that. The more another is present in me, the more I am present in myself. And that creates a third state of being. Have I got it right? Yes I have. We're doing it all the time. The minute you create a new friend you create a third state of being. That's obvious, isn't it? But then it's in that third state that societies live, move, and have their being; where they flourish or fail. Like the congregation in Montgomeryshire. It's a central part of the mystery of existence. Oh dear. Mental effort is so tiring. I need to take a shower. Or should I take a bath?'

Arnot was in the bathroom studying the equipment rather than listening to his mother. He recommended the bath as simpler. In their own room Lisa and Arnot wondered about his mother's high spirits.

'She's up to something,' Lisa said. 'Do you think she's fallen in love?'

Arnot was embarrassed by the thought.

'We don't change all that much do we?' Lisa said. 'She had to find somebody to laugh at all his jokes and love him to distraction. That's the way she was originally constructed and now she's reverted to it. She's right, you know. The meaning is in the mystery of meeting. And the only light you've got in the dark is the spark of love.'

'I don't know.'

Arnot gave a deep sigh and rested his chin on the back of his hand. He looked like a lawyer daunted by the mountain of evidence suddenly dropped on his desk.

'I don't think you've got it right,' he said. 'I've seen the things she's had to struggle through. She found a way to a level of detachment as much through meditation as anything else. She had to. There was no other way. That's where she found her strength. That's what kept her going.'

He sounded cross with himself.

'I don't think it's necessary for us all to be such an amazing mystery. Honestly I don't. There has to be a level where everything is reasonable and straight forward. Otherwise we'll all end in a messy chaos. Absolute hell.'

Lisa was laughing at him with an affection that was almost motherly. She ruffled his close-cropped curly hair and kissed the top of his head. There was the problem of Chateau de L'Epine that still had to be brought to Menna's attention and they had to consider the best way in which it could be done. Arnot favoured a blunt approach without any subtleties. To humour him, Lisa agreed. But on their way down to supper he held her by the waist with a warning hug. When they sat at the table opposite her, Menna said she had an announcement to make.

'It's a journey that never ends,' she said.' 'Like talking to yourself. That's why you two are so lucky.'

Her smile and her finger tips stretched towards her son and his wife in a gesture of benediction.

'You don't need me at all,' she said. 'Which is better than just as well. It's marvellous. Now I have to tell you my news. I'm adopting two little girls. As it happens they're twins.'

Their astonished reaction amused her so much, she burst out laughing like someone who'd won a prize.

'They are in a refugee camp on the borders of the Sudan. Their

parents have been killed in the Civil War. They have no close rela-
tives. They are nearly three years old. All I've got so far is a
polaroid picture.'

The picture was not very helpful. Dark faces unsmiling and white
soulful eyes. Arnot and Lisa stared at it in turn, still unable to
conceal their amazement.

'Nerys and Mari,' Menna said. 'Why have they got Welsh
names? Two little Nubians. Because the refugee orphanage is run
by a Welsh couple. Missionaries we used to call them. Qualified
relief workers. A doctor and a nurse. Bishop Bob is lost in admira-
tion for them. He's been there twice. And now I'm going there. The
week after next.'

Arnot was blunt when he recovered from his surprise.

'Are you sure you know what you're doing?' he said. 'And why
are you doing it?'

He leaned over the table in an attitude or cross-examination. His
mother reached out a hand to cover his.

'My boy,' Menna said. 'He's been such a tower of strength. Even
when he was small. Carrying such a load of responsibility. He kept
me going. And now you can both keep each other going. That's
wonderful.'

'Your age,' Arnot said. At your age.'

'I know,' Menna said. 'I can't claim to have thought it through
all the way. But I've got the main outline. The rest is faith. I
suppose that's the best thing to call it. Talking of faith, Bishop Bob
says I must visit the Cistercian abbey at La Chapelle-St. Martin. It's
not so far from here. There's some connection with an Abbot of
Llantarnam. He would like a book if I can get one. Or at least a
brochure. Do you think we could make a trip there tomorrow?'

## XV

'Is he disturbed do you think?'

Arnot had left Lisa and Menna in the nave of the abbey church
to go for a walk on his own. Menna was concerned and Lisa took
her arm to reassure her.

'He misses his running,' she said. 'Sitting at the wheel all day for
hundreds of kilometres. I'm ashamed to admit I let him do all the
driving.'

'So he should. He's your coachman. He likes doing it.'

The great building had a soothing effect on their spirits. They gazed and drifted around convinced that so much architectural harmony had many pleasing secrets to reveal. Lisa drew attention to the cunning control of light. It was a convenient way of introducing her new found interest in Bonaventura. The rose window was plainly designed to capture messages in the form of light from heaven and when you looked at it your effort was the equivalent of the intellect grasping at some aspect of the truth. As far as the stained glass was concerned it was not only the parable of the Prodigal Son or the Good Samaritan: even more than the story and the colour, it was the light shining through them. Menna listened closely and nodded her approval.

They rested in the cool of a Gothic cloister, sitting together on a stone bench.

'What happened to your heretics?' Menna said.

'Ah...'

Lisa paused to show she had much to tell and was intent on arriving at the best way of telling it.

'I think first of all I was seduced by the thirteenth century,' she said. 'And by this brilliant young chap called Bonaventura. And I think you were right. Catharism was an essentially southern, Mediterranean, misunderstanding of the true meaning of spirituality.'

'My goodness! Did I say that?'

'Maybe not in so many words. But you made me see it.'

'My poor old diary. Have you burnt it yet?'

Menna was looking her straight in the eye and Lisa sat up as if she had realised this was one of Menna's dangerously innocent questions.

'I hope you will,' Menna said. 'When you've finished with it. You can write what you like about that poor creature. It must have been me, but it's no one I would want to protect any more. Has it been of any use?'

'I want to start earlier. When you were both young and in love. As a point of departure. In the fictional sense the beginning of a relationship. It could help to give the piece better shape.'

Lisa spoke slowly so that her appeal for more knowledge emerged in the pauses between her spoken word. In the silence of the cloister she wanted to join Menna in a contemplation of her past.

'I can see her now. A little creature obsessed by love.'

Menna was able to smile.

'I suppose most girls are of course. In my case, about what it meant even more than what it was. And of course what it was, was absorbing enough. He used to be so cross with me for not giving in. Protecting my precious little virginity. Even then it was considered hopelessly old-fashioned. Reg just couldn't understand it. As if I were being deliberately selfish, putting up my price. I remember one day we had gone on our bicycles towards Llancarfan. We were in a bluebell wood and I was going on about being careful. He lost his temper completely. "It's all rubbish," he said. "Religion is all rubbish. When you're dead you're dead, and that's all there is to it." There was an outcrop behind us. A rock with the strata lying horizontally. He was so angry he banged his head against it and there was blood on his forehead. He wiped it on the rock. "This was mud once," he said. "Now at least it's rock. That's more than we'll ever be." Poor Reg. I think from that moment on I was afraid of him. But that didn't stop me. And he never found out that somewhere inside me there were great reservoirs of loving kindness untapped. Even before we were married he would tell me to stop being so bloody grateful. "Grateful for what?" he said. "You've got to grab what you can get while you've still got the strength to grab it" Still, it's Reg I have to thank for Arnot. And by extension for you. So it couldn't all have been wasted.'

The cloisters were an invitation to walk and meditate. In the garden a lay-brother was trimming a pattern of low hedges and the rhythmic clipping reverberated in the silence. Lisa had decided on her approach to the question of the Chateau de L'Epine. Her mother-in-law would be thrilled to learn of a French Count who doted on the sound of Welsh and longed to live in a cottage on the shores of Bala lake. But she could see at a glance that Menna was pre-occupied with her own intentions. To adopt would be to embrace another way of life. The careful steps she took in the cloister reflected her apprehensions.

'I hope I'm not being selfish,' she said. 'Not just looking for a fresh outlet for the untapped reservoir I was going on about. Or maybe you can be selfish if what satisfies you best is trying to safeguard the welfare of others. Words are a waste of time for creatures like me anyway. But not for you my dear Lisa. It's what you do best. Your medium for creating a miniature world of music and colour and light to give pleasure to others. Those two little girls need all the love and care I can give them. They will give me the strength of a new purpose. And I will give them all the care, like

Ann Griffiths' tree, planted green and fresh alongside the living waters. Listen to me. I sound just like Bishop Bob.'

Arm in arm they walked like old friends to meet Arnot at the west front of the abbey church.


# XVI

It was after a polite struggle, followed by a burst of laughter, that Lisa was able to compel Menna to sit in the passenger seat alongside her son. Somehow or other, without the fax map they would find the way to the Chateau L'Epine. Lisa was able to sit forward and chatter cheerfully to the two in front, her mouth within comfortable distance of their ears. They were both happy to listen to her customary fanciful speculations more or less without interruption.

'He's not as ridiculous as he looks,' Lisa said. 'He doesn't think clothes matter. Or maybe he does? Maybe he thinks we should all invent our own costumes and that would be the only way for us to cease to be slaves of fashion. He's striking a blow for liberty. Everyman becomes his own élite and satisfy himself with manipulating his trousers and his waistcoat. And I think the idea of a Philosophy Centre is marvellous anyway. I really do. It's all about acorns and oak trees. Anyway how did your lovely Cistercians start except by making baskets out of a sea of reeds. Do you think your Sir Merfyn Yoreth would be interested?'

'Interested in what, dear?'

It cost Menna some effort to concentrate on the incessant murmur of Lisa's voice next to her ear.

'A Philosophy Centre. As a core. And then around that a Cultural Centre devoted to the Arts among the Lesser Spoken Languages. That sounds good. That would be sure to appeal to him.'

Menna raised a warning finger.

'You write for him first,' she said. 'You let him publish your next piece and then you could really talk to him.'

Lisa pretended to a degree of despondency.

'You think I'm in too much of a hurry,' she said. 'And yet if I'm not, I'll never get anywhere. You know what I mean? This desperate balance between the impatience of the moment and the patience that can last a lifetime. You know we went exploring orchards?

Looking for the ghost of the heretic virgin. See her caught in the trap. A commissar of the Thought Police dressed as a monk using his sneaky little power to try and seduce her. Did she burn or make a miraculous escape? You spend ages in historical research but in the end the story has to leap out of your subconscious like the witches' thread flying up through the window.'

'Well there you are,' Menna said. 'You write it all down and Merfyn Yoreth will be delighted to publish it.'

'You know these two brothers, Guy and Roland are twins.'

'Are they really?'

Menna showed no more than polite interest.

'Not exactly Castor and Pollux. Roland looks backward, but it's quite possible he's a bit of a genius. If that is the right word. He belongs to this new sub-species of humanity who have plugged themselves into computers in order to avoid the nastier aspects of daily life. If you decide to have a war I'll watch it on the monitor. You could say he was over-protected. Guy worries himself stiff about him, doesn't he?'

Lisa nudged Arnot to gain his support. His lack of enthusiasm made her bid for more concentrated attention. Perhaps his mother would have responded more readily to the subtleties she had to offer.

'You could say we were all twins in a sense. Consciousness is a dialogue most of the time and the definition of a dialogue is two persons talking. There are always two selves involved in talking to yourself. Was it a deliberate choice? To adopt twins?'

The tone of voice was sweetened as if to anticipate any objection to the bold directness of the question. Arnot said nothing. His mother held her head to one side as if this was an aspect of her intentions she had not considered at all.

'Company for each other,' she said. 'That's what I thought. Coming to live in a totally new environment. It would have had to be two. As it happens they were twins. Whatever happens, pain or pleasure, it's easier to bear if you can share it.'

Menna spoke with that familiar calm certainty that reduced Lisa to a respectful silence. Any lingering longing for a displaced twin could have been no part of Menna's decision, whatever part the notion played in Lisa's imaginative excursions. There seemed to be abundant food for thought around for all three to ponder as they drove through the forest. This time there was no gendarme on guard by the gate pillars. With the car windows lowered Arnot drove with deliberate caution down the overgrown drive.

Before the corner where they had encountered the police van, Lisa murmured in his ear.

'Are you going to blow your slug-horn?'

He looked around as the Chateau came into sight, disturbed by the silence. Menna and Lisa waited by the entrance steps while Arnot strode around looking for signs of life.

'It's odd,' Lisa said. 'I imagined Guy would be marching up and down looking for us. He was so keen on meeting you.'

Arnot gave the door bell another pull. It was possible to hear it reverberating in the interior. They were considering abandoning the visit when the door opened and the old woman they had seen previously washing vegetables in the kitchen, stood in the doorway. Her grand-daughter lurked in the shadow behind her, twitching with nervous curiosity. Lisa did the talking. Menna and Arnot remained on the steps below her. The old woman's accent was difficult to understand and she was reluctant to be responsible for imparting anything more than the minimum information. Lisa was so shocked she questioned the old woman again.

'My God.'

Her face was white as she turned to speak to Menna and Arnot. The old woman studied their reactions with open curiosity.

'Roland hanged himself yesterday. In the Tower Room. Guy is in hospital being treated for shock. I can't get much sense out of this old creature. What can we do?'

The enormity of the news turned everyone around the doorway into pillars of silence. The large unwieldy Chateau was transformed into an inhospitable mausoleum. At last Arnot sighed and shook his head.

'There isn't much we can do,' he said.


## XVIII

The Count lay back on his pile of pillows mildly sedated. An enterprising therapist had provided him with a jigsaw puzzle on a tray. He paid no attention to it. His gaze was fixed on the sky through the window as though he were expecting a visitation. When Lisa was admitted to the private ward he stared at her as someone he did not recognise. This gave the nursing sister standing in the doorway much satisfaction. The foreign woman had been excessively persistent. As she led her down the corridor she muttered that the

Count had been put in a private room for his own protection and visits in this wing of the hospital were limited strictly to twenty minutes.

'*Bala dirion deg.*'

Lisa stood where the Count could see her without moving his head as she recited the words of the folk song he had claimed to be familiar with during the encounter at Brou. First he smiled as the recollection came flooding back then his eyes flooded with tears and his long features broke up in sorrow. The nursing sister was on the point of ordering Lisa to leave. The Count recovered sufficient composure to wave the woman away. He made her close the door. Then he offered a hand to Lisa and she took it to console him.

'All he did...'

The words were barely audible as the Count spelt them out.

'Was ruffle her hair. That's all he did. And those awful people accused him of raping a child. She was changing her costume in the studio. He told me. All he did was ruffle her hair. He loved innocence and purity. And this was the accusation. He did away with himself. He hanged himself with one of his cable wires. Roland, who wouldn't harm a fly.'

He shook with uncontrollable sobbing. Lisa removed the jig-saw and offered him a glass of water.

'I must control myself,' he said. 'You have to see through these things. They put them up to it. I'm sure they did. And this nursing sister. You can't trust her. I can see their plan you know. I can see it clearly. They want to have me put away. Put in care they call it and then they can do what they like with the Chateau. I've got to fight back. I must. It's a law of life. If you don't fight back you'll be driven under. Will you help me?'

He wanted to take her hand again. She moved out of his reach, shaking her head.

'We have to go back,' she said. 'Arnot is due back in his office. We both have our work.'

'They will bring more accusations,' he said. 'More and more. To blacken our name. He loved photographing children. What was the harm in that?'

Lisa was shaking her head in mute sympathy.

'Your mother. Will she help? Something good could come out of all this horror. My poor Roland. Hanging himself for the sake of the family name. When I think of his sacrifice and how he felt. What can I do? Alone?'

Lisa drew in a deep breath and made a series of judicious gestures as she paced about the room.

'Arnot thinks you should engage a good lawyer. A really good lawyer. And I think so too. We have to get back I'm afraid. But Arnot says I am to give you our address. So that if you come to Wales again, you must be sure to visit us.'

The Count struggled to compose himself. He tried to apologise for his emotional outburst. Lisa's gestures implied that she hated to leave him: that she was torn, but what could she do? The Count for his part drew on all his reserves to allow his charming visitor a well behaved and polite withdrawal.

## XIX

The blue sky and the pleasing calm of the landscape found little reflection in the interior of the B.M.W. driving north. Lisa in the back was immersed in gloomy silence. Arnot grasped the steering wheel with the firm resolve of a man inseparably attached to his duty. His mother, alongside, when she was not sighing and wishing herself elsewhere, closed her eyes and attempted to take refuge in meditation. In an effort at reconciliation she had brought up the idea of Miranda and how she suffered with those she saw suffer and her unhappiness at not being able to do anything about it. Neither her son or her daughter-in-law found this any contribution to solving their difficulties with each other or the situation in which they found themselves. They were separated by barriers of unspoken reproaches. There appeared to be no solutions, real or imaginary. Arnot was uncompromisingly pragmatic until Lisa accused him of being too smugly pleased with their inability to act. His resentment drove him into silence. Lisa declared she would sit in the back and join the society of bleeding hearts.

At a roundabout on the outskirts of Chaumont their smooth progress was brought to an abrupt halt. They were confronted by an organised blockade of heavy lorries. In a matter of seconds it was impossible to go forward or backward. The knights of the road were equipped with placards and were providing themselves with sustenance for a long siege. Some of them drifted among the motorists, their mouths stuffed with panini and sustaining baguette sandwiches. They were ready to elaborate on their position and portion out tit-bits of information. They met protest or sympathy with equal equanimity.

'This is impossible,' Arnot said. 'We're trapped.'

'Just like poor old Guy.'

Lisa was quick to respond. Arnot was stung by the stubborn irrelevance of the comment. He looked about for any prospect of movement as he delivered his version of the brutal truth.

'It wasn't just a one-off,' he said. 'It had happened before. The authorities had to do something about it. The poor chap wasn't as harmless as he looked.'

'You'll be saying next you knew all the time,' Lisa said. 'Your marvellous lawyer's nose for trouble. You smelt a rat at Brou. And the poor old rat hanged itself in Chateau de L'Epine. They don't matter anyway. Just some more strangers in a train.'

'I never said they don't matter,' Arnot said. 'All I'm saying is you can't take on all the world's sorrows on your own shoulders. It's as simple as that really. Look, we're moving.'

The routiers had contrived a narrow passage among the lorries so that cars with foreign registration numbers could pass through in single file. It needed a great deal of shouting and manouvering. Once it was achieved the relief was only temporary. Arnot tapped the petrol gauge.

'We need petrol,' he said. 'And we need it soon. The question is whether to get back on the autoroute or stick to the Route Nationale'

As they passed through the suburbs they saw queues of cars at filling stations. When Arnot thought they had found a place, the owners had scribbled out a notice rationing each car to a limit of fifty francs worth of fuel. Even as they read it an old car slipped into the space in front of them.

'God! Every man for himself,' Arnot said.

He jumped out and for a moment it appeared he was about to vent his anger on the moustached farmer who had stolen his place. As the old man lifted the bonnet of his ancient Renault, smoke billowed out and it became a matter of some urgency to push the vehicle away from the petrol pump queue. The old man waved his hands helplessly. Arnot took charge of the pushing and pulling that landed the old decrepit machine on a piece of waste land well away from the garage. Menna and Lisa watched the drama as it unfolded.

'I can see the ghost of the father in the son,' Menna said.

'You don't think I should be so cross with him?'

Lisa was murmuring a form of apology.

'It must have been some student protest,' Menna said. 'Vietnam perhaps. I don't really remember. A caravan with placards all over it went on fire. They said someone was inside. Reg poured water all over his jacket, put it over his head and smashed his way in. There was no one in there as it happened. I was overwhelmed with hero worship. Funny little thing that I was. I thought he was so brave. And of course he was.'

'At the hospital. Why didn't you come in with me?'

'I thought about it. And I decided Arnot was right. What could I have done? Except raise the man's hopes. It isn't always wise to confuse dreams and reality.'

'You think I should never have encouraged him.'

'You weren't to know what was going to happen. We never do. I don't know now, do I? I've made a commitment. That is different from a pipe dream. I have to follow it through. And just pray I find the strength to do so.'

'I was wrong then.'

Menna turned to smile at a contrite daughter-in-law.

'You meant well.'

'Oh yes. The paving stones to hell.'

'And you can keep in touch with him. The last of the Fronsiac de L'Epines. Make him welcome if he turns up on your doorstep.'

## XX

Ten days later, at Heathrow, Lisa and Menna were shunted into a new coffee bar while Arnot and Bishop Bob bustled off to check on the whereabouts of an extra consignment of medical supplies for the orphanage at Lokichokio. Menna was nervous and it was Lisa who was there to comfort her and put her at her ease. She closed her eyes and pushed the coffee cup away as though the vapour rising to her nostrils gave her nausea. Her confidence and conviction were evaporating. Lisa tried to make her smile.

'You must be one of them,' she said.

'One of what?'

Menna reacted as though she had been accused of something.

'One of Bishop Bob's collection of special people.'

Menna apologised.

'He is a bit overwhelming isn't he?'

She fidgeted in her chair, identifying yet another defect in her arrangements. There had been no need, she insisted, for Arnot and Lisa to come all the way to Heathrow to see her off. She wanted them to enjoy her absence. She would be more than enough trouble when she returned with a Nubian piccaninny under each arm. The potential for disruption was yet another defect to be concerned about. Lisa persisted in her effort to make Menna smile.

'Bang-bang Bob,' she said. 'Bless him. He put me right in my place anyway. "To the making of books there is no end," he said. The booming implication being that there were more than enough in the world already and I was a bit of an idiot trying to add to them!'

Menna tried and failed to share the joke.

'Really. He can be so tactless. It's those big feet of his.'

Lisa began to tick off the Bishop's roster of special people.

'Apart from you, there's Berwyn. Son of a pastry-cook who kicked the drugs and went off to Kenya and married a Kikuyu nurse. And there's that ageing chum of his called Spiros Papadakis who's wearing himself out and risking his life trying to create oases of humanity in Bosnia. Those are the people worth writing about.'

'Don't you take any notice of him,' Menna said. 'You've got your own words and music to think about. You are writing, aren't you?'

Menna's question was stern and direct.

'I'd be a fool if I didn't,' Lisa said. 'There's no place like home for really putting pen to paper. And it's a wonderful home. And it's you that gave it to us. I've never been grateful enough.'

Menna smiled at last and patted her arm.

'You'll create something all colour and light. I'm sure you will.'

'It's curious isn't it,' Lisa said. 'The vestiges of faith in oneself one clings to.'

'We have to.'

Menna nodded her agreement. It was deeply felt.

'I'm back to square one,' Lisa said. 'It's got to be the heretic maiden and your diary. Which I promise to burn at the stake when I've finished. Promise. I've got to find a way though the labyrinth and not care in the least how long it takes me.'

Menna raised a clenched fist.

'That's the spirit,' she said.

Lisa moved her head closer to share a secret.

'Can I tell you something? I haven't told Arnot yet. It's a bit soon... but since you're going away. I think I'm pregnant.'

Menna jumped in her chair and then checked her own excitement.

She controlled herself to show a depth of concern.

'Are you sure it's what you want?'

Lisa raised her hands in the air in a gesture of relief.

'It doesn't matter any more what I want,' she said.

# Penrhyn Hen

## I

There they are, standing above the deserted harbour. Two attractive figures. He has a haversack on his back. He is smiling as a man who has reduced the world to more agreeable proportions. The broad beach is devoid of tourists and across the water snow lies on the mainland hilltops like icing on a cake. The same morning sunlight transforms the hair of the girl alongside him from red to gold. She looks as reluctant as he is eager. The cold she is prepared to complain of rises from inside her.

'This is the place! I feel it so strongly.'

He raised a clenched fist. He placed his other arm over her shoulder so that she could share his enthusiasm.

'Things don't change all that much. *Aros mae'r mynyddau mawr...* Empires rise and fall. Remnants escape and discover safe havens. I think that's the way it has to be now. I really do. People of goodwill have to escape from networks of destruction. Electronic networks are even more insidious. They can destroy from within while ghostly satellites watch us from above.'

His manner was ebullient and jovial, but she knew he wasn't joking.

'Be like the curlew,' he said. 'Build a nest that's hard to find.'

They belong to each other. This entailed a flow of communication from him not easy to interrupt.

'It's not the nuclear holocaust. That was yesterday's nightmare. We are confronted with something far more subtle. Cultural pollution. A spiritual greenhouse effect. The disease that rots from within and all that sort of business.'

She freed herself from the weight of his arm on her shoulder.

'You get carried away,' she said. 'There's no point in getting carried away.'

He gazed at her with unqualified respect and admiration. She was the fulcrum of common sense. And more than that, the focal point of the beauty of their surroundings. The shallow water left behind by the ebb tide was a burnished mirror made to reflect his Sioned's hair. Bryn Williams and Sioned Anwyl. Together they could feed off the strength of his convictions.

'Everything sparkles!'

He moved closer to the edge of the harbour wall. Herring gulls found little to scavenge in the caravan park tucked away in the disued limestone quarry. They circled above the silted harbour, yelping and wailing their disappointment.

'I've got to say it or burst,' he said. 'Here, here you know you can inherit the earth.'

Sioned shook her head angrily.

'I've told you and I tell you again, don't talk like that.'

'Sioned. She's your sister. She's dying to see you.'

'You don't know what you're talking about. You've never even seen her.'

'Her letters tell me everything. What more can you ask? She writes wonderful letters. And my cousin Carys Haf says she's a wonderful woman – "Malan Roberts is in the forefront of the struggle" – What more can you ask?'

'I don't want to go near the place.'

Sioned sank down on a stone bench, her hands thrust deep in her coat pockets. How could she continue to cherish his affection and at the same time suffer the restrictions it placed upon her. She had to listen to the compelling force of his arguments like a favourite pupil kept back in class by an over zealous teacher. In a determined effort to make her smile he knelt in front of her and lifted her chin with his finger.

' "What part do you come from then?" '

The first words they ever spoke to each other. An unexpected exercise of their native tongue in the social room of a public library on a wet Midlands night: flat enough to begin with but transformed into a talismanic canticle once the sexual spark had crossed the gap.

' "What part do you come from then?" '

She was obliged to smile at him. After all he was her choice and every choice involves concession.

'It was chance,' he said. 'The way we met. Just an accident.'

He touched her cheek.

'Nothing is an accident once it's happened,' she said.

'Well there you are then...'

They were in agreement and it made him want to kiss her. She restrained him even though there could have been no-one watching. They were there by choice. Two figures marooned in a spectacular landscape.

'Mind you, you mustn't think I couldn't cope,' he said. 'You mustn't think that.'

He was powerfully built. He stretched himself to his full height. He would derive extra strength from their immediate surroundings. This was his own, his native land.

'They are changing the law to allow policemen into schools,' he said. 'It's come to that. Not that Walsall East Comprehensive was ever that bad. In any case the threat of violence is a positive stimulant.'

'I don't know whether your Head would agree with you there. Poor chap is still in hospital.'

Bryn would not allow his train of thought to be diverted.

'The thing is, in the end, if you stay there you have to assimilate. Or become a professional exile. Either way you become something else. You become a unit with a wafer thin identity.'

Sioned shook her head to show how confused and uncertain she felt.

'People can only live as best they can wherever they happen to be,' she said.

II

His neck was broken and his speech impaired. The bed had been tilted so that he could see through the window. As slowly as his eyes swivelled toy ships crawled along the horizon until the headland blocked them for ever out of his sight. His wife Malan bustled into the bedroom carrying an enamelled jug of hot water and towels over her arm. The white walled room was sparsely furnished. His eyes followed her movements with canine apprehension. Her sleeves were rolled up to reveal strong forearms. Her voice was loud and cheerful.

'They're coming, Ritchie Roberts,' she said. 'We must look our best mustn't we?'

There was work to be done. A tough black beard to be shaved. The bedclothes thrown back, the top and then the bottom of his pyjamas removed. She was vigorous but not uncaring. The interest she took in the condition of his white skin and his genitals was intent but professional. While she combed his damp hair, his head rested on her breast and she was able to speak softly close to his ear.

'She's coming back, Ritchie. Sioned is coming back. All we need is patience. You never believed did you? You never listened. And I never listened to my mother. My goodness the things she said – "That Ritchie Roberts will turn this place into a thieves' kitchen..." – and she was right, wasn't she? You did your best with your cara-vans and your car-boot sales. I was so hurt when she called you Ritchie Rwtsh. But she was right wasn't she? Little Ritchie Rubbish. You were always a naughty boy. And she was always right. And I would never listen to her. I listened to you. The serpent whistling in the garden. It takes a whole lifetime to learn. I thought you were the son of the morning. The light of a new day. All you brought was darkness and night.'

'You're mad.'

She understood the noise in his throat and was able to smile forgivingly. She plumped his pillows and eased his head back on them.

'She was meant to have a second chance,' she said. 'My little sister Sioned. And maybe you too. Ritchie. In some way or other miracles can always happen.'

III

Sioned hung back as Bryn pushed open the cafe door and slipped the haversack off his shoulder. The place was empty. He nodded towards a table in a bay window which had an uninterrupted view of the bay and the slipway from the lifeboat station.

'Come on,' he said. 'What you need is a nice hot drink.'

Sioned was fumbling in her bag. He was puzzled by her behav-iour.

'That girl,' she said. 'Behind the counter. She knows me. I was in school with her.'

'So?'

Sioned put on a woolly cap and dark glasses.

'You don't have to talk to her,' he said. 'You make for the table and I'll bring you coffee. Or would you rather hot chocolate?'

He enjoyed being in charge of the operation. He was intent as ever on being positive. He had sufficient conviction for both of them, but the precise verbal expressions he needed were too often outside his reach. He was reduced to blurting out quotations that were no more than rough indication on the point he was trying to make.

' *"In the war I mean to stay/ In the front line take my place..."* '

'War? What war? What are you talking about?'

'It is very strange you know. You've got to admit it.'

'Admit what?'

Sioned removed her eye shades to stare moodily at the in-coming tide. She shifted in her chair so that her back was turned to the young woman yawning between the coffee machine and the glass cake-stand. Bryn was large and bulky and protective, but his enthusiasm kept drawing her into places where she would have preferred not to be.

'How did she know I was a great-grandson of Seth William, Erw Wen? The amazing fact is Sioned, Penrhyn Hen, you and I are distantly related. Just think of that! *Here lie the tombs of our ancestors / And here let our children laugh and play.*'

'Keep your voice down.'

Sioned muttered urgently.

'You've no idea how penetrating your voice can be. You're getting into the habit of shouting all the time.'

She passed a hand over her forehead. It appalled him to realise his voice could give her a headache. There was hurt as well as apology showing on his broad face. How could he be so thoughtless as to give pain to the one person he loved best. She touched his hand on the table, but quickly withdrew hers before he could clutch at it.

'Everyone is related, if you go back far enough,' she said.

They sipped their hot coffee in silence. In order to bring himself closer to Sioned and lower his voice, Bryn hunched over the little table in an attitude of dedicated sincerity.

'She has this way of expressing herself, your sister. A command of the language you could call it. A bit old-fashioned perhaps, but full of a certain authority. That's important. When a language loses that, it loses everything. You know what I mean? It has to be capable of "Thus saith the Lord..." if it's going to have any effect. I mean if there is a message left it must have the capacity to transmit it.'

At the counter a hoarse-voiced woman was buying a packet of cigarettes and leaning against the counter to gossip. Sioned frowned with the effort of trying to catch the drift of their talk. Bryn realised that she was nervous and uncomfortable. He leaned even closer to ask her a question.

'Are you scared of her, Sioned? If you are, you must tell me.'

'Afraid of Malan? Good Lord, no.'

'Well there you are then.'

All was well with the world. He stretched back in his chair to give her a radiant smile.

'She wants you to have the place. She says so. It's all down in black and white.'

'Bryn. I've told you. Keep your voice down.'

He obeyed but persisted with his conviction in a throaty whisper.

'It's basic really. There can be no decent civilisation unless we respect and cherish our inheritance.'

'Finish your drink. I can't bear this place a moment longer.'

Intent on not being recognised she reached the door in his shadow. She waited outside the drab cafe trembling with impatience while he paid the bill.

'Let's get out of here,' she said. 'This horrid little place.'

Bryn took in the picturesque fishing village that had developed haphazardly into a tourist resort.

'I can't stand it. Full of nosey-parker people.'

She crouched down in the passenger seat of his battered Ford Fiesta. He took his place at the wheel and tried to take account of the depth of her objections.

'It can't be that bad, can it? They're mostly natives, judging by the talk. And there's a choir here. Did you see that poster advertising a Whitsun Eisteddfod?'

Sioned snorted her contempt.

IV

Malan stood in the open doorway, her arms folded, contemplating the invalid in the bed.

' "Keep an eye on him." That's what she always said. "Watch out for him, my girl. You never know what he'll get up to." '

There was no reproof in her voice. Or gloating. Only wonder touched with awe at the way things had turned out. This was something he could share with her if only he could make the effort. She noted all his reactions. His jaw was working with what could have been anger or frustration or both: but his eyes were glistening with a plea for mercy.

'In that same bed she was. We used to make fun of her. Do you remember? "Poor old Mrs Anwyl, Penrhyn Hen. Longing all her life to get into bed, and now unable to get out of it." And I was no better. Ready to laugh at anything you said. I was so impressed by your courage and your daring. "Foolish Love" my mother called it. Is there any other? When I closed my eyes tightly enough I would be one with the sands of the beach and you riding your motor-bike backwards and forwards all over it. Now the best I can do is wipe the dribble from your mouth.'

Malan was admired locally as a woman devoted to cleanliness and service. The house reflected her character people said. She kept it bare and devoid of the comfort of labour-saving devices. Every surface was polished and free of dust. It had the chilly perfection of a period house in an open air folk museum. She prepared her husband's porridge in a cooking-pot suspended on a chain over an open fire. The invalid was provided with plain but wholesome food. His bed linen was spotless. His feeding bibs were washed and ironed every day.

She drew up a chair so that she could help him feed himself. Her hand gripped his. He resented her help. Her hand was the stronger. She spoke in a soothing tone to distract him from the futile struggle.

'We have to think about sin, don't we?' she said. 'It's a word people don't like using. Sin. What is it, they say? "Selfishness," old Adda James used to say in Sunday School. "What about the others?" Maggie Whist would pipe up. She always had plenty to say for herself even when she was small. "What about the others Mr. James. Aren't there seven deadly sins?" "Selfishness," he mumbled in his beard.. "That's what they all boil down to." '

Malan held back the spoon and looked her husband in the eye to make sure he appreciated the humour underlying the truth.

'I used to sit in chapel, you know, worrying about it for hours on end. There are forbidden degrees you see. A woman may not marry her brother. A man may not marry his mother and so on. It's all written down there for everyone to see. "With a pen of iron and the point of a diamond... The heart is deceitful above all things and desperately wicked: who can know it..." You could have told me. Why didn't you tell me?'

When he had difficulty in breathing, she witheld the spoon until he recovered. Her disciplined measured approach obliged him to swallow without choking. It was feeding time. There was also a learning process in progress that she was prepared to prolong with infinite patience.

'God sees all our shabby little subterfuges. We don't always realise that. He sees everything. And yet he forgives. He loves us more than a mother loves her child. Can you imagine that? So what else can I do Ritchie? Tell me that. You know for most of our lives we sit in our own shadow and we bar ourselves form the light. Did you think I wouldn't find out in the end? You didn't think. That's always the trouble. I'd gone to chapel. My mother was bed-ridden upstairs and my little Sioned. My sister. My pearl beyond price was sitting in the parlour doing her homework, and she was your victim. A prize you couldn't resist taking. It wasn't love. It was greed. It was lust. But then you were a victim just as much as she was. That's what I had to learn. I could have killed you. But I didn't. It was a bitter lesson. I think you have had enough, don't you?'

She wiped his lips carefully before removing his bib.

'I must get on. There's so much to be done. Sioned is coming back. When you make a welcome it has to be so much more than words.'

In the doorway she turned to check that everything was in order behind her. She shook her head sadly to see how her husband was glaring at her.

'We have to learn forgiveness,' she said. 'All of us. You have to think what is the use of it. All that concentrated helpless hate.'


V


'I mean just look at it! Just look!'

Driven by his enthusiasm Bryn scrambled up the steep bank on the left side of the narrow road to command a better view. The Ford Fiesta was parked at a tilted angle on the grass verge. Sioned leaned against it, her arms folded in a resolute sulk. Bryn carried his old-fashioned camera. He held it up to keep his balance, slipping about on the damp grass as he attempted adjustments to the focal length. Penrhyn Hen nestled under the gorse-covered outcrop on the north side of the headland. The slate roofs of the house and the outbuildings glistened through a screen of trees in early leaf.

There were so many things for him to look at. Out to sea a rocky island with a ruined tower. Above the yellow shore and the silted estuary an expanse of woodland hid a church with a spire. Tiny ships were balanced on the horizon. Bryn encouraged his efforts at photography with bouts of speculation.

'Do you know what I think?'

He claimed Sioned's attention and support.

'If there is such a thing as a spiritual world – a pretty big 'if' I agree – what more convenient way of revealing it to the human race than through the world around us? "There is a poetry that walks these sacred hills..." Ancient? Sacred? Why sacred you may ask? Because they are outward and visible signs of a benevolent universe, that's why. And the sea. What's sinister about the sea? Just look at it. The cloud shadow chasing the brilliance. All the grey and the blue. Could you find a better symbol of eternity? The sea I mean. The same yesterday today and tomorrow. All that water in which to wash our little microscopic blobs of understanding.'

'I don't have to listen to you.'

Sioned marched away in the direction of a path that led down to the nearest shore. Bryn watched her through the lens of his camera as her figure stalked through pools of sunlight down the leafy lane. He abandoned his photography to set off in hot pursuit, overtaking the wayward girl where the incoming tide lapped at the smooth sand. His large hands descended on her shoulders and compelled her to turn and face him.

'Listen,' he said. 'I love you and it isn't easy to make stern noises. You mustn't be so gloomy.'

'Mustn't I?'

'No, you mustn't. Your sister loves you. For that you must forgive her anything.'

'Must I?'

'Yes you must.'

She confronted him with a tense silence before she allowed her lips to part in a tolerant smile.

'You know what's wrong with you, Bryn Williams. You should have been a preacher, not a teacher.'

'What's the difference?'

'The difference.'

Sioned considered the problem.

'The preacher is safe in his pulpit. Above the dust and strife on the classroom floor. I suppose that's the difference.'

'Time to go home, Sioned. Time to see the blue of the sea and the sky in your eyes. Time to dispel old troubles like sea-spray on the breeze.'

## VI

He waved his hands above the meal spread out on the kitchen table. There was home-cured ham, scones and cakes and barabrith and above all home-baked white bread. He took a slice and brought it close to his nose to savour the distinct aroma.

'*Bara cartref*,' he said. 'Scented with blessings. Like manna from heaven.'

'It was the best time of day for me,' Malan said. 'Always.'

She looked first at Bryn and then at Sioned. Frank and yet confiding.

'When my little sister came home from school and we sat around the table. She was always so hungry. Ready to gobble up half a loaf.'

'I don't blame her,' Bryn said. 'I would have swallowed the loaf whole!'

Malan warmed to his response. She smiled at him as though she had acquired a new friend with whom to share her thoughts.

'There's something I want to show you,' she said.

It was her habit to sit on the side of her chair to allow her to get up quickly to her feet. They watched her march briskly out of the room. Sioned uncertain as to what her sister might do next: Bryn prepared to transfer his admiration from the woman to the house that appeared to him an extension of her uncompromising personality.

'Just as it should be,' he said. 'Spick and span and yet alive with an awareness of its eighteenth century origins.'

'Seventeenth in fact.'

He assumed Sioned's precision marked an outburst of spontaneous pride in her old home and this delighted him. He made more expansive gestures as he spoke in a voice subdued with respect.

'So much loving care... What else can you call it?'

'A prison.'

Sioned was staring at the polished stone floor.

'So much unstinting affection. It's so obvious, Sioned. She thinks the world of you. She would give you anything.'

He spoke in a hurry. There was more he wanted to say before Malan came back.

'Surely you can see it? She takes so much pride in you.'

'Me?'

'Yes you, Miss Anwyl.'

He wanted to persuade her to accept the situation as they had found it in a more relaxed frame of mind. This was her home. She was a native who had returned. She was entitled to enjoy the welcome. The farmhouse tea was the equivalent of the fatted calf.

'We've got to get away from here,' Sioned said. 'As soon as we can. It's suffocating. I can hardly breathe.'

'Can't you see how much she loves you?'

'Me? Or some ghost that happens to live in her head.'

Malan came back into the kitchen. She would not allow the bulk of the family Bible she was carrying to impede her triumphant progress. She was out of breath as she dumped the heavy book on a clear corner of the long kitchen table.

'There's a family tree too,' she said. 'A big thing. I've been working on it. I'll show it to you later. We'll have to spread it all out on the parlour floor.'

Bryn was ready to show how pleased he was to agree to anything she proposed.

'Anyway, this Bible believe it or not. It used to belong to your great-great-grandmother, Mr. Williams.'

'Bryn.'

'Well. Bryn then. There's her writing for you. Isn't it beautiful. *Margaret Wiliam, Erw Wen, is the one owner of this book. Read with reverence and respect.*'

Bryn shuffled to his feet to make a closer inspection of the handwriting. His mouth stayed open to denote his amazement. This after all was a message direct from an immediate ancestor. She was long gone, but her handwriting remained. As though in obedience to her instruction he opened the book and fingered the stiff pages with respect.

'You would never guess how it came here.'

Malan anticipated the pleasure of being able to reveal the mystery.

'A car-boot sale. This little art teacher on his holidays. Bald head and beard and full of himself. That's where he picked it up for a few pence. "Have you got any more of these, Mrs Roberts?" he said. Standing just by where you're standing now. Insignificant you would think. But he was bold as brass. "I'm an artist" – marching right in without a word of invitation. "I'm collecting them, to make painted sculpture. I chew them up and glue them. A blow lamp down the right side and paint spray in seven different colours. Rainbow Resurrection I call it." I'll give you rainbow, I said. Black and blue more like. He shot off like a rabbit and I haven't seen him since.'

Her outrage ran out of steam and she burst out laughing. Even Sioned was prepared to smile.

'So now I can return it to you.'

With deep approval she watched Bryn open the Bible and pass his hands over the printed page.

'Do you know what my grandmother used to do? I can see her doing it now. On that very table. First Sunday of the month. With a sewing needle. Close her eyes and pick out a verse. And she had a rhyme she would recite as she did it - *Break through the blindness of my sight / With signals of perpetual light.* That was before she lost her memory. She ended up in that rocking chair mumbling to herself. You wouldn't remember, Sioned. You couldn't have been more than two when she died. I'll look it up. It's not good is it, Bryn, to forget the past?'

'Good heavens no,' he said. 'It's all we've got. People who've lost an interest in their own past are more or less finished and done with.'

Malan showed she was in a brisk and purposeful mood.

'All the same we should not allow ourselves to be weighed down by it. Do you know what I suggest?'

She smiled with benevolent authority and Bryn paid her close attention.

'I think it's time for Sioned to go upstairs and have a word with poor Ritchie.'

'Well of course.'

Bryn was eager to agree. Sioned sat with her eyes closed and one hand clutching the edge of the table. There was an uncomfortable silence.

'My little sister. She could never bear to see anyone in pain. Man or animal. A tender nature as you would expect in such a sensitive plant. That's the way of it. We have to get used to suffering in this life sooner or later. Take the maim and the infirm in our stride. That's what we all are in the end. There is no health in us.'


VII


As she stood in the doorway he managed a smile and to mutter her name. On a tray Sioned carried an invalid cup with a spout, and a fresh bib. He raised two white hands in a feeble gesture of welcome.

'Well now then,' she said. 'No need to be afraid is there. No need to be shy. Remember how you used to stand over me? I was afraid of your shadow. Remember how you took your time, Ritchie Rwtsh? Telling me to relax. Telling me to forget everything. Telling me not to worry. Now here I am and I don't worry any more.'

'Malan...'

He began to tremble as Sioned moved closer to the bed.

'You don't have to worry about Malan. Remember what you used to say? "You leave poor old Malan to me." Master of all ceremonies. King of the kitchen. King of the car-boot sales. King of the caravans. Whichever way I turned you were liable to be there, waiting to trap me. And she had no idea. Malan had no idea. Until that last day when she caught us. And now look where you are. So helpless. I don't need to wait until you're asleep. I could cut it off with a rusty razor.'

With elaborate care Sioned laid down the tray and sat in the chair close enough to Ritchie to be able to feed him.

'What's the best feed for a sick stallion? But you're not a stallion any more are you, Ritchie Rwtsh? Only a rat in the rubbish. Just open your mouth.'

Too frightened to disobey the invalid sucked at the porcelain spout. He seemed to find some comfort in the action.

'Oh what a handsome figure you were, striding about in your riding breeches. Malan on her knees polishing your boots and your leggings. What an adventurer! What a hero! And here lies the mighty man fallen. You were never anything better than a rat. A hungry rat. Ready to eat or destroy anything within reach.'

She withdrew the feeding cup in order to examine the contents with close attention.

'What do we have in here, Ritchie? I think it's rat poison. How about a little more. Feel it burn in your guts. Out of this loving cup.'

The brown liquid dribbled down his chin as he failed to swallow it. Sioned found a rag to wipe the mess.

'Mustn't let Malan see your dirty mouth, Mr. Roberts. And all the dirt that came out of it. I wouldn't bother to poison you. I've got a better life to live and a better man to love me. You lie there and live with that. Mind you, you've got a lot to be thankful for. You can be glad that it's Malan taking care of you and not me.'

## VIII

The caravan was almost hidden at the bottom of the orchard. It was painted a dull green and surrounded on two sides by an overgrown privet hedge. Malan and Bryn approached it avoiding the wet droppings of the geese that cropped the orchard grass. Bryn was ready to marvel at anything Malan chose to show him. Inside the caravan a single bed had been made up. A small calor gas stove was lit to keep the place warm.

'It should be warm enough,' Malan said. 'All those stories about ministers getting rheumatism by sleeping in damp beds.'

They smiled at each other in recognition of their shared knowledge of this piece of nonconformist folk lore.

'This is where I wanted Sioned to have peace and quiet to study. I always wanted the best for her!'

'Of course you did.'

He nodded vigorously wanting her to see how much he appreciated her goodness. In every respect she was a remarkable woman.

'And now you can make use of it.'

She clasped her rough hands together. There was a whole field of understanding that had to grow between them.

'I want to thank you very much for your letters.'

'Not nearly as good as yours,' he said. 'I used to tell Sioned that her sister was a natural born stylist.'

'Very old fashioned. "Annwyl Mr. Williams..." and so on. But then we'd never met, had we?'

'Only in the spirit,' Bryn said.

The sound of his laughter pleased her. He was a responsible man who could also be relaxed and jovial.

'How is that poor man your headmaster?'

'I'm afraid he's still in hospital, Mr. Ackroyd,' Bryn said. 'Fractured skull.'

Malan sighed with profound sympathy. She shook her head.

'Sometimes it seems we are on the brink of another Dark Age.'

She was quick to anticipate his reaction.

'You think I'm exaggerating?'

'No indeed. I think I see what you mean.'

'It's what happens when you live alone. Great issues become simplified. The poor man was knocked off his bicycle on his way to school. An apostle of racial harmony struck down by the very people he was struggling to serve. Lying there unconscious and his bicycle trampled to bits in a frenzy of destruction. I could understand how much it disturbed you.'

'It certainly made me think. You could say I haven't stopped thinking since.'

'It led you back here,' she said. 'You brought Sioned back. However wicked it was, some good came of it in my little world.'

There was more of the property she wanted him to see. She spoke lightly of features of antiquarian interest. There was a stone window in what was now an outhouse that belonged to an earlier house built in 1587.

'It collapsed apparently,' Malan said. 'Bad foundations. I heard them say that when I was a little girl. I thought it had something to do with the house built on sand. And the story of the three bears came into it too.'

The farmyard was in a dormant state. Grass grew in unexpected places. The stables and the cowsheds were empty. An ancient tractor stood like a museum piece in the open coach-house. Malan led the way and Bryn followed.

'You ought to see it all,' she said. 'The extent of the inheritance.'

It was odd she should take satisfaction in the stagnant state they were looking at, unless she was urging him to consider the potential of the place. It was also possible that she was witnessing things that were outside his field of vision. He was anxious to understand. As they walked about the remarks she made were often gnomic and inconsequential. No sooner had he pondered the meaning of one than she moved on to another.

'We live through years of darkness. Then meaning descends on us like a lightning flash and burns us up.'

They stood at the bottom of a stone staircase leading up a gable wall to the granary. Moss grew between the stones.

'I was a woman of no consequence. Ground down between my mother and my husband. I should have been more demanding. It wasn't in my nature. Are you a Christian?'

She gave him time to answer.

'I would like to be,' he said. 'I can't imagine anything better to be.'

'How lost we would be if there wasn't another world. And a better one. How utterly lost.'

She pointed at the stairs. At the same time she sighed and showed a reluctance to climb them.

'We are what we are. I was never satisfied with myself. Neither was my mother. Our old minister told me not to worry about it. "We come in all shapes and sizes *merch i*, and there's little we can do about it. By taking thought we cannot add one cubit to our stature." '

Bryn stopped smiling when he noted how serious she was.

'And yet we have to change our natures. Our religion says so. I used to think it was so difficult.'

'You were right,' Bryn said. 'It is.'

They stood side by side at the top of the steps. The granary door was closed. It was bleached for want of paint and rotting along the bottom edge. Malan hesitated to open it. She turned her back on the door to gaze longingly at the expanse of sea beyond the headland. Bryn understood there was a view to be admired.

'Do you approve of confession, Mr. Williams? Bryn I mean.'

'Good for the soul sort of thing,' he said. 'I suppose I do.'

She used her shoulder to push open the door that was sagging on its hinges. In the dim light beyond her he could see a row of unwashed sheepskins hanging over the central rafter.

'This is where he fell.'

Her whisper reverberated between the bare walls. She pointed to a jagged hole in the worm eaten floorboards. Approaching it gingerly Bryn could see heavy farm machinery rusting in the outhouse below.

'Broke his neck. Because I tried to kill him.'

Bryn shifted back to the open doorway before turning to look at the view in order to hide his unease and embarrassment.

'The hymn says you can throw your burden of guilt off your shoulders. It doesn't happen to me. It goes heavier with every day that passes. You can't see it of course. It's not visible. The weight is crushing me all the same. And I'm the only one that can carry it.'

From outside the door Bryn kept a nervous eye on her, uncertain what she might do or say next. She stood with her arms folded studying the condition of the floor. She could have been considering the best way to go about repairs. When she turned to ask him a question he was surprised to see a calm smile on her face.

'What is the difference between cunning and wisdom, Mr. Williams?'

He was being cross-examined from a distance, and he had no answer prepared.

'There must be a difference,' he said. 'I can see that.'

'It's very simple. Wisdom belongs to God. Cunning comes from the devil. And yet we can't live without cunning. I spend most of my time thinking about it. Why are words so slippery? One moment you think you've caught their meaning at last. And the next minute it's gone. Why do the Children of Light need to be more cunning than the Children of Darkness? There can only be one reason. There is a better life beyond this one. The whole point of living is just to learn that. And that can only mean that it is after death we start to live.'

'My goodness me...'

Bryn rapped his forehead with his knuckles.

'I don't know that I can follow you. I'm out of my depth to tell you the truth.'

'I'm so grateful you came. There is much for you to understand of course. There you are you see. Words. I don't mean understand. I mean forgive.'

She tugged at the creaking door with all her strength until it closed behind her.

'I couldn't bear to go in there. And now I've been and I've seen, it's nothing. Just a dead space. But it's where I saw them lying together. Ritchie and Sioned. Man and wife are one flesh. That is how we are created. Two are better than one says the Book of the Preacher. But I saw it as rape. I was carrying a sickle. He tried to make a joke of it. "Oh dear look at me caught with my trousers down." That's how he was poor Ritchie. Everything was a joke. Life was a giggle, he said. Just a game really and the thing was to be sure to win. I slashed at him with the sickle. He stepped back and he fell through the floor... He stopped laughing.'

'Sioned and Ritchie.'

Coupling the names together was as difficult for him as taking in what the woman was saying.

'I've asked myself ever since why I stood in their way. I meant well, mind you. Sioned was always the light of my life. From the very beginning. I used to be so proud when she said her verses. The light shone in her hair. Like a little angel. And all those Eisteddfod prizes she won. She was so bright and so good at her studies. I did my best. But my best wasn't good enough. I think my love was too much of a burden for her. I was ready to bring up the baby as my own. But she said she wouldn't have it. She just had to get away.'

She studied his face. She was full of sympathy for his evident distress.

'We are what we are, Mr. Williams,' Malan said. 'You have done a great service bringing my little sister back to where she belongs. It worried me so much that she should be deprived of her inheritance. And deprived of the joy of motherhood. Both at the same time. We are as we are made and we are what we make. That is the extent of the tether. There has to be a degree of compulsion. You must explain it all to her in a language that she can understand. You are a man of science. You are a teacher. You can find the proper degree of detachment.'

He watched her walk away. His head was shaking and his legs refused to move. He was unable to follow her. He saw her pace quicken as she passed through the open gate and took the lane that led along the cliff to the shore.


## IX

Each time she called out her sister's name the sound spread out on the evening air more forlorn than the cry of the curlew.

'Ma-lan! Ma-lan!'

It was an appeal for help. Penrhyn Hen was a settlement created for the bustle of daily labour, all the noise and business of wresting a living from the land. This pathetic voice and the absence of response created an atmosphere of cold desolation. The farmstead was obsolete, sterile, deserted.

'Malan! Malan!'

Impatience became desperation and then anger. When he heard the sound Bryn escaped through the orchard towards the green caravan. He clambered in and locked the door as if it was his last refuge.

Now it was his name she called as she strode about the yard. She wore an old overcoat of her sister's against the chill evening air.

'Bryn! What's the matter with you? Why don't you answer? Where's Malan? Where did she go?'

Sioned searched the whole extent of the premises. There was no way she could find of putting an end to her isolation. Everything she saw and every step she took intensified her distress and her fear. A brittle network of relationships had somehow collapsed while she was not looking. The caravan in the orchard became a target of disapproval. She ran towards it through the wet grass. She grasped the door handle and shook it. When she realised it was locked she slid down to sit on the step. She could only wait for his question.

'Sioned. Is it true?'

Such a childlike whimper from a grown man; from the voice she was so accustomed to hear full of theories and opinions.

'Is what true?'

'About you and Ritchie. And the child.'

'Of course it's true. You are a big stupid fool. That's all you are. Why wouldn't you listen to me. Why do you think I was so unwilling to come back to this dreadful place? You never listen.'

'Listen?'

He was bewildered by her fierce denunciation.

'Not to what I was saying. What I was feeling and not saying. Look at you now. Locking yourself up in this horrid little caravan. And what were you doing before? Locking yourself up in a dream of a Wales that never was on land or sea.'

She lowered her head in an effort to make her tears come. They would not flow. She waited until she heard the door open and he stood above her, his large body filling the narrow doorway.

'Did you love him?'

She found his question pathetic. The shadow of his presence was neither a protection nor a threat: only an irritation.

'What's love got to do with it?'

'Man and wife are one flesh. That's what Malan said.'

' "Malan said." ...Can't you see what's in front of your eyes? She lures you here with her fancy Welsh and a lot of claptrap about the great inheritance, and where does it leave us in the end? You understand nothing. It's a trap. That's all it is. A trap.'

'What happened? Sioned, come inside. Tell me what happened. You tell me.'

He tried to exert gentle strength. She shook her arm free.

'How could I tell what was happening? I was only a schoolgirl. Was it all supposed to be my fault?'

'I just want to understand,' he said.

'Can't you see what she's up to, my wonderful sister? She wants me here to wait hand and foot on that filthy bed-ridden creature. That's all. And you've done your best to help her. You stupid schoolteacher stuffed with stupid quotations. Where is she? Can you tell me? She can't just vanish. Where is she?'

'The child,' Bryn said. 'What happened?'

'What child?'

'You could have told me. I would have tried to understand. Why didn't you tell me?'

165

'Tell you? You only listen to what you want to hear.'

'Sioned...'

She moved away and he blundered after her eager to show an open mind and a willingness to listen. He followed her to the end of a neglected flower garden. Brambles had been cut back recently when they threatened to encroach on a small grave. In front of an inconspicuous wooden cross there was an empty flower vase.

'There you are, Brynmor Williams. All your questions lying unanswered. We should have brought flowers. And heaps of quotations. They make a difference. There must be something to make ground sacred.'

His lips were moving but no words emerged. She left him staring at the tilted cross as though deciding whether or not to get on his knees and straighten it.

## X

Alone in the cavernous kitchen Sioned gave vent to her frustration by talking aloud and at intervals shouting her sister's name. Her surroundings were only too familiar and yet she seemed unable to find anything she wanted: even matches to light the lamps. The switch on the wall was useless. Malan had stopped using electricity. Or the telephone. The power was cut off. It was her quiet boast that she could manage perfectly well without them.

Sioned found the matches in the cutlery drawer. She went on muttering angrily as she lit the lamp.

'The woman must be mad. Trying to plant the Past where the Present should be... As if she were trying to cast a spell over the place. It's not natural. She's not natural. And that precious Ritchie of hers... Who on earth would want him? A wreck lying on his back and governing all our lives... Why should he?'

She held the lamp high above her head as she climbed the stone staircase. She spoke up in a teasing threatening voice.

'Now who's the rabbit and who's the stoat? What is the penalty for raping a schoolgirl? A life sentence or death? And don't you try blaming the girl. Half your size. Half your strength. What does an innocent schoolgirl know about lust and male aggression and animal cunning?'

In the doorway of his room she held the lamp so that the light should fall on her face in the most alarming manner possible.

'I'm strong enough to put a pillow over your face, Ritchie Rwtsh. And I've got a perfect right to do it.'

Sioned could see his white sleeves fluttering helplessly in the gloom.

'I tell you something. I've got a man strong enough to squeeze your head between his finger and thumb. The trouble is he's not like you. He wouldn't do it.'

'Malan. Malan.'

This seemed as much as the man could manage to say.

'No use crying for Malan. She's not here. Nobody here to save you now...'

Ritchie pointed excitedly towards the window.

'What is it then? Dear me. It must be the ghost of your misdeeds.'

'Read,' he said. 'Read.'

'Read what Mr. Roberts?'

'For you... To read... You read.'

The black notebook lay on the windowsill. Ritchie made agonising attempts to persuade her to pick it up. She opened it and recognised her sister's familiar handwriting sloping freely across the lined pages. Once Sioned had sat in the corner to read by the light of the lamp, he was able to lie back and close his eyes.

Sioned, my very dear sister, this is for your eyes alone when I am gone... I long for you to think of my life as I have been obliged to live it. I was born to obedience. It was my intention to save you from that: to make sure you had a proper education and a free choice. These were denied to me. My mother was against choice. She called it the "weakness of the age". I tried to change the word. Not choice, I said, just an opportunity, a chance. She disapproved of that even more. "Submit," she said. "Bow to Providence my girl. How many times do I have to tell you? You must discipline the body and bend your will for the sake of your soul. And you are old enough now to know which for a woman is the most dangerous of all the sins. That source of sorrow and corruption. Lust of the flesh"... She told me to strive for purity of heart and learn the language of repentance. You see we have both inherited bitterness from the same source.

She liked to insist that service was the only true form of freedom and of course it suited her to accept my service. All I wanted was to open my heart so that a tide of love could flood into it. Until Ritchie came I felt I was living in a house without a door or a window. I loved him from the moment he touched me. It was as if a door had opened and he was standing there in the sunlight waiting for me to worship him.

I was corrupted by my love. I acquired a new form of intelligence and a talent to manipulate and deceive. You could call it a perverted form of artistry. My mother hated Ritchie. He was afraid of her and hated any form of responsibility. And yet I managed to make them live together. I gave him the illusion he could become master of Penrhyn Hen by marrying me and still be able to enjoy racing motor-bikes and car-boot sales. The more work I took on the more power I exerted over both of them. By the sweet sweat of labour I overcame my mother's legacy of bitterness and disappointment.

As you grew up, Sioned, my faith grew in the prospect of new forms of art and life that could emerge from innocence and a child-like joy of living. You became the light of my life. So I invested everything in your presence: you were beautiful, my sister, and no-one could avoid seeing it. He seduced you and you accepted him. How often I don't know, and it doesn't matter. I have to declare my interest without subterfuge or polite fictions. He is yours because you took him. He belongs to you and you belong to him. You will treat him as the child I never had and you should have had. I must not stand in your way or prevent you fulfilling your destiny. It is the impossible things we do that make a new life possible. The earth will once again become a tapestry woven in front of your eyes. The day before I knew you were coming I saw the standing stone begin to sway in the damp wind from the sea and I thought it was danc-ing without moving its feet. Our skulls are shaped to contain our fantasies. Under the dead farm the grass and the soil state with equal firmness an outline of the bedrock of reality. You will come to revive it and your voice in this place will be a message as power-ful as heaven's command.

Sioned raised her head and saw that Ritchie's eyes were wide open. He was smiling at her. In her anger she hurled the note-book across the room. It caught the spout of the feeding-cup on the bedside locker. The cup smashed on the floor. She grasped him by the shoulders and shook him with all her strength.

'You know where she is. Tell me or I'll kill you.'

It was a futile threat. She was not strong enough even to hold his dead weight and she let him go.

XI

Through the rain-blurred window of Malan's bedroom Sioned could stare at the pale light in the caravan at the bottom of the orchard. The rain was heavy: sufficient to provide the hero with an excuse to continue sulking in his tent. Malan's bedroom was furnished with spartan simplicity. At her bedside was another black notebook and a plump leather-bound copy of Richard Morris's 1746 Bible that also contained the Book of Common Prayer and Edmund Prys's Metrical Psalms. Even her reading had to be in keeping with her vision of the antiquity of their home.

An unlikely adornment was an enlarged photograph of their mother, Bessie Anwyl, taken in the late thirties when she was a girl of fourteen, and still able to gaze with the wide-eyed eagerness and a faint smile at the camera as if it were a better future. It was not thus that they remembered her. When she was still alive and complaining and bed-ridden by choice rather than by necessity, the sisters would marvel and even joke at the difference between the photograph and the mother they knew. Sioned sat on her sister's bed to gaze at the framed photograph on the wall as though it were an artefact that contained a hidden meaning, and looked at long enough would explain the contradictions of their existence. She stared so hard that the image began to merge into the faded wallpaper.

She was too disturbed to attempt to sleep. The choice of reading was limited. At least Malan's bold flowing hand was easier to decipher in the lamplight than the cramped eighteenth century print, and it seemed more immediately relevant. The notebook recorded the daily details of the business of making both ends meet at Penrhyn Hen: bills and records were interspersed with reflections, unexpected comments and cries from the heart.

> This morning, seeing a white gull circling above the headland made me shiver. There was something beyond it that made my blood race and my hands shake like the hands of a prisoner shaking the bars of his cell... My breath clouds the window of my room as if it existed to restrict my understanding. This house is a black pit of silence. It is possible to spend all the days of your life among strangers without moving from your hearth... There are mornings when I wake to a darkness breaking instead of a dawn and then I give thanks for all the work that awaits me... I have to remember he rejects what I have to offer. His ears close like steel doors merely at the sound of my voice... Pain is a strange phenomenon. It can't remember any condition when it did not exist and it can't offer any future except more of itself. You could say it was able to kill without being

able to die... Nothing is impossible for the person who is prepared to suffer. I shall prepare the way for a day of reconciliation. He will come again and his face will shine perpetually on a sea of glass...

Carrying the lamp, Sioned wandered aimlessly through the empty house. On the parlour floor she saw a family tree spread out like a large map. Her sister had intended to have them on their knees tracing their ancestry like excited children on a treasure hunt. The whole house was cold and repulsive and made her shiver so that the hand that held the lamp was shaking. She opened the back door and watched the rainwater streaming across the farm yard. It cut off any hope of escape. To reach the caravan, even with a rain-coat and a lantern she would have arrived soaking wet and uncertain of the reception she would receive. Her own bedroom had been kept by her sister exactly as she had left it so many years ago. The ridiculous dolls in ethnic costumes she had once collected still stood in a row of cellophane cylinders on the mantlepiece. This room was the most unbearable part of an unbearable house. It was a bed she could not hope to sleep in. She returned to Malan's room and lay awake on her bed. When at last she dozed off she saw an image of her sister beyond the window, the beatific smile on her face dissolving in the rain.

## XII

In the cold morning light a shambling and shamed-faced figure appeared in the open doorway of the kitchen. Bryn was hungry and the bottoms of his trousers were soaking wet. He lingered outside waiting to be invited in. Sioned was kneeling in front of the kitchen grate trying to coax the fire into more vigorous life. She took her time to acknowledge his presence.

'There's nothing to eat,' she said. 'You'll have to wait.'

He gave a feeble smile and seized on the curt announcement as a permit to enter the kitchen. He found a place to sit at an angle from the bare table. Without Malan the house had become alien territory: inexplicable and unexplored. His hands dangled between his legs and he looked like an unwilling visitor to an outpatient's waiting room.

'I've had time to think,' he said.

He opened the palm of a hand and stared at it as though he had discovered something to be grateful for after a long unhappy night.

'You were right,' he said. 'Of course you were.'

Sioned was busying herself with all the menial tasks her sister had been accustomed to attend to. Nothing was convenient. Nothing easy.

'That's nice,' she said. 'What was I right about I wonder?'

He breathed deeply. Having admitted his mistake he had to muster the strength to demonstrate a new resolve.

'You were quite right of course. We should never have come in the first place.'

She said nothing. He pressed on assuming she was restraining herself from making a sharp retort.

'Of course we had to face the truth,' he said. 'I realise that. I understand why you couldn't tell me...'

'Tell you? Tell you what?'

'About the baby and so on. It doesn't matter, Sioned. Between you and me it doesn't make any difference.'

'Oh. So you've forgiven me.'

She paused in her labours to confront him with a bread knife in her hand.

'What a relief,' she said.

'I didn't mean it like that... Not at all.'

'So how did you mean it? I seem to remember you saying the world needs to learn to be more precise with language. You know, like my sister. Precision. That's what you were keen on.'

'We have to get away from here as soon as we decently can.'

'Dear me. Abandon the earthly paradise already? Where to I wonder?'

He struggled to ignore her sarcasm.

'Somewhere where we can make a fresh start.'

'How about Seattle?' Sioned said. 'Weren't you offered a teaching job there, Mr. Williams, Chem? No. They speak English there. That won't do.'

'We need time to talk,' Bryn said. 'That's all I'm saying.'

'Talk away,' she said. 'I can listen while I get on with the work.'

She moved now with greater speed. The domestic tasks she undertook were becoming more familiar to her. Perhaps because he was watching so closely she demonstrated greater competence. Now she seemed to know without any question where everything was kept. More than once his mouth opened and closed without saying anything. He followed her around as if standing closer to her would free his tongue. He mumbled apologies when he got in her way.

'How old was the baby?'

He had managed to speak at last. He pulled a face to show he regretted the bluntness of the question.

'I had a pet once,' Sioned said. 'A lovely little dog. Muffy his name was. We buried him in the garden. Didn't Malan tell you about it? How sad I was. And the song I sang. She must have told you. Those wonderful letters of hers. Good enough to deposit in the National Library you said. For the edification of future generations. She sparked you off, didn't she? Maybe it was Malan you should have been in love with, not me.'

He was provoked more by her smile than by her teasing.

'Was it an abortion or a miscarriage?'

Sioned sat down to show exaggerated shock.

'Well my goodness,' she said. 'The great scientist. The great detective. The truth, the whole truth and nothing but the truth.'

Her mood changed. She wanted to justify herself to herself more than to her companion.

'I wanted a life governed by reason. That's all. Was that too much to ask?'

He could find no answer to her question. She leaned across the table to look him straight in the eye.

'An abortion. An act of unforgivable selfishness I'm told. What's your opinion Mr. Williams?'

He had no opinion. His face flushed with misery and confusion. His fingers twitched in the air as though in search of something to hold on to. The silence that closed in on them was thicker than the walls of the old house.


## XIII


Sioned heard his pathetic moaning before she reached Ritchie's bedroom. She found him on the floor clutching a heap of bedclothes. He had made an effort to reach the commode before collapsing. Now he lay helpless stained with shit and urine. She hung back in the doorway repelled by the smell and uncertain what to do and where to begin. She retreated down the corridor to call for help. There was no reply. Exasperated she rushed downstairs and into a farmyard that was still glistening wet in the bright sunlight. She found Bryn sitting disconsolately on the outside steps to the granary.

'Don't sit there,' she said. 'Come and help me.'

The clatter echoed through the house as he raced up the stairs after her. Any form of action was a relief. He stood aghast in the doorway.

'Poor sod,' he said. 'Poor sod.'

He was seeing Ritchie for the first time. The discrepancy between the man's lurid reputation and this pathetic reality was unnerving. Sioned shook Bryn's arm to break his trance. Together with concentrated efficiency they set-to to clear up the mess. He lifted Ritchie's body in his arms while Sioned worked with bucket and mop and disinfectant. Ritchie's eyes swivelled in his head with the effort of trying to keep up with everything they were doing. Gurgling noises emerged from his throat that sounded like grotesque distortions of an infant being dealt with under similar circumstances. When at last he was restored to a clean bed Sioned and Bryn sat down at a distance from each other to recover their breath and survey their handiwork.

'How on earth does she do it,' Bryn said. 'How does she manage?'

'It's too ridiculous. So absurd.'

Sioned appeared to be talking about something else. She was not listening to Bryn's practical proposals.

'She must get the power back,' he said. 'That's the first priority. Electricity, power and light. The first thing she should do. It's so elementary.'

In bed Ritchie looked pleased to have their presence in his room. He wanted them to see he was enjoying their company even though they spoke as if he were not there.

'To think I wanted to kill him,' Sioned said. 'In any case what could I do to make things worse for him than they are already?'

Bryn shifted uneasily on his chair.

'He should be in a Home, surely. He needs specialist care.'

'It was my fault as much as his,' Sioned said. 'More my fault probably. There's no such a thing as innocence. We always run away from the truth. It's too awful to have to face it.'

The silence did not embarrass her. She was determined to talk and have both men listen to what she had to say.

'All she wanted was the baby, and I wouldn't give it to her. That was all she wanted. Poor Malan. She must come back. I want to stay here and make it up to her. That's what I want. Now you can see what I'm like. Always ready to blame everyone except myself. That's what I'm like.'

She sat petrified by an awareness of her own irreparable short-comings. Both men looked at her as if she were a graven image, a strange likeness set up in the shadowed corner of the room.


## XIV

The policeman knocked politely at the open door, removing his helmet as he entered the kitchen. He passed a hand over his thinning white hair. In contrast his eyebrows were so thick and black they made his eyes glitter with a benevolent light. He had duties to perform that restrained his natural inclination to be agreeable.

'Miss Sioned Anwyl.' he said. 'I don't know whether you remember me? Katie Blodwen's father. She was in the same class as you.'

Sioned was seated at the kitchen table. Bryn was clearing up after their meal.

The policeman waited for some response. There was none forthcoming. He sighed deeply and began to finger the notebook in the breast pocket of his tunic.

'I don't know how I'm going to tell you this, Sioned fach. It's one of the worst duties that fall to a policeman's lot. It's time I retired, I can tell you that much. We don't know yet how it happened.'

Already Sioned had buried her face in her hands.

'The body was washed up on Dulas beach. Mrs Roberts, your sister. A terrible loss of course. To you and to the community. And all the good causes. How it happened of course it is too soon to say.'

Sioned pushed back her chair and rushed out of the room. As she ran up the stairs they could hear her howling her sister's name.

'Malan! Malan!'

The sound reverberated weirdly through the whole house. It distressed the policeman so much he lifted both hands in a vain gesture as though in front of a disturbance pleading for calm and quiet. He accepted Bryn's presence as someone he could talk to on an intimate level. The colleague waiting in the police car was a newcomer with little local knowledge.

'She was a very religious woman, you know, Mrs. Roberts. Malan, Penrhyn Hen. It's true she never went to chapel nowadays. But she never failed to contribute. She was widely respected. She had some extreme views in certain respects, but she always stood up for what she believed in.'

He seemed to realise he was after all a policeman, and his duty required him to identify the young man standing in the kitchen, and if necessary acquire some official notion of where he stood and even what he believed in.

'Are you a member of the family Mr...?'

'Williams,' Bryn said. 'Brynmor Williams.'

'Not related?'

'Not really. A visitor. I'm a teacher. I teach Chemistry in Walsall East.'

'A friend of the family? Can I say that?'

'Of course. This is my first visit. I didn't really know Mrs. Roberts very well.'

The policeman's jaw stretched as he considered the range of difficulties ahead. It was his nature as well as his duty to offer help on more than one level.

'There'll be problems here,' he said. 'No question about it. Poor Ritchie Roberts. You should have seen him on his motor-bike. Good enough for the T.T. any day. And look at him now. Life is very strange. No two ways about that.'

He became aware of Bryn's uncomfortable silence. The young man was standing stiffly in front of him as though to emphasise his detachment. The policeman straightened his back into an official stance.

'We have to let these things take their course,' he said. 'What other way is there. You'll be here when she comes down?'

Bryn nodded.

'Just tell her I'll be back. Tell her we'll take our problems on as we meet them. One at a time. Tell her I'm here to help her.'


## XV


Sioned found Bryn standing on raised ground in a field overlooking the estuary. Out to sea she could see the rocky island with a ruined tower. When he knew Sioned was watching him he lifted his arms towards the sky as though demanding attention and even sympathy for his predicament. Sioned walked up the field carrying Malan's black notebook in her hand.

'Bryn, I've been looking everywhere for you. Didn't you hear me?'

He turned to face her and provide a lame excuse.

'I had no idea it would be like this, ' he said.

Even the view seemed something he could no longer approve of let alone enthuse about. Focused on Sioned his voice was thick with disapproval. His appeal was desperate.

'We can't stay here,' he said. 'It's impossible. It would poison us. He would be lying up there day in day out governing our lives. You could sell the place. Put the place on the market and put him in a home. That would be the obvious solution. It's reasonable enough. People would see that.'

'I wanted you to see Malan's notebook. You were right you know. It is marvellous the way she writes. Look.'

She offered him the book. He gazed at it with deep suspicion.

'It's wonderful, the way her mind works,' Sioned said. 'I never realised it before, you can see for yourself. She seems to have fore-seen everything and forgiven everything. When you think of the kind of life she had to live and how she was able to transform it. It's overwhelming.'

She watched him finger the book and stare her sister's handwriting with ill concealed distaste.

'She wanted us to have the place. You know. The way you used to talk about. Carry on the tradition. It's the least I can do.'

'I couldn't stand it!'

Sioned shook her head and smiled. His petulant outburst seemed no more than a source of mild surprise. He was disappointed of course and upset, but she still had reason to believe he would recover the essence of his original vision.

'That creature upstairs,' he said. 'He ruined your life. Remember that? How can you let your life be governed by the fantasies of an unbalanced woman. You could see from the moment we arrived here how strange she was. You said so yourself. Take this book and lock it up somewhere. We've got to get away from here as soon as we decently can.'

'I'm twenty seven years old,' she said. 'It's time to take charge of myself.'

'By staying here to look after that creature? I don't believe it.'

'It's amazing the things she writes,' Sioned said. 'She says humans have to believe in sacrifice. Otherwise everything is God's magic and you don't have to be responsible for anything. Do you see what she means?'

Her calmness fuelled his anger.

'Responsible? Staying here to look after that creature?...'

'It seems so. We have to wait and bend our will and listen. That's what she says. If we are not prepared to suffer the crucifixion becomes a conjuring trick. It was only a ghost on the cross.'

'Rubbish! I've just told you. You saw for yourself the woman was unhinged. Deranged would be the only word for it.'

'My sister? I don't think so.'

'What about us, Sioned? What about us?'

He could see her smiling at him as if he were already becoming a memory she would always cherish.

'Don't worry Brynmor. Mr. Ackroyd will be glad to have you back. And the cricket team. And the Library Players. I'm not laughing at you. I mean it.'

'Good God,' he said. 'You mean you prefer him to me. That's what you mean.'

He threw Malan's notebook at Sioned's feet.

'Take this wretched book and burn it,' he said. 'The ravings of an unbalanced woman. That's what it's come to.'

She bent to pick up her sister's book wiping the wet grass from the covers.

'It's an unbalanced world we live in,' she said. 'Better for you to get back on course Mr. Williams, Chem.'

They stood for a while held in a stubborn silence. There was nothing left they could say to each other. She walked to the old house without looking back.

# THE AUTHOR

Emyr Humphreys is the doyen of Welsh writers. He is the author of more than twenty novels, plus volumes of poetry, stories and a history of Wales, *The Taliesin Tradition*. He is a winner of the Hawthornden Prize; his most recent novel, *Gift of a Daughter*, was Arts Council of Wales Book of the Year 1999. A native of north-east Wales his career as a teacher, and later a television producer, took him to London and to Cardiff. He now lives on Anglesey.